Inspired by one
of the longest manhunts
in Canadian history

ON SCENE

Kate Kading

One Printers Way
Altona, MB R0G 0B0
Canada

www.friesenpress.com

Copyright © 2021 by Kate Kading
First Edition — 2021

While inspired by true events, this is a work of fiction. Any and all resemblance to real life people or situations is coincidental unless otherwise noted.

Author photo by Julie Cortens Photography.

All rights reserved.

No part of this publication may be reproduced in any form, or by any means, electronic or mechanical, including photocopying, recording, or any information browsing, storage, or retrieval system, without permission in writing from FriesenPress.

ISBN
978-1-03-910706-9 (Hardcover)
978-1-03-910705-2 (Paperback)
978-1-03-910707-6 (eBook)

1. FICTION, CRIME

Distributed to the trade by The Ingram Book Company

For Sarge and our boys

Chapter One

```
Friday, October 9, 1970
MacDowall, Saskatchewan
Before dawn
```

Wilfred Stanley Robertson didn't know if his wife was cheating on him…again.

Or maybe he did.

Maybe he didn't want to know.

His weathered hands gripped the battered steering wheel tighter than necessary, bits of dry, cracked calluses grinding against the rough spots. He'd hauled a double load of wood to the city that day, from well before sun up, and it was past midnight now but he didn't hesitate to face the long road home. His mind was on what he'd find there—or wouldn't find. Staying the night in Saskatoon would have killed him. He unclenched one hand, reaching up to squeeze the back of his neck; it did little to relieve the strain there. The slivers in his palm scratched against his skin, an uncomfortable shiver running down his back with the slight pain.

Some said Ruth married too young. Others said she wasn't quite right in the head. He was cut from a stricter cloth. His French mother and inscrutable Cree father hadn't shown a lot of affection, but he'd learned his role as a husband and father. And what Ruth's role should be as a wife. When Stanley married, he married for life, for richer, for poorer, in sickness, and in health.

If having eight children to care for didn't stop her from gallivanting, likely nothing he said would make a damn bit of difference either.

A thin stream of crisp night air snaked in through the lowered window, stroking his face with icy fingers. He turned his head a fraction to the left, breathing in the freshness. Fall on the prairies had a certain smell at night. Old leaves? No, that wasn't right. Fall was short here; the leaves never got a chance to grow old. The air smelled of comfort and familiarity. Like pulling heavy quilts out of the cedar chest before the cold set in. It was a thick, woodsy smell that preceded the bite of winter. As familiar as it was, it did nothing to settle him.

The people around town were respectful enough to whisper about them behind closed doors, but whisper they did. It wasn't the first time they found entertainment in discussing his private matters. Knowing Ruth, it wouldn't be the last.

The yard was darker than the highway, tucked back into the bush away from prying eyes. The old truck's headlights swept across his house and his father's in turn, just catching the side of his uncle's small cabin beyond. With no central light in the family yard, only the not-quite-full moon prevented the thick pine trees behind from swallowing the houses whole. Stanley cut the engine, sighing on the last sputter, empty eyes staring at the shadowed outline of the dashboard. Mindful of his parents, his uncle's family, and his own children sleeping close by, he got out and carefully closed the truck door. His few steps towards the house were silent and without thought he avoided the first porch step that always yawned in protest. Just as carefully, he eased open the rickety wooden door of his house. In his fog of thought he didn't immediately miss the warm puff of wood smoke that normally greeted him upon entering the house. They weren't fancy but they were fed and warm.

In his mind, there was nothing else to want.

Ruth disagreed.

Shedding his jacket, he hung it on the hook and stepped into the bedroom. No need to disturb the wife. Any awkward talk could wait until morning.

Moonlight filtered in through the single pane window, bathing the still-smooth bed in a foreboding glow. It looked exactly as it had after Ruth made it early the previous morning. The emptiness tore through him like a dry prairie wind storm, leaving nothing good in its wake. The chill of the bedroom gripped his neck and held on tight. He strode over to the stove and laid a hand on the surface. Not a wisp of warmth remained; must have gone out hours ago. He noticed the cold now, pressing in on all sides.

He reached up to claw at the top button of his shirt, gasping for a full breath, and went into the next room to check on the children. He counted over and over, a mantra of security, one through eight in the three beds. They were all there, but Ruth wasn't. A red wave of anger and embarrassment crashed from one ear to the other. He gripped the corner of the wall for support, his dark hair falling limp over his brow. He raked it back.

The wave receded and left him with a terrifying stillness. He didn't slam the door or yell or curse. He quietly closed the children's door, put his jacket back on and got his rifle from the front closet. The weight of it in his hands was the only thing that made sense.

Taking the steps back down to the deserted yard, he got into his truck, turned the key and pumped the gas pedal, waiting as the old thing went through its customary coughs and sputters. It roared to life and he jammed it into gear, pulling out onto the road as softly as his racing mind would allow. There were the children to think of.

He still couldn't catch a deep breath through the iron band compressing his chest. Finding them alone well past the middle of the night…his hands shook and he clenched and unclenched them trying to bring some warmth back. Less than two miles to town and he knew where Ruth would be. Who she'd be with. What she'd been doing.

Fran's Café would be abuzz in the morning.

"Have you heard?"

"Did you know?"

The two questions he detested most and wished he could silence forever. He'd quietly go get Ruth and bring her home, where she belonged.

The dim light from the truck's dirty headlights bounced along the rough road, heading north to MacDowall through scrubby bush and nearly bare trees. The truck wasn't fast but she was steady. Why couldn't Ruth be steady? There wasn't anything wrong with a quiet life.

He shifted uncomfortably. Grinding his grip on the top of the steering wheel with one hand, he picked at a scab near his thumb where he'd pulled out a bigger than average sliver. A drop of blood welled up and he picked at it harder, not flinching at the physical pain. It was the mental pain that he couldn't bear.

Stanley didn't know if the roaring in his ears was the sound of the truck or the clutter in his own head. Immersed in the 'what ifs', the outline of a parked truck jumped out at him like a deer at dawn. Heart hammering, he leaned heavily on his brake, stopping just short of the other vehicle.

His headlights were enough to illuminate awkward fumbling in the cab before him, and he averted his eyes as shirts were buttoned haphazardly. Shutting off his rumbling truck, Stanley closed his eyes for a fraction of a second, wishing for strength and patience and a calm he didn't feel. His eyes flew open at the creak of a door.

"What in Sam hell?" Standing on the running board of his truck, the driver threw a hand up to shield his eyes from the assault of the headlights.

Stanley opened his door and stepped out onto his own running board. From this higher vantage point he saw Ruth still struggling with her clothes. He ground his thin top lip between his teeth to block the rage from coming out. Three breaths. Maybe four. He reached up to rub at the deep indent across his lip, pulling his finger away to see if he was bleeding. Not yet.

"Mr. Nelson. I'll be taking my wife home now." Stanley had ignored the truth of the matter for a long while. Being in the bar with this man was far more to Ruth's liking than being cooped up in the house with all their kids. He couldn't ignore it anymore, but they could just turn their backs on this situation, right now, and go home.

"Get out, Ruth," Stanley called firmly, silently willing her to obey and end this. She didn't look any more ready to move than a forgotten hay bale frozen to an icy field.

Don Nelson leaned his head down into the truck, scrubbing at his shaggy blond hair. If he said something to Ruth, it was quiet enough to be lost in the space between. It was the longest moment of Stanley's life and he didn't know whether to order her to his truck again or wait some more. The humiliation ate him.

"Good Goddamn, woman," Don snapped. "We don't need a scene."

He'd never known Don to be fearful, but a smart man knew when he was in the wrong.

What would the folks at Fran's say about being on a deserted road in the middle of the night with another man's wife? They were two sides of a precariously balanced coin. He didn't want to deal with the gossip, and from the look on his face, Don plainly didn't want to deal with Stanley.

Arms crossed over her chest, Ruth stared belligerently at Stanley, then looked over at Don. Seeing that movement, his wife looking to another man for go ahead, Stanley felt something break inside him.

He was at Don's truck before he realized what he was doing, wrenching Ruth out by the arm. She was having none of it. Twisting at an unnatural angle, she bucked her thin body violently in his single-handed grip, raking her fingernails down his cheek and beating any part of him she could reach with her one free fist. Stanley stayed still but didn't let go. Ruth kicked and screeched as he dragged her out of the truck.

He gently closed the door behind them, exaggerating the slow movement. It was important to be quiet.

Ruth had never learned that.

Don remained rooted to his driver side running board. Stanley spared him no more attention as he tried to deposit Ruth into his own truck. With the amount of cooperation she was giving him, the gap between the closely parked vehicles felt like a million miles. Stanley hauled her up by the arm and brought her close to his face. She huffed at him and he smelled the beer and cigarettes on her breath. His disgust bloomed.

"Stop it. We're going home," he hissed low through clenched teeth, trying to keep some semblance of privacy between them. Ruth didn't seem interested in privacy and tried, without success, to twist away again.

"I'll go home when I'm good and ready," she said, words penetrating the dark cocoon around them.

He wondered how far her voice was travelling. And who could hear her.

A bark of nervous laughter erupted behind them and Stanley's head sprang up, eyes narrowing at Don. He could see the man immediately regretted the laugh. Stanley's hand loosened a fraction on Ruth's upper arm and she took advantage, wrenching away and toppling sideways between the two front bumpers.

Stanley lost all sense. Reaching down, he grabbed a handful of Ruth's thick dark hair, squeezing his fist as hard as he could, dragging her forward as she screamed and clawed at his hand. The strands of hair wrapped around his fingers as he pulled, the sensation making him rejoice and shudder at the same time. He would succeed in hurting her as much as she hurt him.

Don jumped down from his perch on the running board. "Hey now, no need for this. Let's just all get on home and forget this happened." He held out his hands, palms up, looking suspiciously like he was going to try to help Ruth.

Stanley didn't care what this philanderer thought of what he was doing just now. Viciously shaking his wife by the hair, he looked down at her, pathetic in her mewling. She was crying now, alternating between wailing sobs and softer pleading. He dragged her the few feet left to the driver's side of his truck, his rage heating his body, increasing his strength. She was taller than he was, everyone was, but he'd always been stronger. He tossed her inside and she landed in a heap. She sat up and brushed her matted hair off her face.

"You're a bastard," she seethed. Their eyes met for a brief moment in the dimness of the truck. This wasn't like the other times.

Bracing his forearms on the top of the open door, Stanley squeezed his eyes shut, pressing his forehead into his arms, trying to block out everything this night had to offer. He would take her home—just quietly take her home and it would all go away.

"Stanley, come on. No harm done, right? Leave her be." Don made the grave mistake of walking forward between the trucks, arm extended as if to say good-bye with a handshake. He laid a hand on the hood of the truck, eyes pleading.

ON SCENE

Cousin or not, Stanley had had enough of Don. His eyes darted over to his .30-06 lying across the top of the truck seat. With deft hands and unmatched skill, he grabbed the rifle in one fluid motion, stepped back up onto his running board, levelled the gun directly at Don Nelson's head and fired.

Massive Hunt Under Way For MacDowall Area Man-*The biggest police manhunt in the history of Saskatchewan was being concentrated today in the MacDowall area, 20 miles south west of Prince Albert…*

Headline and excerpt, Prince Albert Daily Herald (Saturday, October 10, 1970)

Chapter Two

Friday, October 9, 1970
Dense bush near Melfort, Saskatchewan
1600hrs

Sergeant Walter Regitnig might have been one of the best dogmasters in the Royal Canadian Mounted Police, but that didn't mean he liked getting called out on card night. His partner, Bruce, paced the length of the back seat of the car, whining and dripping with the drool of anticipation.

"Yeah, well, if I don't get to eat yet, neither do you. Catch this asshole fast so we can get back." He pulled the car off to the side of the narrow grid road, easing the passenger side tires onto the bush line and parking with the doors inaccessibly pushed into the trees. The story he heard his rookie year about the fugitive who circled around and snuck into the back seat of the dogmaster's car stuck with him like a bad aftertaste that even 20 years in the force couldn't erase.

His every movement was quick and measured. No time to lose but nothing to be missed with careless hurry, either. He threw open his door and without thinking reached down as he swung his heavy booted foot to the ground. The broken handle of the hood release caught on his boot laces if he wasn't careful and when he hit the ground there was no time for lollygagging. He opened the back door and Bruce leaped out, circling around Wally's legs, whining and yipping, hurrying him to give the command. It was time to work.

ON SCENE

Wally smoothed the part in his brown hair and reached across the seat for his hat. He flipped the Stetson on with one practiced hand, sliding the leather strap in place at the back of his head with his other hand. He pulled it down low, but not too low, with the perfect tilt to the right. He didn't bother with his coat. The khaki wool of his uniform would be stifling within a quarter mile. The extra jacket was a waste. In this in-between time in Saskatchewan, you could have the heater on in the car in the morning and by lunch you were half hanging out the window trying to catch a cool breeze. Not every October was like that, but this one was. Freezing temperatures at night and afternoons warm enough to make you want to rip the brass buttons off your uniform.

The beginning of a track like this was never very eventful; they weren't chasing a mastermind. You had to have a few screws loose to run from the police after being caught in a stolen car. Wally grunted and caught a passing glance at his watch before his arm was extended almost beyond its capacity. The dog surged to the end of his line, ready. They could still make it if they hurried.

A job like this wasn't just a job; it was your whole life. And sometimes there was precious little to look forward to. They all ruthlessly protected card night. If they missed it, something big was happening and likely they all missed it. This car thief didn't qualify as something big. Not big enough to miss his wife's pie and the laughter in the Schrader house. Last week had been one of those nights the laughter should well have lifted the roof off the house.

A crash that rattled the good dishes in the sideboard of Connie's kitchen landed Wally with a lapful of yelping wife and meringue sticking to his hair and sliding down the front of his shirt. He'd left Bruce in charge of the five Schrader kids in the living room and now the walls were shaking.

The raucous laughter was deafening but typical for a Friday night. A half dozen of the guys crowded around Sergeant Bob Schrader's kitchen table, the officers swapping cards and stories with the three wives standing at the counter chatting over their heads and pouring coffee. Bob and Connie took in officers like elderly ladies took in stray cats. They fed and cared for all of them. Wally loved that about his best friend. No man was left behind, especially when the Missus had a meatloaf in the oven. The cigarettes were plentiful, the food always good, and even if they never did more than exchange a few glances across the kitchen, Wally took comfort in his wife's quiet presence. Dolores had just handed him a piece of her award winning lemon meringue pie when all hell broke loose. He wasn't overly comforted now, just sticky.

"Arries!" Connie Schrader shouted, stabbing her cigarette into the ashtray, limping from the kitchen waving a tea towel. Connie's bad leg never stopped her from chasing after her children. Bob had long since discarded the top half of his uniform and pulled at the neck of his white t-shirt with what could only be described as parental exhaustion creasing his genial features. Greying chest hairs poked out the top of the shirt and Wally wondered if his own were showing his wisdom yet? He and Bob were the same age and rank but tended to have different stressors turning their hair grey at different rates. Or what little hair Bob had left, anyway. Wally and Dolores had started their family six years earlier than Bob and Connie, back when the families didn't know each other. Seemed like a lifetime ago. They didn't shoot for the hockey team Bob was intent on; their two kids were both off to college and not wreaking the havoc that followed the Schrader boys.

Wally closed an eye and stuck a finger in his ear at the screech. Dolores up-righted herself, smoothing her slacks, and batted at him. The three young Constables Joe Greenslade, Henry Long, and Danny Cavello were doubled over with laughter. Doug Anson, a senior constable with considerable influence, pinned them with a glare of warning, but Wally noticed the corner of his mouth turn up a notch at the same time. When one of the Schraders yelled out "Arries" it was certain Larry, Barry, Garry, or Terry were up to something that would make a good story later.

A louder, longer shriek came from the living room and Wally raised his eyebrows.

"You better get in there, Bobby. Sounds like a good one gone bad." Wally pointed his cigarette at Bob then took a drag and set it down in the nearest ashtray, preparing for fireworks.

ON SCENE

Bob hung his head, rubbing the bridge of his nose under the heavy black frames of his glasses. His thinning thatch of more salt than pepper hair was as neatly parted as it could be at the end of the work day, but Bob's head hung so low Wally caught a glimpse of the growing shiny spot at the very top. Unconsciously, he reached up and smoothed over his own part. No shiny spot…yet.

"Can't wait to hear the blaming," Bob said, heaving himself off his chair.

Long and Greenslade each threw a dollar bill on the table and said in unison "Barry." Wally snorted on a sip of coffee.

Cavello threw down his dollar. "Connie." Apparently he was changing the bet to who would win the day, not who'd caused the chaos in the first place.

Wally heard Connie curse a blue streak and then heard Bruce's name. "Uh-oh. That's my kid." He winked at Dolores and went in to see just how bad the damage was.

The middle twins, Garry and Barry looked a little banged up but no worse than an average night at the hockey rink. Wally looked around for the more responsible of the bunch. Larry stood in the corner, highly entertained, while his twin Lynn, lounging in her father's armchair, turned back to her book immediately, rolling her eyes as thoroughly as only an almost-sixteen year old girl could. Little Terry was trying to be included in the chaos without actually being blamed for anything in the process. He usually succeeded and Wally admired his spunk.

"Bruce, what did you do?" he boomed out through his smile. Bruce came to heel, guilt written all over his black and tan face.

"Wally, it wasn't me, I swear," Barry said, but Garry yelled over him.

"Was so. He got bored so he told Bruce to get me."

11

Kate Kading

"Did not. An' he wouldn't have anyway, would you ol' boy?" Barry ruffled the hair at Bruce's neck and hugged him hard. A willing partner in crime but not in punishment, Bruce's tongue lolled out, making him look innocent of any and all charges laid against him by the children.

"Dad, he's lying!" Garry thrust an accusing finger at his twin. It was quickly grabbed by his mother. Garry yelped and yanked his finger away.

"I don't care who did what. Look at this." Connie's wide eyes took in the impressive pile of rubble. The stereo cabinet would never be the same. Wally was relieved to see Bob was having a hard time hanging onto his laughter, too. Connie would give them both hell if they didn't keep it together. Wally cleared his throat, the sound drowned out by the arguing.

Connie put a hand on her hip, her face almost matching the red of her hair, and snapped above the din, "Lynn?"

Without glancing up from her book, Lynn murmured, "Barry bet Garry a quarter that he couldn't hide the ball somewhere Bruce wouldn't find it. Garry said yes, he could. Barry was still hanging on to Bruce's collar when he dove behind the stereo." Lynn didn't look up as she turned the page, "Everything went flying."

Bob's laughter burst from him, filling the room. His wife stared daggers at him, and the younger officers, unaccustomed to dodging a formidable woman's wrath, ducked out of the way like there were razor sharp projectiles flying from Connie's eyes. Wally inconspicuously reached out to straighten the family photo hanging at a precarious angle. He heard a snort behind him but kept his eyes forward and didn't know if it was Anson, Cavello, Long, or Greenslade. The detachment boys had a bad habit of cleaning up behind the Schrader kids, both literally and figuratively. They were all guilty of it, Bob included. It took a village to raise children, but it took a detachment of armed policemen to help raise these boys.

Turning her back, Connie wagged her finger at the culprits, threatening no dessert for a week or even worse.

ON SCENE

"You boys clean this up right now. Oh…" Connie's bluster deflated when she turned around and found the mess had disappeared while her back was turned.

The tall snake plant was mostly back in its pot, sitting at a new jaunty angle, the records were stacked in the cabinet, someone had shoved a broken picture frame behind a speaker and the fronts of a couple of shirts looked suspiciously bumpy. Wally hoped Connie wouldn't smack their middles just to prove her point; he was pretty sure Greenslade had pieces of a vase tucked into his waistband.

"They won't learn a thing with you all covering for them. Mark my words." She huffed and turned her deadly finger to the face of each of the rescue crew. The constables skirted out of her reach and allowed themselves to be shooed back to the kitchen.

Wally and Bob hung back, each with a hand on Garry and Barry's shoulders. Both sturdy and nearly as tall as their dad, brown hair buzzed short like most boys their age, that's where their similarities ended. Twins in mischief but individuals in looks. Wally frowned but then winked, "You know you can't hide that ball where Bruce won't find it. No use trying."

Bob nodded, "That's right. Quit destroying the house or I won't sneak you any pie later. You're fourteen now. Maybe time to stop devilling your poor mother." Bob hugged both boys, pounded them on the back in turn, and sent them out the door with Bruce barking in hot pursuit.

"I tell ya, Wally, no use hiding that ball and no use trying to have nice things in this house." Bob leaned over, poking a finger through the hole in the stereo speaker.

"We can't solve the problems of the world right now." Wally opened the kitchen door and was hit with more laughter. "But we can eat pie."

He could almost taste the pie and strong coffee when thrashing brought him back around to the chase like a siren's call.

"Wait."

13

Kate Kading

The dog froze.

Wally closed his eyes. The movement of the forest came at him in waves. His ears defined and discarded the unnecessary: wind, startled birds, and other animals. The only animal he concerned himself with was the dog at his side and the suspect fleeing them.

Bruce pointed his nose first left, then right, searching for the thick scent of fear on the breeze. He jerked his head.

"Go." Direction reset, Wally let out more leash. The dog needed space and he didn't want his arm yanked off. He dragged a hand across his creased face, the cool fall breeze barely keeping the sweat off his forehead. They could run like this for days, but come on. This guy needed to just give up. Wally had better things to do than chase a thief through the forest. He loved a good challenge, but this was not that.

"Find him." He slogged through the spongy undergrowth, jumping over branches and fallen debris, hanging onto his leather duty belt with one hand. Damn thing banged around too much on a good run.

He trusted his partner's slight shift north without hesitation. He could hear the suspect, closer now. Bruce could smell him.

The thrashing reached a recognizable peak and Wally jogged on, reeling in the leash.

"Stop or I'll release the dog."

Bruce's barking nearly drowned out the bellowed warning. The dog was more than ready, the threat was obvious, and if the guy didn't stop…well, that was on him now. Wally yelled the command a second time. He always liked to give them a second chance to do the right thing. They rarely took his charity.

Crouching, Wally grabbed Bruce's collar, the dog straining against his grip. The sound of the clip releasing was like a starter's pistol. Bruce set off like a shot, sailing over another fallen tree; powerful form eating up the distance like it was nothing.

Wally followed the smashed leaves and snapped branches like a roadmap, laying eyes on their target sliding to a stop at a drop off. The man threw a desperate glance over his shoulder, face pouring sweat, chest heaving, a wild look about him. Wally drew down, lightening fast, leveling his gun in a steady, two handed grip.

"Stop, Police!"

He recognized a man weighing his options but still didn't believe his own eyes when the guy pitched himself headlong over the drop off.

Cursing, he knew who was next.

"Aw, hell! Bruce, don't!"

Without hesitation, the dog went over after the suspect. Wally scrambled over to the lip and surveyed the drop. Luckily, it was no steeper than the sledding hill at the park.

The tumble of predator reaching prey sent birds shooting into the air, frenzied barking and growling second to the terrified screaming.

Thrown around like a rag doll at the mercy of eighty-eight pounds of obstinate German shepherd, the suspect screeched like an injured rabbit. "Get him off!"

Wally took his time, picking his way down the short hill, hopping over the impressive gouges of earth made by the sliding body. He coughed on a chuckle; boys on the evidence team would want to see that.

There wasn't much sense in the guy's howling and he'd already wet himself. Wally caught a whiff as he came upon the pile of chaos. Bruce loved this part but Wally could do without the mess.

The suspect was on his back, wailing his apology, trying to put his arms over his head and go limp as Wally instructed. A nearly impossible feat while being yanked and shaken.

"Out, Bruce. Enough." Wally approached and laid a hand on his partner's head. The dog released the suspect's arm and sat inches from him, barking incessantly at the cowering, sobbing man.

"On your stomach. Hands on your head." Gun still drawn, his words held clear authority but in all his years of service he'd yet to see a suspect obey the first time. Between the pain and the barking, it always took them a while to gather what meager wits they had left to obey an order.

Watching for even the slightest movement, Wally slid his gun back into the holster, leaving the snap open, and approached the suspect, cuffs ready. Some RCMP officers found Bruce's barking distracting but it reassured Wally. He knelt on the suspect's back, twisting the man's free hand to snap a cuff down on his wrist. Left hand secure and raised at a sufficiently painful angle to cut off further resistance, he kneeled harder to encourage compliance.

"Give me your other hand or I'll let the dog go again." He pulled harder on the suspect's arm, losing what little patience he had, but the guy had more strength left than Wally expected. The slippery little bastard wrenched free, grabbing at his waistband. Wally struggled madly for control. It was a situation he didn't fear but always dreaded.

Muscles straining, he looped an arm around the suspect's neck, clamping his other hand to his wrist, squeezing his forearm and bicep together.

He pressed his head against the suspect's so the ass couldn't snap his head back and smash Wally in the face. The man stunk like fear and desperation and Wally felt his greasy hair slide against his cheek. It was encounters like these that sent him directly to the shower before kissing his wife when he got home. Wally put some mustard on his grip.

"Stop…resisting," he said, feeling the man gasping in the hold.

Writhing like an eel he rolled into Wally, pulled out a raggedy little pistol and squeezed off a shot. Wally ducked the flailing arm, loose cuff catching him across the neck and narrowly missing his face. If he hadn't ducked the loose cuff, he wasn't sure he would have avoided the shot. His heart hammered harder. Usually these car thieves didn't carry much more than a heavy screwdriver. The odd one had a knife and thought he was a tough guy. What the hell was up with this day?

Bruce launched himself back into the arrest, ripping into the arm that got a second much more accurate shot off. Wally flinched again, hitting the ground with a force that jarred him out of the thoughts of how lucky he'd just been. He didn't need luck. He needed to get a handle on this guy.

Jumping up, he drew his gun and yelled instructions again. He was breathing hard. He hated that.

"Drop it!"

ON SCENE

The gun came flinging out of the growling, screaming pile. Slicking sweat out of his eyes, he kicked the weapon away, keeping his own levelled at the suspect's head. Bruce kept up his end of the business, growling and shaking the guy's whole body.

Then the begging started.

It was tough to roll your eyes and keep watch on someone at the same time. No matter how many years he did this, every criminal was the same. Big man…until the dog got a hold of them.

His hand went to his waist but he felt nothing; there was an empty spot where his radio used to be. "Damn radio, where is it?" he muttered. The cumbersome thing dropped off the belt in a fight, but was a necessary hassle. He didn't often have the luxury of being close to his car.

He kept his gun steady, searching the ground around them and let Bruce hold the would-be fugitive.

The crunch of boots in leaves and a deep murmur of chatter told Wally the rest of the team was coming in behind them.

"Visual on the dogman, he's 10-4. Subject in custody." A voice squawked out of a bush a few feet ahead and Wally brushed aside some branches and picked up his radio. He shook it free of leaves and debris, rubbing the thicker grime off on his pant leg while keeping an eye on the dog.

Two officers came in to cuff the sobbing, stinking mass of regret.

Wally looked down at the dog who abruptly stopped barking, tongue lolling out of his mouth. He pointed a finger at Bruce. "Don't you go telling Bob about this. I'll never live it down."

Bruce barked in response and Wally agreed.

"You're right. I can trust you. It's these guys I may have to bribe into silence." He thrust a chin at the young upstarts sweeping up after him and they both grinned, happy to be included.

"You boys going to haul that out for me?" At closer range, the man smelled like he'd just been chased down by a pack of hell hounds. It wasn't far from the truth.

The officers nodded but looked less than enthusiastic. Wally chuckled. Not a single extra mile involved, but the thrill of the hunt always eliminated any real concept of time or distance. Jogging in was the easy part. Dragging this unwilling mass out of the bush would add a staggering amount of time and effort. Grateful for the help, Wally jerked on the suspect's arm to keep him upright between the two young officers.

"We're not going to carry your ass out of this bush. If you make me miss my card game, you're not getting a smoke."

Straightening up, the suspect put one foot in front of the other and stopped sagging his weight against the officers' grip. In Wally's experience, if the person wasn't strung out on something, their next currency was a cigarette. He gave the officers a nod. Worked every time.

He whistled for Bruce who was nosing around some other officers on scene. A couple of them were really bad for spoiling the police dogs with bits and pieces from whatever they carried in their pockets. Wally was consistently gruff about it, but it was mostly just to keep up his reputation. Deep down, he didn't mind.

There were two sides to Bruce, just like there were two sides to every other officer in the Force. When you were on your own time, you could joke and let loose a bit. Beg beef jerky off the officers. But on the job, they were all business.

Sergeant Walter J. O. Regitnig and PSD Bruce always got their man.

"Regitnig, get up here right now. You're going to want to take this." The NCO's voice carried down the hill on a wave of thinly veiled panic; there was no mistaking his urgency.

Wally jogged up the incline to where a small knot of men stood, some yelling orders, some in conference with their heads drawn close together. Whatever it was, it wasn't good. Then he heard a whisper on the wind.

"10-33."

ON SCENE

RCMP SEEK INFORMATION-*Police asked the public to supply information, no matter how insignificant, which would lead to the arrest of a murder suspect. To assist the investigation and to afford anonymity to persons with information, a post office box has been made available. Letters need not be signed and all information received will be treated with the utmost confidence.*

Headline and excerpt, Winnipeg Free Press
(Thursday, October 22, 1970)

Chapter Three

```
Friday, October 9, 1970
MacDowall back road
Before dawn
```

The wind blew gently through the few leaves left at the very tops of the trees, the sound rippling through Stanley's senses, making it the only thing he heard. He stared, unfocused, at the dirt road ahead of him, choosing to hear the slight scratching noise the leaves made when they rubbed together, rather than the piercing screams. He forced his breath to come evenly, laboured at the task, slowly blinking on the exhale and not stirring to the other noises around him.

A hand touched his shoulder. It didn't startle him, but made him realize he was still clenching the rifle tight to his shoulder, cheek resting against the sight. Stanley lowered the rifle and turned his head.

Did he expect the ghost to come out of the trees and whisk him away into the night? No. It wasn't a ghost. It was the only person who could make him stand and answer for the terrible drama unfolding before his eyes.

"Son." His father's eyes searched Stanley's face. "Heard the trucks," Gordon said, expression unchanging.

Stanley's head lowered a fraction, his eyes focusing on a spot to the left of his father's head. He couldn't bring himself to look him in the eye, this man who had always taught by silent example. He pushed Ruth's screams far to the back, trying to close himself off.

Grasping for some sort of explanation, Stanley cleared his throat and murmured, "Sorry we woke you."

His father's gaze flickered away from Stanley's face to the darkened side of the truck where whimpers mixed with soft cries and snuffling. Had the screams truly stopped or was he just getting better at erasing them?

"S'pose the neighbours heard that shot." It wasn't a question.

Gordon's eyes boring a hole through him, Stanley's discomfort reached a level he hadn't experienced before. The roaring in his head started up again, blood thrumming through his ears, deafening him. He struggled to keep a steady breath. In. Out.

His father always knew when he was suffering. It was a cross quiet men had to bear, packaging their emotions up in tight, neat bundles. Never revealing to anyone how they really felt about any situation. Stanley wanted to package up his current emotions and set them on fire. Never to plague him again.

Placing a light hand on his son's shoulder Gordon whispered low, "Go on home." The fatherly grip brought Stanley back. Slowly, as if coming out of a long, narrowing tunnel, his surroundings came back into focus. He was unaware of how much time had passed. Was it seconds or hours?

Ruth sniffed long and wet, drawing herself up onto the seat.

Gordon squeezed his son's shoulder again, bringing his hard, calloused hand up to cup the back of Stanley's neck. He drew him forward until their foreheads were touching, holding on for several breaths. Stanley could feel his father's pain. Gordon squeezed once more before dropping his hand.

"Maybe it'll be okay."

He melted back into the dark brush. As the crow flew, they were less than a quarter mile from home, through the unkempt forest that hid the houses from the road. The trees barely moved as he cut through.

Stanley thrust his rifle into the cab of the truck and climbed up, pausing on the running board. He surveyed the scene, disbelieving…no, solidly rejecting what he'd done. It wasn't him. Not his fault. It couldn't be.

He started the truck, the engine abrasively loud at this time of night, on a dark back road filled with silent anger. Doing its sole job, with the driver on auto pilot, the truck carried the couple, tumbled with emotions, down the rutted road to the farm house. They didn't speak.

They didn't have to.

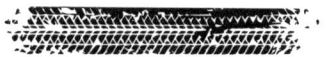

The eerie silence continued on into the morning. The older children were good at sensing when there was trouble with the adults and disappeared early to their chores. Stanley didn't say anything to anyone, pacing in and out of the bedroom. Ruth slept late, as she often did on Saturday mornings.

Stanley had never before been so starkly confronted with what she'd been doing on a Friday night in town. He stood in the doorway, listening to her even breathing.

He knew the moment she woke, felt the air crystallize between them, and the anger in her conscious presence. She rose without a word, dressed, and started breakfast. Stanley wandered back into the bedroom, away from the annoyingly normal domestic sounds. He could hear the little kids murmuring, pots and pans being set on the stove, and dishes set on the table. All normal. The chaos crashing through his head was far from normal.

"Pouting won't do no good."

He heard the statement float in from the kitchen. Was she talking to one of the children? Stanley came to the door, meeting her eyes across the impossibly small room. Kitchen and living areas were separated only by the pot bellied stove, and some wooden furniture that had seen its last days over a decade ago. The walls moved in on him, pressing him closer to his wife. She stared at him, seemingly without remorse, and raised her chin a notch.

"There'll be trouble now. Watch and see." Ruth smoothed the front of her apron several times. Stanley could tell when she was in a state. She was trying to look brave, to put this on him, but it was all for show. She was smoothing her apron.

ON SCENE

Narrowing his eyes at her, he disappeared back into the bedroom and lay down. Still in the same clothes he'd gone out in yesterday, he smelled like sawdust and diesel fuel. He closed his eyes and focused on the smells, catching hints of pine from the forest, and his mind immediately went back to the road. The embarrassment. The shot.

Stanley heard Ruth shuffle across the wood floor to the bedroom but he didn't bother opening his eyes. She whispered, "They're gonna come get you."

His eyes flew open at the statement and he settled an intense stare on her, burning with rage. She faltered for a moment, smoothed her apron again, but to his utter surprise, took a step forward. Her quiet voice pierced his skull, creating a new scene of chaos and punishment.

"You'll go to jail for it. You will." She put her nose in the air and turned away from the door.

Like a striking snake, he was off the bed and gripping her upper arms brutally enough to leave angry red marks.

His father had strict views on how hard you could handle a woman. Discipline was necessary, but leaving marks wasn't acceptable. He'd take his father's disapproving stares. Tears appeared in the corners of Ruth's eyes, but she didn't make a sound.

They stood eye to eye, his anger radiating from his grip on her arms, her head vibrating back and forth with the force. Silently cursing his short stature, he raised his chin to look down on her. Ruth pressed her arms out against his grip, her hands going up to his neck. "Sto—op," she rattled out on an exhale, her dull hair shaking loose from her bun.

Stanley stopped as abruptly as he'd started, dropping his hands to his sides. They remained standing, face to face, noses almost touching, her eyes swimming with unshed tears. His own eyes burned dry as a desert.

Would he go to jail? Immediately after he pulled that trigger, the thought crossed his mind. Jail. Four close walls, bars on the windows, and no fresh air to heal the soul. He couldn't let it happen.

"Where are you going?" Ruth failed to keep the frantic fear from her voice, eyes wide, hair straggling down her neck.

Stanley could barely stand to look at her.

Decision made, he threw on his thick jacket and took up his rifle, slamming the door behind him. Let her think whatever she wanted about what he was up to. He had to go back and collect up the evidence of what he'd done.

Running a hand over his bristly blond military cut, Constable Doug Anson sighed audibly and threw his pen down. The detachment was buzzing, but not any busier than normal. Set on the top two floors above the small post office, the building was an antique, made of stone with creaky wood floors and plaster walls. It smelled of business and age. A hub of the community, on a typical day people came and went all day long and it had never bothered him before.

He felt the crawl of annoyance across his neck and shot up to close the door of the tiny office. He normally brought a methodical patience to his interviews, but this one had him disgusted and fighting the urge to pace.

"Look, Mr. Nelson, I can't help you if you aren't telling me everything there is to say," he said for the third time in the last hour. Eleven years in the Force didn't leave him with a whole lot of faith in the first version of any story… from anyone. Tied up in a neat and tidy package, upon closer inspection this particular story looked like a tattered old fish net in dire need of mending.

"That's it and that's all. He grabbed me out of my truck, threw me on the ground and put a shot into the ground right beside my head. And no reason for it." Don Nelson hunched in his chair and shifted sideways, eyes darting to the left. A snort came from beside him but he ignored it. Danny Cavello's dark head lowered farther into the court files.

Crammed with two desks and four chairs, the office wasn't private but they did their best with what they had. Doug grabbed the unoccupied desk beside Cavello when this Nelson fellow came in with his complaint.

"No reason. No reason at all that you can think of?" He tried valiantly to keep the sarcasm out of his voice but wasn't hiding it overly well. He glanced over at the other desk again and caught Danny's look. He could smell a fish, too.

ON SCENE

Nelson was still stubbornly shaking his head.

Doug let out a longer sigh.

He couldn't let frustration take over this interview. You didn't get anything that way. He drummed out a tune with his pen on the lined pad of paper in front of him. Sometimes silence prompted more nervous talk from a complainant and they ended up saying more than they intended. But Nelson just shifted in his chair, arms crossed over his chest, chin tucked into the collar of his coat.

"Okay, so that's it then? Your complaint is that a Mr. Wilfred Robertson of MacDowall—"

Nelson raised a finger. "Goes by Stanley. Don't forget." He punctuated that bit of information with a nod.

Doug paused in mild disbelief. All the details he was trying to drag out of this stubborn ass and this is what he focuses on? "Right. Can't forget that important detail. So Wilfred *Stanley* Robertson," he paused for effect and waited for Cavello's snort. To his credit, he held it in. Doug was impressed. "Stopped you on the back road south of town, threw you on the ground with no provocation, and fired a shot into the dirt next to your head. For no reason." He finished with a bit of a hand flourish, waiting for laughter. When had Cavello developed so much self control?

"I can't hardly hear out this ear now. Doc says it might be permanent. It ain't right." Nelson shrugged and tucked his chin deeper into the front of his coat.

"That's it? Nobody else there to verify your story?" He didn't need to try very hard to catch Nelson' eyes dart to the side again, knee bouncing.

Tucking deeper into the neck of his coat, and staring at the floor, Nelson mumbled, "Nope. Nobody else."

Anger bubbling just below the surface, Doug stood, bracing his hands on the desk, knuckles cracking with the pressure he put on his hands in an effort to channel his increasing exasperation. He let his piercing stare penetrate Nelson.

"You know it's a crime to lie to the law, right? Best to just get all the facts out, here and now."

The man looked nervous, but shook his head resolutely.

"No, sir. That's it."

Doug rubbed fiercely at his forehead, took a deep breath, and with resignation, turned the paper over to Nelson.

"Fine. If that's your entire statement and you have no more details to add, please sign here."

He hunched over the paper, scribbling, and Cavello shot Anson a questioning look over the man's head. Anson made a face back at Cavello but wiped it off in the blink of an eye when his complainant raised his head from the statement.

When Nelson left the office, Anson closed the door again and collapsed into the hard wooden desk chair with an explosion of breath.

He thrust a booted toe at Danny's chair. "So?"

"Stinks."

"Yeah, but he wouldn't budge. What do you think happened?" Doug didn't need to catch this file right now with three days leave almost in his grasp. Vallarena would be disappointed if they couldn't leave for Pierceland tonight, and disappointing his wife wasn't an option.

"Who knows? Relax, Doug. We won't mess up your leave with your pretty new wife." Cavello patted his pockets absentmindedly, smoothed his slick hair back, checked the court basket and, satisfied everything was where it was supposed to be, stood up and started stacking his arms full.

"I have to testify this afternoon. Hold off and we'll talk to the boss when I get back. I can take the file."

Anson's relief was real. He'd owe Danny big time. "Beers on me. See you later."

Cavello grinned at him as he squeezed through the door, cigarette barely hanging from his lip, juggling the boxes and files with an ease only he could pull off. Anson turned back to his desk, intent on clearing up every last bit of paperwork before the weekend, giving their commanding officer less reason to say no. Nothing would stand between the new Mr. and Mrs. and the party the Sharps had planned for them.

ON SCENE

Not surprisingly court ran long, but knowing what was holding Cavello up did nothing to settle Doug's anxiety about this new Robertson file. He glanced at his watch for the tenth time in as many minutes. Almost 1630hrs and nothing to do but wait. The detachment settled down later in the afternoon, people getting their downtown business done before coffee time. The constant racket on the long staircase leading up to the office had ceased. Sergeant Regitnig got called out to chase a car thief near Melfort and after the flurry of that died down, the office fell into a barely audible hum of work. He was thankful for the quiet.

It had been nearly a decade since he was a swim instructor at Depot, but he still tried to keep in shape and was stiff and restless after an entire day in the office. Unfolding his lean body from underneath the desk, he stretched his six foot frame, touching the ceiling in the cramped space. He flung his head back and stared at the ceiling, every scenario running through his head. If the Staff Sergeant said no, maybe he'd have a talk with this farmer, wrap the file up, and they could drive through the night. He'd move a mountain if it meant Vallarena could see her folks.

Damn it, he needed a change of scenery and more patience than he had. Waiting downstairs wouldn't speed things up but at least he'd feel like he was doing something. He came down the long staircase, thumping with authority in his Sam Browns. The tall boots weren't all that comfortable to work in but they came along with a certain presence that Doug liked. You could hear a Mountie coming a mile away, especially on the old hardwood floors. At the bottom of the stairs, Cavello was slapping Bob on the shoulder in obvious appreciation.

"Thanks for the help, sir. Haven't had such a full court docket in a while."

"Yeah well, that's what I'm here for. Anytime." Schrader looked just as worn out as Cavello, but returned the hearty handshake. He pushed his glasses farther up his nose and looked up at Doug.

27

"You look like one of the kids anxiously waiting to ask me for money." His face creased, laugh lines deepening, slightly crooked front tooth appearing. Doug shook his head with a smile; the man just never seemed to frown.

"I only take your money in poker. And if you were a better card player you'd have more money to give the kids at the rink on hockey nights." Poking at Schrader, Doug sat down on the step and lit up a smoke, coughing heartily on his first drag that choked off his laugh.

"Aw Doug, you missed a good one last night. You should've seen Barry come straight up the middle, clear breakaway. Put it right up in the top left corner, goalie didn't see it coming." Schrader crowed at the ceiling of the little foyer, reliving the moment. Hockey excited Bob like no other.

"Little guy has a wrist shot no fourteen year old has any business having. Kid's a firecracker." Cavello dropped his court boxes in the corner and lit a cigarette.

"Sorry I missed it." Doug took another drag on his smoke, aiming to change gears back to work but was cut off with more news from the home front.

"Can you believe the twins turn sixteen tomorrow? Coming by for cake after supper?" Schrader pointed at both Anson and Cavello in turn.

"If I can help it, Vallarena and I'll be off to Pierceland yet tonight." He shot Cavello a questioning look. "But I caught a file while you were off playing lawyer. Danny tell you?" Schrader frowned and shook his head, dropping a heavy booted foot onto the bottom step, his demeanour immediately switching back to professional Sergeant.

Cavello put up a hand in his usual relaxed manner. "Sarge, if it's okay with you, we can just ask the superiors to transfer the file to me. I don't mind taking it so Doug can head out." He took a deep drag on his smoke, popped open the side door and flicked it outside into a half frozen mud puddle. He smoothed his oiled hair back with both hands. Cavello wasn't one to waste time, unless it was on his hair.

Schrader nodded. "See what they say, anyway. Couldn't hurt."

Anson allowed a small flame of hope to ignite at Schrader's agreement. It was almost Thanksgiving weekend. They all shared the promise of an elaborate meal cooked by the wives and a few hands of cards. Time off loomed tantalizingly on the horizon. They could see it, but hadn't quite reached it yet.

There was a slim chance Cavello would be allowed to take the file, but the chance that work would trump family was far larger. It was no secret that Anson had been looking forward to going back to his bride's hometown to celebrate their recent marriage, but that didn't mean the powers that be would take that into consideration. Even with Sergeant Schrader's endorsement.

All three officers thumped up the stairs straight to the offices. Raising his eyebrows at Bob and Danny in silent question, Anson knocked sharply.

> "I've been married to the same lady for 54 years this summer. Doug Anson was the best man at my wedding."
>
> Excerpt of interview with Anson's troopmate
> Lorne Lowe (2016)

Chapter Four

Friday, October 9, 1970
Prince Albert RCMP Detachment
1700hrs

"Let me just get rid of this stuff. You can fill me in on the way." Bob dumped a stack of files onto his desk. He tried to cover his frustration, avoiding eye contact with anyone around him and immediately grabbed the files up again, putting his desk back to rights. He felt nothing but sympathy for the scrape this put Anson in with his wife but he sure didn't need to start anything by letting it show. He wasn't the tantrum throwing sort.

"Nah, it's fine. Your shift ended half an hour ago, you don't have to do that." Anson's not-too-serious attempt to stop him from attending fell firmly on deaf ears.

"No arguments. It's going to take us the better part of a half hour just to get out there; you'll like the company. I'd make Wally do it if he was here." Bob grinned, the sparkle of his blue eyes complementing his deep laugh lines. "You love hearing stories about the kids." He gave Doug a shove but trying to lighten the mood was tough when disappointment hung this heavy in the air. "You can't go alone. Go get the car. That's an order, Constable." He pointed at Anson resolutely. He lifted his gun belt off the back of his chair as Anson headed to the door, throwing a look of gratitude over his shoulder.

ON SCENE

Clearing space in his briefcase, Bob coiled the belt inside as neatly as he could, and snapped the locks closed. Why did they keep Anson on this file? There was no use in questioning these decisions. It very well could have rested on the fact that Cavello had double the work load of most of the other constables already, preparing the court files on top of taking calls. Anson took the statement from the complainant, so Anson would see the file through. Most of day shift was already gone, and night shift wasn't on for another hour. It wasn't a far stretch for Bob to volunteer to back Anson up. Arguing the point or waiting for a night shift member to arrive would have just taken more time. Together they at least had a small window of chance to clear this up before the clock ran out on Anson's leave. Bob loved the Force but there were times over the years that still stuck with him. He'd never really forgotten the disappointment of missing his parents' twenty-fifth wedding anniversary and he wasn't going to see Doug miss his reception dance.

"Ours not to reason why," he muttered, rubbing his thumb over the tiny gold plate under his briefcase handle. A gift from Connie when he made Corporal ten years ago, the engraving had worn smooth but was still visible. *RJS-15445*. He shook off the heavy cloak brought on by hard decisions. He needed to keep a clear head.

He was back downstairs just as Anson pulled the car around. Bob hefted his briefcase behind the passenger seat, the weight of his gun making it an awkward swing, climbed in, and clapped his hands together.

"Ok, let's get this taken care of and get you on your way. We're all happy for you, Vallarena is a real sweetheart." He hoped he was putting enough optimism into the situation but seeing Anson's side eye told him they'd worked together far too long to fool each other.

"Appreciate that. We'll see what we can do." Doug lit another cigarette and pulled into traffic. "How's Connie?"

Bob looked ahead on the main road. Even in what would be considered rush hour, they would still be outside Prince Albert in mere minutes. Hopefully there wasn't a tractor moving from one field to another. Harvest time could slow the highway to a crawl.

"You know Connie, hates when that leg gives her trouble. She finally gave up yesterday and let me take her in." Bob chuckled at Anson's knowing look. "I'll head up to the hospital as soon as we get back. She's going stir crazy already."

"Tell her it's a vacation." Doug's amusement only spoke to how well he knew Connie, and Bob appreciated the backup.

He slapped the dashboard. "Right. That would go over like a lead balloon." He sure admired Doug's ability to discard disappointment and stress as quickly as it came on. His confidence grew that they'd have this tidied up within the hour. "Vallarena like that new carpet?" He pulled the files from the dash, flipping through them.

"Oh, yeah. Installer finished Wednesday. Least I could do for her. I feel bad we didn't have a big wedding but she didn't want a fuss." He shrugged and Bob unconsciously mirrored the action, throwing up a dismissive hand.

"You can never figure women. If a small wedding was what she wanted, it's best you gave it to her. You can let her tangle with her mother over how many people are invited to this dance in Pierceland." A snort escaped him, thinking of mothers…and mothers-in-law. There would be no tangle and he well knew it. Doug would take the brunt of his wife's annoyance behind closed doors, just as Bob did when Connie let her mother have free rein over something. It was just the way of married life and Doug seemed to be adjusting with ease.

Anson gave his flat stomach a pat. "I'm sure everyone within twenty miles of the place is invited tomorrow night and I'm not arguing. Nobody would miss the opportunity to eat my mother-in-law's cooking."

The mention of food reminded Bob he was long overdue for a meal. A packed court day didn't lend time for a decent lunch.

"Well, let's try to get this mess sorted so you can get on the road and I can get back to Connie." He shifted in his seat, waving the thin file. There wasn't a lot to go on. A couple of address sheets, an occurrence summary with a few lines of what happened, and a sadly sparse 1624. "Pretty sad list of actions, here." He scanned the single page.

"Yeah, but until we talk to Robertson, there's no other action to take." Anson's grunt spoke volumes of disgust. "This Nelson comes in at the insistence of his doctor to report the altercation. Says it happened around 0200hrs between him and this Robertson. You know him at all? Robertson, I mean. Had any dealings with him?"

"A ways back I met him up at the dealership that fixes the detachment cars. Seemed like a nice enough fellow, I guess. You check for previous files?" He ran his finger down the 1624 again. He never passed up an opportunity to keep the constables on their toes.

Anson snapped his fingers and pointed at the sheet, a deep furrow between his brows. "You know I did. Got nothing. So I'm hoping we can have a chat, get the real story, give a warning, and we're all home before the wives get mad."

Bob grunted in agreement. He tried to find as much humour as he could in life but the fact was, things often didn't go as planned. It was just best to be prepared for it. He hoped Anson was right though, and all this would amount to was a kitchen table chat.

"Figure we should stop on that road by the bar first. That's where Nelson said it happened. Take a look around and see what's what."

Bob absently murmured, "Yeah, absolutely," and kept thumbing through the file, scanning the statement over again. He twisted his wedding ring as he read; a habit he had when deep in thought. No previous history for anyone involved. That wasn't usual in a file like this. If a gun really was involved, someone, somewhere, would have had a chat with the police at some point. You didn't just all of a sudden decide to shoot at someone; there were always at least a few previous run-ins. His mind searched for more between the lines of the statement. Land dispute, maybe? Neighbours could get right into it over land.

"What're you thinking?" He snapped the file closed and tossed it on the dash. Pulling his knee up, he rested his boot on the bottom edge of the door, elbow on his knee, face in his hand, eyeing Anson.

"Thinking about what?" Anson quirked an eyebrow.

"Don't pull that with me. You can sniff out dishonesty in people faster than Bruce can find them in the bush." Bob saw a brief hesitation, but knew Doug was dying to talk it out. That was just how he operated.

His ice blue eyes flicked over to Bob and then back to the road. A burst of breath and he was off and running. "Here's the kicker, Sarge. Why? If you just take what Nelson handed me, there's no why and that doesn't make any sense. It's a net full of holes and it stinks." His eyes were on the road but Bob could see his mind was on the case. Anson clenched his jaw muscle whenever he was mentally chewing on something. The muscle jumped now. An investigator to the core, Doug often skipped a few steps and still came to the correct conclusion. The man had a quick mind.

"Those two are squabbling over something. I was thinking maybe land?"

Pleased Doug had come up with the same theory as he had, he nodded. "Could be. Usually what gets people riled up around here. We'll see what we find on the road."

Anson took the quick dogleg at the restaurant that would lead them past the MacDowall bar not a quarter mile down. Everything in the town of MacDowall was within spitting distance of Fran's Café and the '66 Garage. Good food, a telephone, a gas pump, cigarettes, and a few convenience items kept the place busy from sun up to well past supper.

The town appeared sleepy, like all towns boasting a lot less than a hundred people, but Schrader knew there were eyes on them the second they took that turn off the highway. Nothing started the talk more than a police cruiser rolling into town.

The bar came into view and Anson slowed. Bob was not surprised to see the owner already waving from the step. Anson threw the car into park and cranked the window down.

"Hey there, officers. What can I do ya for?" Friendly with a helpful nature, Jim had always been easy to deal with but didn't accept disrespect from his patrons. He and Doug had been to the bar for coffee on more than one occasion but had never been called there for trouble. Generally, Rosthern Detachment took care of MacDowall but most times Prince Albert was closer if someone had to come to the office for something.

"Hi, Jim. Just passing through, patrolling some of the back roads." Doug returned the friendly smile and leaned back as Jim reached his arm in through the window to shake hands with Bob.

ON SCENE

"Sergeant Schrader, haven't seen you around here in a long while. Good to see you." The bar owner jarred Bob's arm from fingertips to shoulder. He exchanged a good natured glance with Anson. Pleasantries were all a part of the job, no matter what kind of hurry you were in.

"They finally let me out of the office. Good to see you, too. Thanks for the sponsorship for the boys' hockey team. We sure appreciate it." Bob released the man's hand with a nod.

"Aw, it was nothing. Glad to do it, glad to do it. Keeps them boys out of trouble." Jim flushed a bit around the collar at the thanks.

Bob didn't get out often but he never saw Jim in anything but the same pair of jeans with the one patched knee and the brown button down shirt with creases down the arms despite the obvious age of the garment. He thought Jim's wife must take her ironing pretty seriously.

Jim tugged on his collar. "Can I get you a coffee for the road?"

"Sorry, no time today. But thank you kindly just the same," Anson replied politely, shifting back into drive.

Bob put a quick hand on Doug's arm.

"Hey Jim, you hear anything strange just after close up last night?"

Jim's balding head had one thatch of greying hair still desperately holding on and he smoothed it back in deep thought. He wasn't given to unnecessary smiling but was friendly enough with anyone passing through whether it was an officer on patrol or a thirsty traveller.

The corners of his mouth turned down as he frowned and shook his head slowly. "No, sir. Nothing but me and an owl or two at closing. Something wrong?" Jim asked, curiosity narrowing his already small eyes. Small towns did love a good story.

Doug put the car back into park. "Nothing wrong." He took over the casual questioning without missing a beat. "Was Don Nelson here last night?" Taking Bob's subtle cue, he was not in such a hurry to leave anymore.

"Oh yeah, that I know for sure. Don was here for a good long while. You need him? I can go get him for you." Jim looked like he was ready to set off across the field that second to retrieve anyone they needed.

"No, that won't be necessary, but thank you. What was he doing?" Bob encouraged, treading carefully, lest he inadvertently start any would-be rumours. None of the usual firing off of questions one after the other. That questioning had its place, but not here.

"He was drinking with his cousin, Albert. Mostly kept to themselves..." Jim trailed off, enough uncertainty in his voice that Bob gently prodded a second time.

"Mostly?" He waited. He could feel something coming. Maybe Anson would catch a smelly fish in his net full of holes, after all.

Jim crossed his arms over his chest, fingers picking compulsively at his sleeve. "I never want to tell another man his business, sir. I ain't no gossipin' ninny." Shaking his head he backed up a step, eagerness slipping from him faster than a man could blink.

"Nah, course not." Anson motioned for Jim to come closer to the cruiser, lowering his voice in confidence. "Just the facts, Jim. Nothing more, nothing less." Anson's words were calming and smooth, in direct contrast to Jim's shifting eyes and fidgeting fingers. He looked like he was at war with himself, but honesty won out.

"That Ruth Robertson was with them. By herself." Jim stretched out the last word with an elaborate raising of eyebrows and roll of his eyes. "But I ain't trying to tell a man his business," he repeated, hands going up in supplication.

"We know that, Jim. You're a good man." Bob took the lead back with a smile and deep nod, leaning into Anson to see out the driver's window better. "What happened? When did they leave?"

"Like I said, they all mostly kept to themselves. The usual. Left around one, I suppose." Jim shrugged and squinted.

Anson thanked Jim and gave him a slow salute. "We'll take a rain check on that coffee." He rolled up the window against the sudden chill in the air and pulled away. Jim stepped back, arm raised in farewell.

"Drinking with a married woman," Bob muttered, staring down at the signed statement in his hand. His gaze went straight through the document, insides blazing at the thought of his Connie, in a bar, with another man.

ON SCENE

"Yeah. Just the usual." Anson's dry words ate at the small space inside the car. The holes in his net were getting smaller. He narrowed his eyes. "With no reason at all for the altercation."

Bob harrumphed. "No reason."

They meandered down the narrow, bumpy road as slowly as the cruiser could roll, on the lookout for the spot Don Nelson reported in his statement. It wasn't hard to find. They got out of the car about a mile down from the bar where long tire depressions, half in the shallow ditch, were easy to see in the firm mud of the prairie fall.

Bob pointed up ahead. "Looks like someone hit the brakes pretty hard." He stood still, squinting at the ground, lost in the movie scene playing out in his mind. "You think there's any truth to this? Robertson pulling a shot off beside Nelson's head?"

"I didn't think so before. By all accounts this Robertson is a pretty quiet guy. But now?" Doug scrubbed at the whiskers starting to shadow his sharp jaw. "Can't say what I'd do in the same situation. Maybe he did try to warn him off."

Bob pressed his lips together, contemplating how far someone would go to cover up some pretty serious sins. "Think he would lie to the doctor? Just to throw some trouble in Robertson's path?"

Doug made a noncommittal noise in his throat.

They stood an arm's length from each other and walked a grid back and forth between the two sets of tire treads. Eyes glued to the ground, they searched for anything that didn't belong. An untrained eye could spot where the trucks pulled up but it was the keen eye of an investigator that would dig up the dirt on this incident.

Bob continued his part of the grid, eyes never leaving the ground. "If I've learned anything on this job, it's that you always trust your gut. If you think he's holding back, of course he was." He stopped dead in his tracks, reaching down to pluck a substantial chunk of what looked like human hair from the rocks in the road. He whistled long and low. "Looky, here." He held the clump up with the end of his pen. "What the hell went on?"

Anson's face changed from disbelief to analyzing in a blink. "That's a sight too long to belong to either of those men."

Bob put the chunk of dark hair on the dash of the car and went back to his spot on their makeshift grid. They continued scanning the ground and came up with some cigarette butts and beer bottle caps. Both not uncommon just down the road from a small-town bar, but any little thing could turn important as more information was uncovered. They carefully collected it all.

Anson put the items on the dash with the clump of hair and got back into the car. Bob stayed in the same spot where he picked up the hair. Something was wrong. Where was the rest of it?

"You got something else?" Anson called from the open car window. "We should get going."

"No. It's what we don't have." He backed up, pacing the ground where the tire tracks met. "He said he was pulled from his truck," he pointed a finger at the deep tire treads half in the ditch, following them to where there was a disturbance in the dirt, "then there was a shot pulled off into the ground by his head. Robertson would have been…," his eyes tracked over to the end of the skid marks where a different set of tire marks ended in the middle of the narrow road. "There. Right there. If this Nelson is telling the truth, there should be a shell casing somewhere here where his truck was parked. Even if he's lying about getting pulled out of the truck, we'd still find the casing over there somewhere." He swept his arm in an arc, encompassing an imaginary area around their imaginary truck.

Anson made a face he reserved for when Cavello passed gas in the car. "Unless there was no shot at all. Hence, no bullet casing, and we're wasting our time."

Bob had a number of grunts in his communication repertoire, all different, and every one of them got their point across with startling effectiveness. He loaded a whopping dose of annoyance and no little distaste into this grunt. "We're going to find out, one way or the other. Let's go." He got into the car and slammed the door.

ON SCENE

POLICE INTESIFY SEARCH IN SASK. MANHUNT-*Police intensified one of the largest manhunts in the province's history Thursday sending 50 men and seven tracking dogs into heavy bush.*

Headline and excerpt, Winnipeg Free Press (Friday, October 16, 1970)

Chapter Five

Friday, October 9, 1970
Robertson yard
1730hrs

The farmyard was typical for the area, if a bit poorer than most. They spotted an old work truck parked parallel to the house as they slowly pulled up the long, uneven drive. The massive thing had rust on every available surface, with tall wooden slats banded with metal rising up from the sides of the box.

There were several children scattered about playing with the dogs. They had sturdy, if well-worn shoes on, jackets, and two had knit caps pulled low over their ears. They didn't look cheerful but none of them bore the pinched look of poverty that some in these parts had. A few chickens scratched out what they could find on the edge of the bush line and Bob saw a garden beyond one outbuilding. Dry corn stalks waved in the wind and a wilting scarecrow said a last goodbye to his summer occupation. The entire property was surrounded by trees and bush so dense the ambient light got a bit greyer as they drove up to the house. Not much penetrated the thick vegetation. Bob felt like they were cut off from the rest of the world here.

Anson passed the truck and a few of the children at a crawl, waving as they passed. The children went back to what they were doing, not returning the wave. Bob frowned. His own kids, their friends, and any other kids on the

ON SCENE

streets of Prince Albert would have swarmed the car, excited to see the officers and begging them to turn the siren on. Sometimes he handed out gum but he doubted that would be well received here after they stated their business. Anson turned the wheel sharply, pulled a one-eighty, and parked the car on the opposite corner of the house, headlights facing the road exit. None of the kids moved so much as an inch.

"Might as well see if you can find anything in the truck. I'll go up and knock. Glad he's home, at least." Anson had the car in park and the door open almost before Bob could agree. He strode with purpose up to the porch while Bob got out and went to the driver's window of the run down truck. Hearing the front door of the house creak open, he tore his gaze away from Doug's back and cupped his hands around his eyes, pressing his face to the dingy window. There was nothing. Not so much as a tissue. He tried the handle and, not surprisingly, the door popped open. Nobody ever locked anything around here. He hauled the heavy door open wide and leaned across the torn seat to get a better look at the passenger side. Smells of oil and sawdust wafted from tattered seat covers. The truck was empty of everything: tools of the man's trade, garbage, a discarded lunch box, there was nothing that he'd normally expect to see in a work truck. Even the rear gun rack was empty. He got out and slammed the door. Upon closer inspection, the truck had been black once upon a time. The long box sides were as high as his shoulder, and he looked up at the wooden slats towering far above his head. Peeking between the slats into the truck bed, he saw a blanket of wood chips. The truck would hold a lot of wood. It would take a heck of a lot of work to fill it.

A worn down mouse of a woman with a messy pile of dark hair tied up on top of her head stood on the porch with a blank look on her face.

"Is Stanley here, Mrs. Robertson?" Anson patted his jacket pockets, shoulders lowering in defeat.

The woman's staring eyes didn't react and Bob pressed in closer to the truck to see better. "Darn it, just a minute," Anson looked back at the cruiser. "I'm sorry, be right back." He ran down the few steps, threw open the police car door and rummaged around in the front seat. Staying out of the woman's line of sight, Bob kept his eyes on Mrs. Robertson as she smoothed the front of her apron down her legs over and over again.

He caught Anson's eye when he turned away from the cruiser, pointed at the truck and shook his head. Anson nodded once and took the four rickety porch steps in two long strides. Bob paced down the side of the truck, looking in the back and underneath. He stayed out of sight of the nearest window, but kept a clear view of Doug.

"There, sorry about that." Anson held up the pen and notebook for the woman to see. "Is Stanley home?" She stepped aside and Doug went into the house, allowing the creaking door to gently swing shut behind him, the dirt on the window and the sun's glare obscuring Bob's view.

"What does he want?" A voice echoed from inside the house.

There was no discernible reply.

Every hair on Bob's neck prickled.

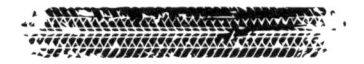

Standing in the doorway, Doug's eyes met Mrs. Robertson's for a split second before the gunshot to his chest wheeled him around.

Was there apology in those non-descript eyes? Triumph?

He didn't know.

A pen and his zippered case slipped from his grasp and hit the floor. He staggered towards the door, reaching out for the handle.

His shouted warning to Schrader came out in a strangled gurgle.

The second shot hit him square in the back, propelling him forward through the front door and off the step. His last breath left him like a gentle breeze and he hit the ground.

Pure police instinct made Bob react with the first shot. Intense shock not slowing his instant crouch, eyes surveying the integrity of the surrounding cover, his hand going to his right hip. The emptiness there wrenched his heart

ON SCENE

and his hand squeezed into a fist. Diving around the side of the truck, he saw Anson facing him through the open front door. Where had the shot come from? He stood cautiously, taking a step towards Doug.

"Run."

The word he thought came from Anson's mouth wasn't loud enough to hear but the intensity reverberated through him.

Their eyes met but there was no time to react.

A second shot sent Anson hurling off the porch, arms outstretched in a silent plea for help. He landed face down in the dirt in front of the step, papers fluttering down around him, the wool of his uniform darkening from brown to black.

Bob's body convulsed and he hit the ground, slid through the dirt, taking cover behind the truck. He was too far from Anson to help him, too far from the cruiser to get his gun, and too helpless for his mind to comprehend.

"Stay down, Anson!" he ordered in a bellow that carried clear across the yard, then flattened himself against the side of the truck, keeping one eye on the door, judging the distance between himself and the car. He squeezed his hand closed again, willing the heaviness of his gun to magically appear there but this was real life. There was no such thing as magic.

After the second blast everything in the yard froze. Children, dogs, chickens. Everything. Only the dust in front of the porch moved, kicked up in a body-shaped cloud when Anson hit the ground. It settled on him in the ensuing silence.

Bob saw the barrel of a gun poke through the door. Any chance of reaching the police car was abandoned. He couldn't help Doug if he got himself shot trying to get to his weapon.

Seeing more cover near some decrepit grain bins behind him, he slid around the back of the truck and noted the single boarded up window on this side of the house. Making a run for it, he grabbed a little girl, her long, untied hair blowing in his face and wrapping around his neck as he clutched her. He shoved her behind a tree halfway between the truck and the bins. Whoever was shooting from inside the house surely wouldn't shoot a child?

"Doug. Anson! Answer me, son." Bob debated the intelligence of drawing attention to his location with his shouts, but on the other hand, it would take the shooter's aim away from Doug. He turned to make the run from the tree to the grain bins when a shot took a sizeable chunk out of the tree above his head. He ducked, hands protecting his face and the little girl from flying splinters. She never uttered a sound.

"Hold your fire. I have to help my man!" Leaving the child in the cover of the tree, Bob rose from his crouched position, running to the grain bins, breath coming in short gasps, lungs burning in the cold air. Another shot and he hit the dirt, crawling for cover. In decent shape even for a desk Sergeant, the cramp he got the last few feet took him by surprise. He grabbed at the front of his uniform, low on his stomach. His hand came away warm and slippery.

A monotone voice called out from the partially open door, but Bob couldn't quite make it out. His mind otherwise occupied, conversation was not high on his priority list.

Bob pressed on his stomach, welcoming the pain that kept him alert. Somewhere, a baby cried. It transported him for a second to the first time he heard each of his children cry. Their noise hadn't stopped, just changed in volume. He wanted nothing more than to hear that noise again.

Pressing farther back in between the grain bins, he picked up his head, eyeing the two children he could see, and motioned for them to stay where they were. They stared at him like he was a foreign object.

Eyes darting every which way, brain moving even faster, he tried to take in everything at once. Two more children, a boy and a girl, calmly walked up the steps and into the house like their mother had just called them in for supper. It was boggling but he had to focus on what was in his control. There was more cover directly behind him over a fence and through the trees. It was just over a mile to town. He could run that easy, even injured, and call for backup.

Considering, he closed his eyes and rested his head against the cold wood, hearing the far off wailing of the baby again.

No.

A plan to escape hadn't even fully formulated in his head before he put it aside. He wouldn't leave these children. He wouldn't leave Anson.

ON SCENE

Getting back to his feet, he glanced around the side of the rickety building, trying to get a glimpse of who was shooting. When he moved his head, he caught sight of the little girl he pushed behind the tree, peering out at her siblings, grubby thumb planted firmly in her mouth. Bob waved his hand frantically, trying to silently order her back behind the tree. She flinched, her lip quivering, and stared with impossibly wide eyes at her older brother by the truck. The boy, who looked about the same age as Terry, beckoned to his sister. Schrader waved his arms again, shaking his head violently so she didn't dash into the open where bullets were finding their mark with frightening accuracy.

Gathering courage around him like armour, he put one foot under him and struggled up. Weakening before he could get steady, he fell back, head thumping painfully against the wood. The girl pulled her thumb out of her mouth. She was going to run. He took two deep breaths and jerked his leg under himself again, gripping the side of the bin and steadying his other foot firmly beneath him before letting go. He needed another deep, deliberate breath to hold onto that armour before moving but the child bolted. Sprinting, he grabbed the girl on the fly and all but threw her behind the truck. Hands slick with sweat and blood and gasping for breath, he gripped the side of the truck box to steady himself. The child clung to her brother, staring up at Bob with a silent fear he didn't understand. She looked nothing like his Lynn, but he felt a fierce need to protect this child, whether she trusted that or not.

He couldn't protect Anson. The realization knocked out what little breath he had left. His chest ached and it took him what felt like a full minute to suck in another full breath. The children stared at him, one with fear, the other with what could be written off as hate but Bob saw an overriding curiosity in the older boy's eyes. There were dark circles there, like he'd seen too much work in his few years on earth. A scar near his mouth twitched and he used the tail of his shirt to wipe a smear of blood off his sister's chin. He looked at Bob again, making Bob look down. The blood had taken over the lower half of his jacket. He forced his eyes away from the spreading stain. Questions clouded the boy's eyes but he still didn't speak.

From his vantage point behind the truck, Bob could see Doug still face down by the porch. He hadn't moved and part of Bob died. He made a guttural noise of determination, more for his own resolve than anything else. The far side of the house was closer to the police car than where he stood now. To get to the cruiser from here, he would have to cross the front of the house, the open door, and a window, but if he looped around the back of the house, came in from the west side, he might be able to reach his radio. That is, if there were no windows at the back of the house, or on the west side.

Those were big bloody 'ifs'.

Glancing around to make sure no one else was in harm's way, he retraced his steps back to the cover of the bins. His limbs felt heavy; his brain was functioning far faster than his body could respond. In his mind, he had already made it to the grain bins, but in reality he had only gone a few steps when he stumbled, faltering to one knee. He crawled the rest of the way to the tree. Sitting with his back against it, legs splayed out in front of him, he reached under his glasses to wipe the sweat from his eyes. Pulling his hand away, he squinted. It was red and sticky and his vision blurred. He took off his glasses and used his sleeve to swipe at his burning eyes, then put his glasses back on. Reaching down he pushed hard on his injury, willing more pain to keep him sharp and alert. Good cover looked a million miles away.

Breathing hard he gasped, "Come on, Bob."

Getting to his knees, he laboured to his feet, hugging the tree for support. He was going to make it to the grain bins and around the back of the house. He would call for help on the radio. He wanted the chance to take this shooter down.

You're going to make it. You're going to get him.

Staggering across the uneven ground, he tensed, fighting off the fingers of fear trailing up his back. He saw the sanctuary of the space between the grain bins and lurched forward, throwing himself between them with a groan of pain.

Not wanting to stop for long, knowing the throbbing would hold him down if he gave in to it, he got his feet under him again and peered out from the other side of his cover. Abandoned pieces of ancient farm equipment dotted the landscape between him and the far northwest corner of the house. Tall grass grew up around the machinery, creating another hiding spot if he crouched low enough behind the rusted, jutting metal.

ON SCENE

Ready in mind and spirit, he set off towards the next bit of cover but his body was slow to cooperate. His left leg went out from under him and he fell to his knee, inner thigh of his right leg exposed.

It was the only opening the shooter needed.

He yelled and fell, clutching his leg. He rolled onto his side, dragging himself a few feet. "Stop! We aren't armed. Let the children go…please." Writhing to his other side, he pulled himself another foot or two, trying to reach the cover of the abandoned machinery. The stark reality of the situation blurred in his mind's eye, and he thought maybe he was within a stone's throw of cover. Safety. He dragged himself another foot, hands clawing at the clumps of grass.

Strength running out, he fumbled to feel where he'd been hit the second time. There was too much blood to see anything and it all felt warm and slick. Already lying down, he turned over and collapsed fully on an exhale, banging the back of his head on the ground.

He roared at the sky and slammed his head back again, revelling in any feeling he had left. His lower half was going numb, part pins and needles and part…nothing at all.

The sun was fat, sitting on the horizon, just thinking about starting its disappearing act. Suppertime in the fall, your eyes played tricks on you. Edges blurred with golden light, and his vision shifted in and out of focus.

He never had the opportunity to face the shooter, but the last shot belonged to him.

Whether he wanted it or not.

He would not accept it willingly and screamed his objection at the setting sun.

Search Continues For Robertson-*Neighbours described Robertson as a quiet man who worked hard to support his wife and eight children and who was 'more a woodsman than a farmer.' They said he…was an 'A-1 marksman.'*

Headline and excerpt, Saskatoon StarPhoenix (Friday, October 16, 1970)

Chapter Six

Friday, October 9, 1970
Robertson yard
Just after 5:30pm

Nobody moved. Nothing stirred inside the house. Nothing stirred outside the house. After the first two shots were fired, and for the space of at least two breaths, nothing happened. When the officer fell off the step, the children in the yard disappeared behind trees and farm equipment; the ones still sitting in the kitchen were silently staring down at their supper plates. The baby was crying, if only because her mother clutched her far too tightly.

A yell from outside startled Stanley so violently his weapon slipped from his sweaty hand. Tightening his hold before it hit the floor he whispered, "There's another one?" Storming over to a boarded up window in the bedroom, he reached into his pocket for more ammunition. Methodically reloading his rifle, he watched, heart pounding.

A second officer. Double the death. How many more were there?

"He'll get you." The whisper floated from a corner of the kitchen and he whipped around to stare at Ruth through the bedroom door. She pointed a finger at him but didn't say anything else, lowering the finger to cup the baby's head with a shaking hand. Her dry eyes had no life but spoke volumes to him.

ON SCENE

She finally won.

Another yell drew his attention and he ran back to the door where the first Mountie lay, trying to zero in on the new target. Faced with the real possibility of being arrested, he needed to get rid of the threat. It would be fine. He would just stay quiet. He wouldn't bother anyone. After this, he'd just keep quietly working and the law would leave him alone. He peeked through the narrow sliver of daylight between the hinges on the open door. Nothing. He left the front door and went back to the boarded up bedroom window, peering carefully through slats that didn't quite meet. They were far enough apart to get a good shot off.

Two of his children stood stock still by the truck. They weren't in danger. He moved a hair to his left and saw his daughter peeking out from behind the tree. She was a lot shorter than his target. He pulled off a third round above the Mountie's head, driving him away from the child.

"Hold your fire! I have to help my man!"

He saw his mark disappear out of his line of sight when the officer ran for the grain bins around the back. He came out of the bedroom and crossed the floor, closing the gap to the back door in just a few strides.

Things weren't as crisp at this time of day, the sun casting a glow on everything, but he could make out the darkness of the officer's uniform jacket against the faded grey of the grain bins and squeezed off another shot.

"I'll help your man. I'll help you, too." His voice sounded foreign to his own ears. That fourth shot met its mark, he was sure, but the officer got himself into the tight space before Stanley could pull the trigger again. He knew the man was hit. He never missed, even when the target was never meant to be a target at all. By habit, he stooped and picked up the shell casing, dropping it into his front jacket pocket.

Then he waited.

Any hunter who knew anything would wait for an injured animal to make their move. They would either try to escape, or just give up and die. Stanley didn't get the impression this man had a habit of giving up.

He cracked the door open a little farther, just enough to see that his daughter wanted to go to her brother over by the truck.

The girl darted out under his watchful eye, the area still lined up and steady in his sight.

"Fast," Stanley mumbled, jerking his finger off the trigger, laying it alongside. He watched the officer run to his daughter, grab her, and carry her to the truck. Surely the idiot didn't think he would shoot his own daughter?

The officer let go of the little girl and got down before Stanley could put him back in the rifle sight.

He hesitated. A family man himself, in his mind everything he did was for the good of his children. He loathed killing a man with the same values. A man who would put a stranger's children before his own safety. He shook his head sharply; it didn't make sense. This Mountie needed killing, or Stanley would end up rotting in a cell.

It was either kill quickly, or be killed agonizingly slowly.

Decision made, he turned back to the front door where he'd have a better view of the truck at the side of the house but stopped short. Ruth stood in the same spot, clutching the baby to her apron front. The three younger children sat at the table, none of them looking up. The hesitation was miniscule but there, a stutter in his step to the front door. He acknowledged they were there, but had nothing else. There was no coming back from this. No apologies.

He got to the front door in time to see the officer make another play for the back of the house. He wheeled around and retraced his path to the back door, throwing it open wide this time. If the officer hadn't fired back by now, he wasn't going to. Stanley pressed the butt of his rifle tight into his shoulder and eyed the sight. The officer made it back to the tree but lost his footing, dragging himself behind the thick trunk. Stanley waited to see what he would do. Barely breathing, the smell of gunpowder burned his nose but comforted him at the same time.

He waited, eye twitching, ear resting on his shoulder, listening to his own breathing. There was a catch every now and again that he didn't like. Not a hiccup, just a…catch. An awful marker that he didn't want to be here doing this thing. He drew another breath and held it.

There it was. A flurry of movement and the officer was up again, running back to the grain bins. Stanley missed his chance to fire, his mind wandering a line of thought he never had while hunting. What was this man doing? He was unarmed, that much was clear, but still stayed to make sure the children were secure. It confused Stanley more than why his woman wouldn't stay home at night.

He didn't have more time to consider the officer's motive, following him as he came out from his cover again.

Standing in the doorway, he tracked the officer, seeming large as life in his sight as he wasn't but twenty yards away. The man staggered with a will Stanley wondered if he ever possessed himself. He could almost admire him, if he wasn't so scared of what the officer would do to him if Stanley allowed him to live.

Even in the gathering dusk, he could easily make out the bright yellow stripe on the man's uniform pants. The officer faltered again, went down on one knee, exposing the inside of his leg.

He ignored the man's will, his concern for a stranger's children, and zeroed in on this one vulnerability.

The fifth shot laid the officer out on the ground, thrashing like a wounded bear. Stanley inhaled, not realizing he was still holding his breath. Was it over?

The officer was kicking up a ruckus.

He set his rifle down against the wall and covered his ears, but nothing could block out the sound. The blood-chilling yell grabbed Stanley's fear with a mighty squeeze. He rocked back and forth, clenching his eyes shut, pressing his hands harder over his ears, but the screaming went on.

This man fought. He fought empty-handed, for his own life, his partner's life, and the lives of children he didn't know.

A low moaning started, not quite a sob. He squeezed tighter and tighter but couldn't cover his ears hard enough.

Kate Kading

It took him a long while to realize he couldn't block it out because the sound was coming from deep inside himself.

> *"If I think of anything else to help, I'll let you know. I don't understand what got into him to do a thing like that. If I'd knew they quarrelled, I'd understand what got into him but he never quarrelled."* Refused to sign his statement saying *"My word is as good as I say it is."*
>
> *Excerpt from interview with Robertson's father-in-law, Albert Dallman (Oct 1970)*

Chapter Seven

Friday, October 9, 1970
Prince Albert, Saskatchewan
RCMP Detachment
1803hrs

"Prince Albert RCMP, Constable Cavello speaking." Danny should have left an hour before, but the pile of paperwork on his desk wasn't going to take care of itself. Phone calls after office hours were uncommon so he didn't mind answering. It was usually someone looking for the Sergeant or wanting to report loose cattle. All he heard was rapid breathing.

"Hello? This is the RCMP. How can I help you?" He tapped his pen on the desk, impatient but trying to hang on to a measure of courtesy. "Hello? Anyone there?" He shrugged and pulled the receiver away from his ear, hand already on the way to hanging up.

"I need…" a thin female voice and some static caught his attention and he jerked the phone back up to his ear. Another pause. "…he—help. I need help." The caller stuttered on her few words, and at the end of the faltering sentence he thought he heard the word 'dead.' Every hair on the back of his neck stood up. Ears tuned for the smallest sound, he sat perfectly still, waiting for more. Nothing came.

"Hello? Ma'am, are you there? Say that again?" He pressed his ear closer to the receiver, his whole body straining to hear what he thought he heard. His heart banged away in his head, the loud racket impairing his senses.

The voice on the other end of the line had been tinny, quiet on the first use but came through firm this time. "Them cops is dead. He shot 'em." A ragged intake of breath and the line went silent again.

"Where? What cops? What's your name?" Danny's entire body thumped in tune with his hammering heart. He strained to hear the voice over his body's reaction.

A pause long enough for the bile to rise in his throat, and then, "Robertson. The name's Robertson. Out MacDowall way. Two police shot. You better come." The voice went soft again, but the direction was clear. There was sadness in the echo, desolation in the hesitation between words. A click, and the dial tone followed.

Hand on the radio as he hung up the phone, there was no pause in his actions. No panic, either. He needed his strong, deep voice to reach out from the radio and grab hold of every RCMP officer in the vicinity.

"10-33." He put the radio mouthpiece to his forehead and blinked hard for the barest hint of a second. Dragging it back to his mouth, he pushed the words from tight lips. "10-33 MacDowall, shots fired. Location to follow." He threw down the handset, stomped through the office with the purpose of a freight train, grabbed his gear, and unlocked the rifle cabinet.

He didn't get far before the phone rang again. In the breath it took him to acknowledge the phone, a passing thought urged him to ignore it. Get to the scene. But it could be his superior officers, wanting an explanation. There'd be a lot of overturned supper plates and Mounties heading for the door. Spinning on his heel, he went back to the desk.

"Cavello," he yelled into the receiver. He listened to the caller for a moment before a wave of nausea had him bracing a forearm on the counter. They were asking for Sergeant Schrader.

"He's busy," he shouted, slamming the receiver down, vowing to atone for his actions later.

ON SCENE

He stormed the gun cabinet like a rampaging monster, anything unnecessary flung to the floor. With three .308 rifles under his arm, and as much ammunition as he could carry, he came down the stairs, boots sounding like rapid repeating gunshots. Each one tore through his head where the ten-code ricocheted around.

10-33. *Help me quick.*

Only used in extreme emergencies, it was the ten-code no officer wanted to hear. Or use. 10-33 would bring the cavalry.

Armed.

Ready for anything.

He could hear distant sirens as he threw everything into the police car and tore out of the parking lot. He flipped on his light and siren, careening with controlled precision down the main road leading out of town.

A few blocks from the detachment he saw a uniform walking away from him and jerked the wheel, screeching to a stop.

The officer swung around, confusion stark on his face as he yanked open the passenger door of the cruiser. "What are you doing, Cavello?" Brent Jette yelled over the siren. "For fuck's sake."

"Get in. 33."

Jette did a double take but took no time to react. He stuck his cigarette between his lips, slipped the baton off his belt, threw it into the car, and jumped in after it.

Danny hammered on the gas and was away from the curb before Jette closed the door.

He swerved in and out of traffic until they hit the open highway, two more cars blaring their presence behind them. He could just make out the top of an ambulance several cars back in his rear view mirror.

"Alpha two-one-two, you have a 20?"

Danny didn't recognize the member on the radio but he didn't care. All hands on deck.

"Robertson place. Anyone know where that is?" His question burst out louder than he intended but if that was the only by-product of the adrenaline pumping through his body, he would take it and run. Jette's dark, heavy eyebrows shot through his hairline.

"Anson?" he asked.

Danny shrugged the shoulder closest to Jette, keeping his eyes on the road and his ear on the radio.

"10-4. I'm right behind you, Cavello." He recognized the voice of one of their commanding officers, Staff Sergeant Al Mosher. Danny breathed easier. "Hit the road into MacDowall, go past the bar, and straight south less than two miles. All units, confirm. I'm first on scene." 10-4s rang out one after the other. A slice of fear was replaced with confidence.

A drive that should have taken nearly half an hour was cut in half. Vehicles trundling down Highway 11 south cleared a path for the convoy of wailing sirens. Besides the few questions Danny could answer about the what and the who, Jette knew enough to keep the why questions to himself. They didn't speak, listening to the radio chatter the rest of the way.

"Silent entry. Lead car, block visual." Even over the crackling radio, Staff Sergeant Mosher's voice was steady and commanding. As they approached the MacDowall access sign, one by one each car turned their top light and siren off, not slowing or hesitating for a moment. The dogleg into town past the café and gas station should have been taken slower, but Cavello didn't let up on the gas pedal. Jette kept a firm grip on the dash with one hand, and the roof with the other as three cars took the curve in a shower of gravel and dust.

The back road was unforgiving but the police cars were built to withstand a terrible beating and keep on going. That's what they did.

The first car in the line up, Danny saw the break in the trees for the yard approach.

"Hold on," he said, stomping on the brakes and skidding into the opening, ass end of the car swinging in behind, he spun the wheel in the opposite direction to compensate and straightened out on the narrow driveway.

ON SCENE

Slowing considerably, they both craned their necks, eyes alert and searching for movement. The long driveway was only wide enough for one car, a stand of spindly trees and brush lining both sides with open fields visible beyond.

He eyed Jette and figured they both had the same thought.

They were leading everyone into the complete unknown.

"Hold up, Alpha two-one-two."

Mosher's voice was tight and Danny's attention zeroed in on the order. He reacted without thinking, stopping the car halfway up to the house.

"10-4." There was a pause but not silence. They heard rustling and murmuring over the radio.

Mosher's voice came back strong. "Back cars, move ahead. I need a blockade here." The cars crept into position at Mosher's command. They flanked Cavello's car in a rough triangle, driving over bush and forcing it aside. The screech of unforgiving branches scraping the metal of the vehicles reached Danny through his open window, making him shudder.

Rolling forward, they stayed in formation, waiting for the direct order to stop. Danny slid the car into park and leaned forward as far as he could, squinting at the front part of the yard.

"You see anything?" he whispered at Jette.

"Nothing useful. Can't see past that truck."

It was the point of dusk where you weren't quite sure what you were looking at. Not dark, but not entirely light either. The space in between. Dusk, with ghosts waiting in the wings. The trees cast long shadows, hiding sins and shame.

"I want someone on that back door, one directly across from the front door, one on that truck, and one covering from the rear. Nothing holstered." Mosher's voice was quick and clipped, leaving no room for side thought.

They threw open their doors nearly in unison. Without knowing who would do what, the team fanned out in uniform formation, weapons drawn and ready.

"Back clear."

"Shotgun covering from the rear."

"4. Truck clear."

"Shed across from the house, clear. I can see something in the yard. Gonna need some lights soon." Danny took up his position on the corner of a dilapidated shed on the edge of the yard straight across from the main door of the house. He sat maybe twenty long paces from the doorstep with a decent view of the immediate yard. Not six feet from him a small toy car lay on its side, abandoned by its owner. Scanning farther out, trying to get as many details embedded in his brain before the darkness took over, he could see a pile of something on the ground in front of the steps. In the fast-fading light, the shadows were too long to make it out, and the headlights from his cruiser only illuminated the back of the big, rundown truck which was blocking the light from going any farther.

"Stand by, Cavello. I'm bringing a light. Keep your heads down, could still be an active shooter." Mosher used the cover of the cars to snake his way to Cavello's position with a spotlight from the trunk of one of the vehicles. Just an oversized flashlight, they were good for scaring off poachers or illuminating secret spots in dark alleys in the city where trouble liked to hide.

"Hold your positions," Mosher said.

"We need a dog. Where's Sergeant Regitnig?" Danny asked, voice low as Mosher approached.

"En route. He was chasing for Melfort detachment. Called him the second you put out the 33."

Danny's relief was audible.

When Mosher flipped the switch on the spotlight, the unidentified pile in front of the stairs took shape. The spectacle before them was like nothing Danny had seen before, and nothing he wished to ever see again. Face down, arms askew, the back of the brown wool uniform stained black, papers scattered all around.

It was one of their own.

ON SCENE

"...We could see an object lying on the ground near the door. An Identification Section member arrived with a powerful spotlight as did an ambulance, a doctor, and additional members. Once the light was trained on the object it was obvious that it was one of the members."

Interview with Anson's best friend (April 2016)

Chapter Eight

Friday, October 9, 1970
Prince Albert, Saskatchewan
Schrader house
Suppertime

"Arries, supper." Lynn flung herself around the wall, bellowing up the stairwell at her brothers. There was an awful racket coming from the second floor, crashing to equal a dinosaur coming through the ceiling, but as long as nobody was bleeding, she wasn't going to concern herself with it. Only one day away from her sixteenth birthday, she was in charge of the house while her mother was in the hospital, and she was ticking her evening chores off the list so she could go over to Jeanette's house for an early birthday party.

"Arries, I said supper!" The crashing reached a mind-jarring crescendo and in turn, three of the four 'Arries' came rattling down the stairs, hanging off the banister and banging into walls. Larry, Garry, and Terry pushed past her into the kitchen.

"Where's Barry?" She crossed her arms over her chest, an expectant eyebrow raised at her twin brother.

He shrugged. "How should I know?" Larry's mouth was full of potato, before he even pulled a chair up to the table. She rolled her eyes and grabbed at Garry.

ON SCENE

"Where's your brother? You need to keep track of each other." She was trying to hold onto her patience, but sometimes it was a challenge being the only girl. Garry dodged around her outstretched arm and grabbed a plate and fork from the counter.

"I think he went to Jed's house for supper. Why do I need to keep track of 'im? You don't keep track of Larry." Garry plunked his plate down at the table, cramming meat into his mouth, uncut. Around the mouthful he slurred, "Where's Dad? Think he'll take me over to the rink?"

Lynn looked at the wall clock. It wasn't unusual for their dad to be late, but you could count on the suppertime phone call if something held him up.

"I don't know. Just eat. I'll call the office." She crossed to the phone, jabbed her fingers into the dial one number at a time, and waited for an answer to the jangling.

She jerked slightly at the abruptness of the answer.

"Hi, this is Lynn. Is my dad there?" She didn't often call the detachment, but was always met with a friendly voice on the other end, no matter who was there.

"He's busy." The phone was slammed down with such force she jerked the receiver away from her ear. Frowning, she shook her head.

"Okay, that's weird." She rolled her eyes and hung up the phone. Filling her own plate, she cringed at the mess her brothers were making.

"You guys are so gross. Can't you just be normal?" She put an arm out to stop Garry from throwing a spoon at Terry. The only Schrader child with no twin to back him up, Terry often relied on his older sister for protection. She didn't blink as she smoothly took the spoon, set it beside her plate, and started eating.

The wail of sirens made all four heads snap towards the window. The older three lost interest immediately and turned their attention back to their plates, but Terry jumped from his seat and flattened himself to the huge dining room window in time to see three police cars and an ambulance whiz by.

"Neat!" he exclaimed. Lynn got up and guided him back to the table.

61

"Come on, bud. Eat. I have to get over to Jeanette's. Larry will look after you until Dad gets home. You can go to the hospital and visit Mom later." She gently pressed on his shoulder and he sat, then she went back to her own supper. She smiled at the thought of her best friend, Jeanette. She didn't know what was planned for her early birthday party but she was looking forward to it. If it didn't involve cooking supper or making sure her brothers didn't annihilate each other or any of the neighbours, she'd take it as a successful evening. It had been a busy couple of days holding down the fort.

That morning, her dad had given her a tight hug, whispering in her ear, "One more day, sweetheart." She'd squeezed back with all her might, revelling in the brief attention. She reminded him she'd be heading out after supper, and he was excited for her. He always was when she had something that was just hers. He made such an effort to make sure she knew he was proud of her.

She couldn't wait to tell her dad all about the party. Maybe they'd have a midnight snack together like they often did when he came in late. To that end, after she put her empty plate in the sink, she cut an extra large piece of cake from the dessert she'd baked before supper. From the obnoxious rumblings coming from the dining room, she knew if she didn't set some aside now, there would be nothing left after her brothers got into it. She put it on a plate and strategically hid it behind a big jar of bread and butter pickles on the top shelf in the fridge. Nobody would find it there.

"Just for us," she whispered with a sweet smile. "See you later, Daddy."

Jealous husband shot to death two Mounties--*Schrader was always a peaceable man. He didn't believe in carrying a gun into a domestic situation, especially when children were present. The Robertsons had eight children.*

Headline and excerpt, Prince Albert Daily Herald
(Tuesday October 3, 1995)

Chapter Nine

Friday, October 9, 1970
On Scene
1930hrs

Before the gut wrenching yell could escape him, Danny felt a sharp, painful grip on his arm. Grunting, he tried to jerk free. Staff Sergeant Mosher kept his grip up with one hand and spoke into his radio with the other.

"You all listen good. We have one officer confirmed down and no eyes on a shooter. I don't give a damn what you see, you stand fast and keep your heads down until I give the order. Check in. Relay positions."

"10-4, sir. Greenslade. At the truck."

"Jones here. 10-4. Covering from the rear."

"Yes, sir. Jette here. Back corner of the house. Getting pretty dark out here."

Mosher exhaled sharply. "Stay put, Jette. I have a light coming to you. Cavello is with me. I have eyes on one body—" Mosher was cut off by a loud crackle and he let go of his radio button.

"Responding to the 33, repeat location, over."

The radios blasted with the voice of another member, trying to get on scene. "Goddamn it, I need radio silence. Robertson farm, south of MacDowall. If you don't know where it is, get a fucking rural map and figure it out."

Mosher let the order sink in across the airwaves, keen eyes still on the move, watching all around them. It was the only time Danny had ever witnessed Al Mosher lose his patience.

"Greenslade, you and Cavello go get our man. Jones and I will cover. Stay low, get out fast." Mosher released Danny's arm at the same time as his radio button, face intent, surveying Danny in the cast off glow from the spotlight he had propped up in the dirt. Danny swallowed hard. All the fear, anguish, and doubt forming a heavy ball in his throat. That stuff didn't go down easy.

"I'm good. Cover me." He gripped Mosher's shoulder, taking from the contact, however brief, a bit of the Staff Sergeant's stability and grit. He adjusted his right hand on the grip of his revolver, cupped his other hand underneath, and took a breath to steady himself. He crouched low and ran across the open yard towards Greenslade at the truck. Ducking his head, he spared only quick glances left and right as he ran, intent on his destination.

He rushed up on the truck and pressed his back against it, the solid metal grounding him, but not enough to eliminate the bullseye he felt. "See anything?" he whispered to Greenslade, half crouched beside him. Greenslade shook his head. Danny found it unsettling for the usually outspoken guy to be so silent. He was the kind of man you wanted on your cover. He never missed a thing and had the heart of a lion.

Even through his silence, the look on Greenslade's face spoke volumes. He wanted to know.

"Pop up and look over there." Danny pointed over the front of the truck towards the house and switched spots with Greenslade, adrenaline making his heart skip and jump. He pressed harder into the truck, trying to erase the feeling of eyes on his back.

Greenslade's sharp intake of breath was the only outward sign of upset, but he suppressed it faster than Danny had.

Finding his voice again, he grabbed Danny's sleeve. "Fuck, we have to go now. We have to get him." Greenslade readjusted his grip on his gun, wiping his palms against his pants one after the other. Readying himself at the front end of the truck, he hissed, "You ready?"

ON SCENE

One quick nod was all the go ahead needed. Keeping his weapon up, Danny ran in a crouch on Greenslade's left. They made their way across the yard to the officer face down in the dirt. His skin crawled, the back of his neck burning with the knowledge that it could be in the crosshairs. Danny always felt somewhat invincible in his uniform, but it was ludicrously inadequate against a bullet. He'd never felt so defenceless.

Holstering their weapons beside the body, they threw themselves over the downed man. They waited for a shot. Some form of attack.

A count of three passed and Danny nodded again, not sure if Greenslade could even see him but they didn't falter and each grabbed an arm of the victim, dragging him back to the truck. Danny's heart pounded so ferociously he feared others would hear it, or that it would fail him altogether.

Crouched behind the truck, Greenslade popped his head up again, surveying the darkness left to right, then dropped back down, hand on the neck of the fallen officer. "Can we help him? Who is it?" he whispered. Cavello stopped him from flipping the body over.

"No time, let's get him safe. Take his feet." He knew it was either Schrader or Anson, but didn't allow for the luxury of which to mourn at the moment. The skin on the back of his neck prickled in warning. He still felt like eyes were boring into his back and they sure didn't need another dead Mountie on this farm. He motioned to the other end, gripping the limp officer's arms. The second Greenslade secured the officer's legs, they took off, half carrying, half dragging the body back behind the old shed. Mosher kept the light hidden to give them a measure of cover in the descending darkness.

Only when they had their backs against solid wood again did Danny let his breath out and dare to look and see which of his friends was at his feet. With great care, Mosher turned the body over and put a hand on the officer's head, shining his flashlight on the face.

"10-33. Anson is down." Radio silence broken, the airwaves erupted with responses.

"Rosthern Detachment 17."

"North Battleford, ETA fifteen minutes."

There were a few other snippets, some drowned out by others, all trying to answer at the same time. Location and directions repeated.

Danny sat on the ground, firearm back in his hand, his other hand on Anson's shoulder, the body tucked up beside his leg. Adrenaline drove him, keeping him sharp and aware of his surroundings. He clenched his fist into Anson's jacket and took a deep breath. When he let it out his heart dropped through the bottom of his stomach. The wave of grief was overwhelming for the moment he allowed it.

Like a silent movie, the events of the day played back in his head, daring his thoughts to imagine Doug as anything but vibrantly alive and excited for his wedding dance.

"Oh, God. I'm sorry, Vallarena." His breath caught in his throat and he clenched his fist harder, the rough fabric biting at his palm. Anson's eyes stared up at him, imploring.

Find him.

Questions shot around inside Danny's head like a dozen ping pong balls and he lifted his gaze to Mosher.

"Where's Schrader?"

> "In the close proximity of the front door, where ANSON's body was found, an R.C.M.P. Stetson was lying on the ground. Approximately 2½' East of that was a large pool of blood."
>
> *Excerpt of report by Corporal R.H. Waller, Rosthern Detachment (1970)*

Chapter Ten

```
Friday, October 9, 1970
Robertson yard
5:50pm
```

Stanley didn't look anyone in the eye. The silence punched him, steadily stealing his breath. Never setting down his rifle, he gathered up his jacket and hat and went out the front door, stepping over papers and a leather case scattered on the steps. He stood at the dead officer's feet, glad he was face down and not staring accusations straight into Stanley's eyes. He reached over to yank the officer's gun from the holster, gave it a shake, and tried to pull it free. Eyeing the snap on the side, he put his jacket and hat down, grasped the snap with both thumbs, and flung it off its base, freeing the weapon with a grunt. Coming down so close to the body, his attention centred on some fluttering pages he hadn't noticed before. Neatly written words jumped off the page and slammed Stanley in the head. *Nelson. Gun. Altercation.* He reached across the dead officer and grabbed for the papers. Nobody ever needed to see that.

The body shifted with the movement and Stanley's heart seized with fear. He hastily straightened, backed up, and met his oldest son's quizzical gaze. They stood there, silent, a lifetime of questions flying from the child's eyes. Stanley looked away, gathered his pile of warm clothes and weapons, eyeing the police car parked on an angle in the yard.

The only plan he had was placing one foot in front of the other. Anything past that was a mystery to him.

Eleven. It took him eleven steps to reach the driver side door of the police car. He grasped the door handle and the cold metal jarred him far enough out of his haze to glance up again. Expecting his son to still be staring, questioning, Stanley almost succeeded in averting his eyes, but the urge to look up was stronger than before. He stared past the red dome on top of the police car straight into the eyes of his father. After forty-odd years on the same land, he was used to his father appearing out of nowhere. Always ghost-like, even in the crisp fall leaves. Gordon stepped through the bushes between Stanley's house and his own small cabin, far enough away to let another man mind his business, but close enough to silently ask *why*.

They held that gaze for what felt like an entire day. The old man's disappointment sliced into Stanley like tiny razor blades. One cut not big enough to cause much damage itself, but all together the slices would bleed his soul dry. He still stood with his hand on the car door handle, not knowing if he wasn't physically capable of breaking his father's eye contact, or if he just didn't want to, for fear of what came next.

His father's eyes swept down, along with the corners of his mouth, and he stepped back into the trees, as ethereal as when he stepped out of them.

Broken, Stanley rested his head on top of the car. Where was he? He needed something that made sense.

"What happened?" His head jerked up at the familiar voice of his sister. Jessie came out of the field where she always did, by the fence behind the shed. The area separating the family land from her house as a married woman was not large. Certainly not large enough to erase gunshots.

"Daddy shot two police," her nephew said matter-of-factly, standing beside the officer's body. Jessie rushed over to the boy, her intense eyes finding her brother's on the other side of the car. Eleven steps didn't seem far enough away from the critical eye of his older sister. She looked angry but he knew she would take care of everyone.

Stanley got into the police car and felt around for the keys. Everyone left their keys in the vehicle when they pulled up on someone's property, and to his relief, the cops were no exception. Not used to a vehicle far newer than his own, every movement he made was exaggerated. There was no reason to back up; they'd parked with the front of the car pointing out towards the road, but he reversed away from the body. He couldn't get far enough away from it. He veered to the right in a half circle and when he was sure he'd given a wide enough berth, he straightened out onto the long driveway and left the yard at a crawl. He didn't so much as glance in the rear view mirror for fear of seeing questions in his children's eyes and the truth of his circumstances written all over his sister's face.

> "The police came falling out the door, because he was dead, because he was shot. I knew he was shot because I heard the shot in the house. I don't think he moved. ... Then I ran down into the spruce and I hid behind a big tree. The (older) Policeman was still standing beside the granary when I hid behind the tree."
>
> Excerpt from recorded interview with Robertson child (Saturday, October 10, 1970)

Chapter Eleven

Friday, October 9, 1970
MacDowall, Saskatchewan
On Scene
2000hrs

Dogmasters were notorious for having a lead foot but Wally had never driven like this before. If getting on scene hadn't killed him yet, he wasn't going to let this shooter have a crack at him, either. "Regitnig and Bruce, 17." Wally squeezed the radio button until it bit into his thumb. "Eyes on a shooter? 20 on Schrader?" The radio crackled, cutting Mosher off, and Wally pounded on the side of the metal mounting.

Bruce barked and paced in the backseat, feeding off his master's building rage.

"Neg—" More static and whatever Mosher said was lost in the air. Wally gave the radio another solid punch. "Enter with caution." The last bit came through clearly and it was all he needed.

Bob was still out there.

They'd find him. Then they'd find the shooter. Doubt didn't live in Wally's mind.

He rolled up on the property, silent save for the fierce enthusiasm of his partner.

ON SCENE

"Bruce, be quiet." Wally snapped. The dog silenced instantly, alert and ready. Eyes never still, Wally pulled up behind the cover of three other police cars, got out, and ducked behind his door. He reached over and opened the back door, ordering Bruce to stay low and quiet. The dog hit the ground, slinking in beside Wally.

"I'm 23. Shut up." Wally's voice scraped like gravel across the airwaves. They were already taking a hell of a risk; they didn't need a radio transmission giving away their location.

Mosher stepped out a fraction of an inch from beside the shed, motioning the go ahead. Barely able to see the outline of the officers across the yard, Wally squinted at the horizon. The dream-like haze of the fall sunset would only give them a few more precious minutes of ghostly visibility. They needed to move.

Acknowledging Mosher with a nod, Wally and Bruce came out from behind the door, around the back of the car, hugging the treeline up to the house.

Keeping Bruce leashed, Wally held him in tight check. This situation was a sight different than what they had dealt with just a few hours before. There was no clear-cut chase here. He leaned down to Bruce, loosening his grip just enough for the dog to feel it.

"Where's Bob?" The dog tensed at the question. He yawned and licked his lips, high-pitched whine laced with anxiety. His body vibrated, fur on his withers standing straight up against Wally's forearm.

Bruce woofed softly beside his face. Wally stood up and they set off into the rapidly dying light, moving in behind a truck and making eye contact with the member at the corner of the house. Brent Jette, Wally noted with relief. Steady, reliable, kept his head in a crisis. He stood, revolver at the ready, back against the wall. Wally signalled him to cover as he and Bruce left the safety of the truck, and cleared the open space to the house.

Reaching Jette, he gripped the constable's shoulder and leaned into his ear, "You okay?"

Jette nodded. "Can't see shit." He jerked his head to the dim empty space ahead of them. "Bruce needs to get out there. I got a bad feeling. You know they got Anson?" Jette's green eyes stared intently into Wally's. Fear danced

71

up the back of his neck and he nodded curtly. The 'officer down' had come through loud and clear. It killed him to listen to the recovery of Anson's body over the radio. To not be there. But he was here now.

Wally tucked Bruce into a heel, both of them still but craving action. The soles of his feet prickled. There was a light on in the house, but only a few pale beams showed, reminding Wally of an old smuggler's lantern with its door slightly askew. Light peeked through the curtain of the one functional window they could see, a slice of light shone through a crack in the door, and then on the closest side of the house, slivers were seen around the edges of a boarded up window.

Nothing stirred.

The danger of the situation poked at him. You went an awful long time without breathing when you were trying to keep silent. When your lungs told you enough was enough, the huge gasp you wanted to take could be all an expert needed to find his mark. He gently turned his radio off. Mosher would never squawk it in a situation like this, but he wasn't the only officer here. Anyone could ask a question without thinking and cost him his life.

Not today.

"All right, Chief." Wally's whisper set the dog on edge, low growl rumbling through him. Wally silenced him, gave him a hard pat on the side and whispered, "Find him," before releasing the snap on Bruce's leash.

Off like a black and tan streak, he was swallowed by the shadows within a second.

Wally closed his eyes, willing his ears sharper, and pictured in his mind what Bruce was doing. A stretch of open space directly behind the house was filled with humped grey shapes that could be farm equipment, bushes, maybe pieces of fencing. Bruce would be navigating in and around all of it. Sniffing. Searching. Locating Schrader faster than any of the other officers could ever hope to.

The dying dusk hid the details of the yard, and closely guarded her secrets.

The uncertainty felt like an eternity. The wind kicked up, carrying with it different sounds from the forest. Every snap and whisper drew their attention.

ON SCENE

He heard rustling on the other side of the house. Mosher would want an update. He wanted his men safe and wouldn't get after Wally for turning off his radio, but Mosher's patience only ever stretched so far waiting for the dog.

He tried to convince himself if someone was hiding in the tall grass just beyond where he and Jette took cover, Bruce would have found them. There'd be a racket to beat any shrieks from hell. But Wally couldn't shake the feeling there were eyes on him. And they weren't friendly.

Trying not to brush his arm against any part of his uniform, he slowly reached back and pulled his radio off his belt. The click of the knob was as loud as the cock of a weapon. He swallowed hard. Breathing didn't come easy just now.

Volume on the lowest possible setting, he pressed his ear to the radio and waited.

"Regitnig, report." Expectation was thick in the whispered order.

Wally didn't want to answer.

He stalled to give Bruce just a few more seconds.

"20?" Mosher whispered.

Wally hunched his shoulders, as if they could protect his chest if someone heard him and decided to fire.

On a deep inhale he relented and murmured, "Stand by. I don't see—" He was cut off by a single, short, high pitched whine. Knowing the sound of his partner better than any other, he froze.

Motioning for Jette to stay put and cover him, Wally half crouched, keeping his back to the rough wall of the house. He slid his way around to the back, weapon ready. Every jump his heart made cut off his breath. Even with the wall guarding his back, his body tightened with the threat of attack. Two side steps to the left, he paused and waited for a shot. When none came, his heart started again, and he took two more steps to the left and stopped.

Barely a breath, not even a whisper, he called out "Bruce?" and was met with another single whine.

Forward, straight out from the middle of the back of the house and up to the left some more.

Under the cover of complete darkness now, he glanced over his shoulder at the house. With no functional windows on this side, the menacing gloom was only broken by the slivers of light he saw around the listing back door, hanging slightly crooked on its hinges.

There was no movement at all.

He was about to take a step away from the cover of the wall when his radio sputtered again.

"Regitnig, Rosthern is 23." They were ready. He'd worked with Al long enough to know that as more members rolled up, he would snap orders faster than the officers could draw their weapons. Mosher was a leader who never asked from his members what he wasn't willing to do himself.

Wally just needed another thirty seconds to find Bruce.

"10-4. 20 on Bruce." Feeling like sufficient backup would tackle anything happening inside the house should someone decide to take a shot at him, he made a run for the general area he heard the whine come from. Twenty hasty paces out he stopped, closed his eyes again, and breathed Bruce's name. Another whine met his ears and he turned to the right. No more than ten paces forward, his boot touched something solid. Bruce whined again and nosed his master's leg.

Wally dropped to one knee, the blurred outlines of a body coming into his limited night vision. He reached down and touched it, the rough wool of the uniform reassuring under his fingers. It was theirs. The very same he wore. He didn't have to see the face. His fingers kept travelling, over the name tag pin, a row of metal buttons, and up to his best friend's face. Wally rested there, every good day they ever had together racing through his mind. The hockey games, poker nights, family suppers, and laughs. The laughs had been many.

Wally holstered his weapon and squeezed the bridge of his nose with the same hand. The other hand had come away from the body sticky and cold. Releasing a deep, shaking breath, he halted the images of Connie and the kids that snuck into his mind. They had to clear the house and get Bob out of here.

Wally pressed a hand to the middle of his friend's chest, willing some movement. A whisper. Any evidence of a tiny breath of life that would bring his

ON SCENE

smiling face back. Wally felt his way up to Bob's neck, pressing urgently, praying for the reassuring thump.

It wasn't there.

"We—" he stumbled over his words and cleared his throat. "We…we have Schrader. Clear the house." He kept his hand on Bob. The contact steadied him as crashes and yelling came from the front.

"Move in, I want someone on that east window." Even as low as the volume was, Mosher's orders blasted through Wally's radio and he reached over to turn it off.

The knee of his pants was soaked through with…he didn't want his mind to dwell in that place. He knew what his pants were soaked with but he stayed where he was, protectively bent over his friend, Bruce whining at his side.

"Stay, boy. It's okay." Wally didn't touch the dog but his command was reassuring and eased the strain of wanting to jump into the fray. Bruce leaned into him.

Officers swarmed through the house and out the back door to where Wally knelt. Doors slammed open, boots thundered through the house, furniture was overturned in their search. The racket was a relief. As they got closer, Wally heard the calls through their radios, all clears echoing through the dark yard. But what he wanted to hear was confirmation of a third body.

"Clear."

"Clear."

"North door, clear."

"East window, clear."

"All clear."

Each clear made Wally straighten his back a little harder. The small amount of relief he felt when they stormed the house left him. He and Bruce had someone to find.

A small group of members gathered around him, a couple with flashlights, but none of them gawked. They'd taken up tall stances, their backs to the atrocity before them, forming a straight line in front of Wally, Bruce, and

75

Schrader's body. They offered Wally the last bit of privacy he was ever likely to get with Bob. He knew it would be short lived, and hurried to say the things unsaid. His hand still rested in the middle of Bob's chest.

"Well, friend. I don't know what happened here but I know you'll tell me eventually. I promise you no matter how fast he runs, or how far he goes, we'll find him." Bruce let out a sharp bark. Not one of their guards flinched.

"We had some good times." He sniffed. "Aw, hell. They were all good times. I won't let the kids want for anything." He swallowed the solid lump forming in his throat. "They'll still have someone to root for 'em at every hockey game." Wally swiped the back of his sleeve across his eyes. "I'll tell Connie myself, don't worry."

He gritted his teeth and gathered himself the best he could. It was long past time to go. He turned his radio back up. "We need a stretcher, Mosher. Let's get Bob out of here." He put his other knee on the ground and leaned in closer to Schrader's face, seeing his features clearly for the first time in the cast off from a flashlight. "It's been an honour." Wally reached over with a gentle hand and closed his friend's eyes for the final time.

Two stretcher bearers came trotting in and Wally stood, Bruce jumping to heel.

"Doc is on scene, sir. We'll get him over there." The young members, eager to help, had Schrader loaded on the stretcher and heading over to an ambulance before Wally could tell them there was no need to hurry. The ambulance lights came on, red orbs bouncing off the surrounding trees, illuminating the officers' faces. Wally saw that it was parked behind his own cruiser but dismissed it. He wouldn't need his car yet.

Glancing up at the sky, a few sporadic wet flakes were starting to fall. Any scent to be had would disappear as that snow melted into the ground, making a sopping wet mess that covered tracks better than anything. Immediacy clutched at him.

He grabbed a flashlight from one of the members and held his hand out to another one, palm up.

"Give me all your rounds. And somebody give me a smoke, for Christ's sake." The officers started emptying their pockets, holding out hands full of odds

ON SCENE

and ends. Ammunition, flashlight batteries, twine, a small compass, a watch, a few cigarettes, and a lighter. Wally snatched it all up, not caring what was what, and crammed it into his pockets. All of it might be useful at some point, and he didn't know where this trail would lead. Or if it would lead anywhere at all.

Pressing a fresh cigarette between his lips, he leaned over to light it then snapped Bruce's leash on him. "Let's go, Chief." Exhaling a ghostly cloud that hung in the air, criss-crossing the flashlight beams, Wally turned away from the scene, ignoring the orders being barked out over the radio, and walked straight across the back yard to the trees.

"Uh, Sarge," one member called out, hesitating over his words, "don't you want to wait for anyone else?"

Neither Wally nor Bruce turned around. After a last drag on the cigarette, he dropped it at his feet and crushed it under his boot in the muddy grass.

"No. We won't need anyone else."

> "Wally was always the strong silent type who led by example. He was someone you would not want to cross while at the same time being the biggest supporter of me and my family. I remember one time I got kicked out of high school and went directly to the RCMP detachment to talk to him in hopes that he would be able to talk to my Mom first before I got hell. It turned out he was out looking for Dad's killer in MacDowall and I never did get a hold of him that day."
>
> *Excerpt from interview with Barry Schrader (2016)*

Chapter Twelve

Friday, October 9, 1970
Robertson land
Half an hour after the chaos

Stanley had never driven such a new vehicle before. It felt oddly comforting to make the observation, and put aside the circumstances that put him in the vehicle in the first place. There were a lot of buttons that he was careful not to touch. He didn't need a bunch of lights and sirens turning on. He was barely at a crawl on the back road, leading away from the house. He had to watch carefully for the spot he wanted to turn off, or he would miss it in the twilight. He couldn't stay in the police car; that was pure stupidity. He had to get to his safe place; to the familiarity of the forest where he grew up. To the place his father showed him.

As a child he wondered why he was made so small, but was always told he matched his father so he was eager in his pursuit of the duties his father excelled at. A mini shadow, he learned at his father's knee how to snare and hunt, track, and live rough. This was his place.

At six years old, he shot his first .22 rifle, quickly learning the consequences of kick back. His father had smiled but said nothing, letting his young son try again. Using his hands, rather than words, to guide him. That was always his way. By age eight he was shooting gophers clean through the eye at twenty-five yards on a windy day.

ON SCENE

As he got older, his father showed him the way of his people. Trapping and hunting had kept Stanley's brothers and sisters fed through the winter, and Stanley continued that tradition with a knowledge and respect for the land not many had anymore.

Spotting the break in the stand of poplars, he manoeuvred the police car off the dirt road and onto a path through the trembling trees. It wasn't much of a path, but you could make out where you were going in the early morning light if you headed this way for some fine hunting. Families each had their own spots, kept as a closely guarded secret for generations, each boasting that theirs was the best. Stanley never boasted. Passed from father to son, his father had shown him this secret place the spring he turned thirteen. He planned to bring his own oldest son here in just a few short winter months. The boy would be thirteen come May. His astute words burned Stanley's soul. *Daddy shot two police.*

He inched the car forward, barely crawling over the bumps, tree branches bending and softly scraping the sides, whipping back into position as he went along. The slower you went, the less debris you left behind. His father taught him that.

"Always watch. Put your feet where my feet go. Move here like you are one with the earth." They walked on a narrow deer path for a time, cutting parallel to the house. They hiked slowly for several hours through the dense forest until it broke open at a clearing. New spring flowers and green shoots dotted the vast area. A slight valley-like depression lay at the very centre, perfect for collecting water at its lowest point. He looked at his father and his father smiled at him with a knowing look.

"Come."

They stayed at the treeline around the side of the clearing, the path taking a sharp turn upwards. It got substantially steeper just at that spot, and he wanted to ask his father why they didn't walk up where it wasn't so steep but his father always had a reason, so he'd reined in his teenage impatience and kept walking.

They eventually levelled off again, stepping between two stands of poplars, and there in the middle was a majestic Jack Pine tree. It was surely the biggest tree Stanley had ever seen in his young life. The ends of the branches angled down, nearly touching the ground all the way around, and a grown man could stand up underneath.

His father ducked under the branches and led him inside, turning him around to look through the boughs at the valley below. You could see anything coming in for a drink at that standing water. It was the perfect hunting spot. Their spot.

Stanley's mind galloped back to the present when the car dipped suddenly downwards on the path. He knew when he took the police car that it wasn't a permanent solution, just a means to an end.

He'd arrived where he wanted to hide it.

> *"For record purposes this statement is still missing and possibly in possession of the accused."*
>
> *Excerpt of handwritten note regarding statement given by "Don Nelson" to Constable Anson*

Chapter Thirteen

```
Friday, October 9, 1970
On Scene
2100hrs
```

Bruce headed north, feet eating the miles in an effortless gait only an experienced tracker could maintain, with a strong arm-yanking only a seasoned dogmaster's bicep could easily handle. He kept the dog leashed now, for safety.

The dogmasters called the dogs the tip of the spear. They were the first line of defence. The first to know. But the dark made the terrain hazardous and Wally needed to feel Bruce's reactions through the leash. It was his lifeline. They didn't know where the shooter was but the breeze still held clues. The dog's nose wove through the air, side to side, then something he smelled drew his head down to the ground and he set to work. Wally was thankful for each and every yank on that line.

With Bruce leading him, he acted on pure instinct. Eyes half closed against the spattering of snowflakes, he jogged along behind the dog, the line wrapped around his left hand, ears working harder than any other part of his body. He'd closed off his heart when he closed Bob's eyes. Except for powering the physical needs of his body, his heart would play no part in this mission.

He knew he didn't have much time; he didn't intend to be out long, but didn't bother telling anyone that when he left. His radio crackled now and then with far off commands and questions, but it cut in and out to the point of annoyance and he clicked it off again.

He'd have to head back into the city soon to tell Connie and the kids. Nobody else should do that. It had to be him. Mosher would know.

Flipping through the mental catalogue of possibilities, he let out a few more loops of the leash and Bruce surged on, dragging Wally through dense bush. He seemed to have a destination. Wally noticed the branches weren't grabbing at them as nastily as they had been, but he didn't want to go so far as to say they were on some sort of trail.

The entire area was a ripe hunting spot. *Probably how that poor family kept fed,* he thought. They *were* on a path, of sorts, possibly only known by local hunters tracking fat white-tailed deer to their calculated demise. *Fitting.*

The flashlight beam bounced against the trees surrounding them, Bruce leading the charge with no regard for Wally's height or the branches he had to deal with. Busy trying to keep up and keep the melting snowflakes out of his eyes, he didn't immediately notice the change in the trees. He swiped his sleeve across his brow and called a halt, realizing he wasn't being hit in the face with branches anymore.

"Hold on, back up." They retraced a dozen steps and he swept the light in an arc at eye level. Then at the ground. He saw a second trail start, only two paces from the other, and veered right to see where it originated.

"Right here. Where did this come from?" Following the double line in the bush for only a minute or two, they broke through the trees and came out at train tracks. Over the tracks was a rough, narrow road.

He looked up and down the road, cursing the fact that he didn't have a bigger flashlight.

"MacDowall service road," he murmured, then whistled to Bruce who'd wandered away up the road, nose to the ground, dragging his leash.

"Come." They did an about-face, retracing the double track back to the spot where Wally noticed it merging into the trees. A vehicle had come through here, slowly. No broken branches. Sweeping the flashlight over the area again, he knew they were on the right track. Unforgiving tendrils of fear worked their way into his stomach, battling the adrenaline pulsing through him. He suppressed them into a tiny corner of his mind. He had no time to give in to fear.

"Find him," he whispered to Bruce and they set off at a jog again, like a compass pointing true north. They'd have to abandon this preliminary search soon, but something ate at him. How far could the shooter have gotten? And would there be any kind of trail left for Bruce to follow after the snow and rain had done its damage?

Moonlit bush had played tricks on his eyes before. Movement of animals and birds could throw you off, wind in the branches, or simply the mind running away, creating terrifying scenarios. But after a couple decades as a dogmaster, Wally had learned what to obey and what to ignore.

His flashlight beam reflected a glint of red, and he hit the ground, rolling to the side, weapon drawn. Bruce dropped into the tall grass a full second before Wally reacted. He always knew first.

Breath coming heavy and fast, flashlight tucked under his body, he waited. He heard nothing. Reaching underneath his chest, he pulled out the light and carefully raised the beam several feet above the ground, shining it down the path of tall grass laid smooth by tire treads. He saw the red reflection again and lowered the beam.

Rising into a crouch, weapon cocked and ready in one hand, flashlight in the other, he duck walked forward, trying to stay hidden and get closer for a better look. The tall, stiff prairie grass was wet and grabbed at his face but he ignored it, intent on what was in front of him. Heart pounding erratically he ran his sleeve across his brow again, trying to interrupt the rivulets of sweat running into his eyes. As he approached, the flashlight caught glints of chrome.

He knew what he was looking at.

"Bruce, stand down," he whispered to his partner. No part of him wanted to stand down but this scenario would play out in one of two ways; if the car was still occupied, it was an idiotic cowboy move to approach it alone. And if the car was empty, any scent left behind by whoever took it wouldn't last more than minutes and they'd miss their chance. Looking up at the dark sky, wet splotches hit him in the face every few seconds. Time was not on their side. The only thing he knew for certain was you never left a crime scene unprotected.

The inner struggle between following policy and throwing it out the window was debilitating. He wanted to let Bruce run this killer down like a freight train but the job had to win out over his base instincts, or what the hell were they doing?

He trained his flashlight on a spot where the bush opened up a short distance from the police car and cursed a bloody blue streak. It was too wet already. There wouldn't be anything left for Bruce to pick up.

They retraced their exact steps back through the bush, half crouched, still armed, not truly believing someone would jump out at them, but not willing to take the risk of being caught unaware. Bruce whined, nervous, and paced back and forth on his substantially shortened leash.

"Never mind. We need backup." At the double time pace they set from the house, Wally judged they were about a mile from the Robertson place. Protecting their backs was painfully slow. Backing up at a snail's pace, inch by inch, keeping their eyes on the spot where the car sat, he brought them out at a break in the trees where the tire treads went in, obviously coming off the service road and across the train tracks. They took cover just off the road in a stand of closely set poplars. Turning his radio back on, he waited for a break in the chatter.

"Dogmaster requesting backup." He waited for Mosher to reply.

"Go, Regitnig." Mosher sounded controlled but anxious.

"I'm near the MacDowall service road just over a mile north of the scene. I saw the reflection of taillights in the bush up ahead, possibly the cruiser in question. You wanna send a couple cars?" It wasn't a joking matter but Wally's light tone wasn't lost on Mosher.

"Uh, yeah. 10-4. I might want to do that."

"Send me a car. We're done here. For now." He signed off and hunkered down on a rock at the base of the poplars, staying hidden but still in sight of the pushed over grass trail leading to the police car. Bruce sat unwillingly

ON SCENE

beside him, hopping back and forth on his front paws, whining. He never reacted well to being ordered back, but the melting flakes were falling from the sky at a disappointing rate, and even Bruce's nose couldn't pick up scent in a mud puddle. Their time was better spent elsewhere now.

"We have more important things to do, Chief. We need to tell the families."

Six police cars responded to his call for backup. Four of them blasted past him on the road; dirt, leaves and debris churning into a frantic tornado as they sailed by. Two stopped for orders. Mosher had the scene.

Wally left to make the longest, hardest trip of his life.

> "She said she saw her husband shoot both members. Said he threatened to shoot any policeman who came to his door if she complained about him. Four years ago he beat her up-threatened her with a gun. A terrible temper. A crack shot. She complained to a doctor and he told her to leave him."
>
> *Excerpt, scene map, and handwritten notes by Corporal R.H Waller, Rosthern Detachment*

Chapter Fourteen

Friday, October 9, 1970
On Scene
2130hrs

Officers swarmed like ants around the perimeter of the abandoned car, tucked away in the bush where no car should be. Dark and full of questions. A couple of spotlights gave them more detail on where the car had entered the bush. Danny saw there was no furious path of destruction in its wake. The driver had just crept into this covered spot…and stopped.

Speculation flew through a few low-voiced radio transmissions before they were sharply cut off by the commanding officer. "Radio in the car."

That was all it took to shut the chatter down. The shooter had access to all the equipment inside the cruiser, including guns, ammunition, and the radio. There had been talk among the ranks that everything they'd done to this point could have been overheard. Danny suspected they were about to find out.

He was crouched ten yards from the back of the vehicle, using some rocks and bush as cover. His weapon was drawn but there was nothing to aim at unless you could see in the dark. Staff Sergeant Mosher was still on scene at the Robertson farm, so the dozen officers who responded to this sighting were being directed by Staff Sergeant Anderson. He wasn't an overly imposing man; barely the required five foot eight inches with a ridiculously thin moustache. Danny was sure he measured when he trimmed it to get the policy length spot on. It looked too small for his face. 'Full regalia' was the only description that came to his mind when he looked at the man. The officers always wore their ties and were a clean and pressed lot, but Staff Sergeant Anderson was on a different level of importance, if only in his own mind. He was wearing his hat with the gold bison badge, buttons gleaming all down his front, and to cap it off, shoes polished to a mirror shine. Who wore polished shoes in the bush? Danny didn't know what to think and said as much to Joe Greenslade who hunkered down beside him. Dress and Deportment was important to Greenslade only as far as flying under the radar with the bosses. He wore his light hair a little too long, forgot his tie a little too often, and was the best member to have watching your back. Danny made a little more room so Greenslade could stretch the shoulder that sometimes stiffened up on him in the cold. The old football injury from high school nearly prevented him from getting into the Force.

"What's this guy doing? What're we waiting for?" Danny wasn't hiding his annoyance very well, but nobody but Joe could hear him.

"I don't know. Don't think he's ever been in the field, has he?" Greenslade lowered his weapon to rest on his knee, shifting positions again with a groan. It looked like they would be in a hold pattern for a while as the commander made up his mind as to what to do with a dozen armed officers, sitting in the dark, surrounding a police car that could be hiding a killer.

"I hope he's in there. Get this over with already." His whisper was cut short as Staff Sergeant Anderson came strutting past them, no cover, unarmed, and not looking any more ready to direct them into action than he had twenty minutes ago. Danny caught his attention.

"Sir? I could just go check, see if the car is occupied?" His question was met with a stare that went right through him. Like he'd suggested they storm Fort Knox.

"When I'm ready I'll let you know, Constable." Staff Sergeant Anderson sniffed and raised a hand, making a shooing motion. Danny's shock, mixed with the red hot anger that bubbled up at the shooing motion, made for a formidable monster to control. The Staff Sergeant strolled away, ignorant of the threat to his own personal safety.

Even in the limited silence a dozen armed men can muster, the sound of a weapon being cocked was as loud as a church bell. Danny, Greenslade, and the others near them hit the ground, "I'll see if the bastard's in there," was all they heard before a single shot took out the passenger side mirror of the police car. If the cocking was as loud as a church bell, the shot sounded like a canon fired off during mass. Danny's heart jumped and he was sure everyone else's did, too.

Staff Sergeant Anderson whipped around with a roar. "Who discharged that firearm?" He stomped off down the perimeter pointing his finger at officers, leaving Danny and Greenslade to make their own guesses.

Joe snorted. "If Anderson thinks that shot was what took away his element of surprise," he paused to listen to more of Anderson's yelling, "he's more delusional than I thought."

"It's probably that new guy from North Battleford. Damn greenhorns," Danny murmured.

"I don't care who it was. Maybe it'll light a fire under *someone* to let us do something. I don't know what the hell we're wait--" Joe's question was cut off when Staff Sergeant Anderson came storming back towards them.

"You." He pointed at Danny. "You still want to check the car?" The Staff Sergeant stood, fists on his hips, glaring down at them. Danny bit down on a laugh, lest it escape and end him up in cells for insubordination. The man stood like Wonder Woman.

"Yes, sir. Say the word, sir." Thankful for the shadows cast by the two spotlights now directed at the car, he gave himself the luxury of a good eye roll as he said it. Unfolding himself from his crouched position, he took up a ready stance aimed at the back taillight of the driver's side. At the Staff Sergeant's command, he approached with caution, just able to make out the ghostly shape of his side of the car, the spotlights focused through the back window. Ducking under the line of sight of the driver's side mirror, he pressed his back against the rear quarter panel. Weapon at the ready, he flung the door open.

ON SCENE

Stanley gathered his gear, put on his jacket and hat, loaded his pockets with everything he brought, and added anything of use he saw lying around the police car. The forest swallowed him the second he stepped out, enveloping him like a comforting blanket. He stopped short before shutting the door—waiting for someone to grab him. To just come out of the darkness with metal handcuffs and steal away his freedom. But there was no prickle of warning on the back of his neck. Nobody knew where he was. Yet.

He took his first full, deep breath since early that morning and revelled in the calm of the darkness. It didn't bother him, the darkness. He could find his way to this spot blindfolded. His father made sure of that decades ago.

The only thing the dark did was slow him down, which was fine with him. He was in no hurry. There weren't very many people who could search these woods at night, and he was sure none of them worked for the police. Tonight would be quiet and safe. It would give him some time to think things out.

ROBERTSON, the Hunter, Becomes the Hunted--*Albert Dallman and his son in law were going big game hunting next month. This week the trip was cancelled. Albert Dallman's son in law is Stanley Robertson, 40, of MacDowall the object of one of the biggest manhunts in Western Canadian history.*

Headline and excerpt, Regina Leader Post (Thursday, October 15, 1970)

Chapter Fifteen

Friday, October 9, 1970
Highway 11, North of MacDowall, Saskatchewan
2130hrs

The drive into Prince Albert chipped away at Wally's heart with every mile the car ate up.

"Thanks, Jette. For driving. I just needed…" He rubbed at the spot between his eyes.

Brent was restless too, scrubbing at his dark hair that was just a touch longer than policy dictated. When Wally had opened the car door, he noted blood matting the longer strands behind Jette's right ear. They both had smears of blood soaking into shirt cuffs and pants.

"Yeah, don't think anything of it. I had to do it. For me, ya know?" Jette physically winced. "I'm sorry, that sounds awful."

He put a firm hand on Jette's arm. "Don't apologize. The whole thing is awful and nobody's going to know what to do or say."

"He's just so young. Anson." Jette's voice broke on his friend's name. "And Vallarena. She's so young."

Brent was younger than Doug but Wally didn't voice that thought. The constables were all young. The newlyweds' youth, and love for each other in that youth, had never been lost on him.

ON SCENE

"Damn radio, where is it?" Henry Long had his face screwed up until it was barely recognizable, voice deepened as far as it would go.

Wally vehemently shook his head, taking a heaping plate and fork from his wife and finding his chair again. The kid never told a story right. Went for the laughs every time.

"No, that's not how it was at all." Wally shoved a forkful of pie into his mouth, winked at Dolores in appreciation, then made his rebuttal around his chewing. "You try keeping that radio on your belt in a fight." Long sidestepped Wally's swipe at him. He lived for teaching the kid a thing or two in the field. A relief dogman in his first year, Long smacked of confidence and bravado but that's not what made a great dogmaster. He would be, someday. Great, that is. Wally knew it; he just didn't want Long to know it yet. Better to train him up a bit more. "I don't miss a goddamn thing." He pointed his fork at Bob who was grinning from ear to ear across the table. "And if you keep saying any different, we can step outside."

"Oh hush, you." Dolores batted at him, and smiled conspiratorially at Vallarena. The women dished it out as well as the men sometimes. She passed Vallarena a slice of pie, warmly holding onto the young woman's hand for an extra second. Wally revelled in seeing his wife in these moments.

Vallarena handed the plate on to her husband and Doug affectionately tucked an errant strand of blonde hair behind her ear. Her pretty face flushed slightly and Wally hid his smile behind his coffee cup. The newlyweds were a joy to be around.

His rare tender thoughts were interrupted by more commentary from the peanut gallery on the happenings of the day.

"Sounds to me like maybe you did miss something, Sergeant. I heard Long had to find your radio, too." Anson chuckled and Wally scowled, backing up his chair and catching Anson with the metal leg, the joy of his presence vanishing with Wally's patience.

Doug easily sidestepped the chair, knocking into Brent Jette who had his cup held out to Vallarena for more coffee. Jette was steady as the day was long, shorter than Anson and thicker framed. It was like a willow tree knocking into a solid boulder. It didn't move, and neither did Jette. He laughed, grabbing the cup and wiping his wet wrist on his pants.

"Don't worry, Sarge. Nobody believes a thing these yahoos say." Jette took a sip from his cup, heavy dark brows animated over the rim.

Anson leaned his thin frame against the counter, balancing his plate of pie on his coffee cup and coughed, "Sucking up gets you car cleaning duty." He nudged the back of Jette's knee, the laughter volume bubbling up when Jette faltered and had to wipe his other wet arm on the side of his shirt.

"That's enough out of you, Anson. I think you need car cleaning duty," Wally said.

Anson looked just smug enough to incite Wally's grunt of disapproval and Vallarena slapped her husband playfully on the chest with a shocked look on her face. This set the women off again, a high pitched giggle adding to the deep laughter of the officers. Wally had lost track of who was laughing at whom.

"So what did happen?" Jette put a hand up to still the peanut gallery, giving Wally a chance to tell the real tale.

"Long didn't find my radio." Wally tried to keep his hard scowl while clearing his throat, delaying the punchline. Expectation hung heavy in the silence, everyone waiting on who ultimately found his radio. Jette made a hurry up motion with his hand. Wally hesitated, but knew he wouldn't get out of it easily. Might as well take his lumps.

"Ace did."

The cheer for Henry Long's dog and his success in finding Wally's lost radio rivalled that of a hockey rink full of fans celebrating a home team goal. "Cut it out," Wally bellowed, but he couldn't contain the sheepish grin that split his tough exterior. The truth of the matter was he enjoyed the downtime. It was their own form of debriefing, showing the younger officers how to manage the stress of the job.

He looked at Danny Cavello and Joe Greenslade, both relishing the rare moment of being allowed to rib a higher ranking officer with little consequence. The two constables had a few years' service, and were complete opposites in looks and temperament. Cavello was the dark, quiet work horse. Greenslade, on the other hand, was so fair his eyebrows were nearly invisible above piercing blue eyes that never missed a thing. He was a bit brash, but Wally liked him. Never late with files, he sometimes took his lessons hard.

"I don't know, sir. Sounds like you were having some trouble until Long lent a hand." Greenslade looked sideways at Cavello and grinned. Cavello was obviously more than willing to keep the train going.

"Might have to put you on reporting, improve your skills a bit." Cavello let out a whoop and ducked a chunk of pie that came flying his way. Wally licked his fingers in satisfaction. Cavello looked at his shoulder, wiped cherries off his shirt, then smoothed his oiled hair back.

"Don't worry, Danny. I didn't mess up your hair," Wally said.

The table erupted again.

Wally had never heard the Schrader house quiet, and was at his most relaxed when they were all laughing and yelling at each other.

After a scare, it was Wally's favourite place to be. Leaning down to retrieve his lost radio from Ace had saved him from a bullet that day. He didn't know why, but ribbing each other seemed to be the only way to get through it.

Bob was laughing so hard he had to take his glasses off to wipe the tears streaming down his face. "Look, buddy, glad you're all right, but I think you're getting slow in your old age. I hear that guy was half your size and still put up one hell of a fight. Maybe you need a few lessons in take downs." Bob threw down his cards and grabbed at Wally in the chair beside him. The two were evenly matched in size and stature, but Wally had the advantage of being in the field with nearly one hundred pounds of dog constantly pulling on his arm.

"Lessons from a desk Sergeant who hasn't been in the field in three years?" Wally easily twisted out of his friend's hold, the two of them already breathing hard, straining against each other. "I think maybe it's you who needs a lesson." He reversed the hold on Bob, knocking cards and napkins to the floor. The table shook with more laughter, everyone grabbing their coffee cups and ashtrays before everything upended in the hilarity.

Connie swatted at Wally and Bob with a dish towel but immediately stopped, grabbing at her leg. They settled abruptly, Bob crossing the kitchen in two strides, concern wrinkling his brow. He placed an arm gently around Connie.

"I told you we should get that leg looked at again." He tried to get her to sit down but she pushed him away.

"Oh, I'm fine. They'll just send me home and tell me to rest. With five kids?" She snorted. "This damn leg isn't going to get the better of me." She limped back to her chair muttering under her breath, waving her tea towel at Bob again when he tried to help her. "I said I'm fine. Just quit trying to prove your strength in my kitchen."

"I don't need to prove anything; it's Wally who got shot at today." The words flew out of Bob's mouth, unbidden, and slapped Wally in the face. Connie's eyes widened and she reached out to squeeze Dolores's hand. Bob cleared his throat hard and slammed his hand down on Wally's shoulder even harder.

"Glad you came out okay." It didn't happen often, but Wally saw the emotion in his friend's eyes and looked away. It was a reality of the job they all knew well, but tried to avoid talking about too seriously, if they could help it. A joke was always appreciated more.

"Hey, if I ever get shot at, I can only hope Bruce will be there to save my sorry backside." Bob smiled, lightening the heaviness that had settled over them, and everyone went *back to their cards. Wally didn't miss the kiss Bob gave his wife's hand when she handed him a second piece of pie.*

"Tough to give him hell. Vallarena always looks at Anson like he should be wearing a cape," Wally said.

"Yeah." Jette's voice was thick and he stared straight ahead.

Wally nodded and nudged Brent's arm with his elbow. "You've had my back in the past and you have it now." He stopped talking, scared his grief would flood his words and he'd embarrass himself more than he already had.

Brent jerked a nod.

They spent the rest of the trip to Prince Albert in silence, broken only by a whine or bark from Bruce in the back seat, or the low radio chatter in the background.

Pulling up to the hospital, Wally's stomach lurched and threatened to show him what was still in there from lunch.

Cowboy up, Regitnig. They need you.

He gritted his teeth, swallowed several times, and walked through the emergency doors on the ground floor.

The head night nurse greeted him by name, but he uncharacteristically ignored the pleasantries.

"I need Connie Schrader's room number." With that, the nurse's demeanour changed instantly. She snapped her staff to attention, getting the information Wally needed and sent an orderly to guide him directly to the third floor.

The elevator seemed to take longer than the drive into the city. Every hall they turned down stretched out before them for miles. Seconds dragged by like hours even with Wally's boots tapping the tile floor faster than the orderly could stay ahead of him. After Wally stepped on the orderly's heels a third time, the young man jumped to the side with apologies, pointing ahead of him up the hallway.

"Straight that way, sir. Thirty-two twenty-five." The orderly faded back into the nurses' station, out of Wally's way. He walked directly to the room, raised a fist to knock, but stopped. His heart thumped against the inside of his ribs harder than it ever had before. Harder than the last time he was shot at. Every thump reminded him of the promise he made to his friend.

I'll tell Connie myself, don't worry.

He knocked before he could stop himself again and heard Connie's voice call out to come in. Wally peeked in the door. The closest bed was empty and the far curtain was drawn. The door creaked when he pushed it open enough to walk through.

"A little late aren't you, dear?" Connie's laugh came from the far side of the curtain. Wally raised a hand to rub his eyes and froze. He fought to keep the string of curse words from coming out of his mouth and stepped into the tiny bathroom beside the first bed. There wasn't enough antiseptic soap in the entire hospital to ever wash away the feeling of having his friend's blood on his hands. It might rinse down the drain, but the stain would remain forever. He glanced down at his uniform front, satisfied there was nothing visible there. The dark blue of his pants hid what was soaked into his knees.

"Don't feel like you have to get all gussied up just for me. How're the kids?" Connie's voice floated into the bathroom and Wally heard the curtain slide on the track. He frantically finished rinsing his hands, savagely grabbed at the paper towel in the dispenser and slipped out of the bathroom.

"It—it's me, Connie." Wally wasn't used to stumbling on his words. He was convinced she could smell death on him; the sharp, metallic tang grabbed his nostrils and wouldn't let go. Mixed with the citrus of the hospital soap, it was a smell that warranted its own danger label. The mixture would haunt anyone for the rest of their life.

Connie stared at Wally, her mouth half open. "Oh, hi. Where's Bob?" Sitting on the side of the bed, she tried to close the gap where the snug housecoat fit a little too tightly over her hospital gown. She grasped it at the neck, knuckles turning white. "He's here?"

He shifted from one foot to the other, cleared his throat and flicked at the snap of his holster with one finger, the heel of his hand pressing into the butt of his gun. He sniffed hard.

ON SCENE

"Uh, no darlin'. He's not." His brown eyes started to swim and he stepped forward, holding out a hand. Connie's face blanked, gradually gathering a look of profound doubt.

She shook her head, and twisted the neck of her gown even tighter. "No." Shaking her head harder, she reached out for his extended hand, stumbling on her bad leg, landing in an anguished heap in Wally's arms.

Clasping him around the neck, she glared at him, gasping, "Where is he? What happened? I want to go, right now." Panic was building in her grasp, as well as her words. She begged and pleaded to see Bob. To help him. She stuttered, going between a low insistence, and a high-pitched, demanding order to act. Wally needed to be more definitive.

He grasped her fingers from around his neck, pried them away and held them tight in one hand, the other going to her chin, directing her to focus. "Connie, look at me. Hey! Bob is dead, honey. He's gone. You can't see him right now."

Her insistent panic melted into shaking shock and he put a strong arm around her middle, getting her back to the edge of the narrow bed. Everything was too much. Shaking with a violence he'd never witnessed before, she listed to the side, a broken sob escaping her. Jumping to catch her before she slumped to the floor, he hit the call button, causing a cloud of organized chaos to descend on the room.

"What's happened here?" The head nurse was a robust woman, starched white cap firmly pinned in place, her no-nonsense gait in no way disturbing her tightly coiffed hair. She gave Wally a look that would have stopped a lesser man in his tracks, but the look Wally returned brought her up short. Her stern face softened somewhat, and she called for the doctor, rattling orders off. She allowed Wally to pull her into the hallway.

"Sergeant Schrader's been shot. Pronounced dead on scene. Connie needs to be discharged. Give her something if you have to, but she'll skin me if you knock her out altogether. Don't do it."

He dropped his head at the low wail coming from inside the room. It was the sound of despair. A heart breaking, possibly beyond repair. Raising his head on a long inhale, Wally still fought the scent of citrus and death. Exhaling sharply, nostrils flaring, he met the nurse's eyes again. "See to the discharge. There's a police car with two members waiting for her downstairs. I have to go get her kids."

The nurse grabbed his sleeve, a sharp but quiet gasp escaping her before she reined in her emotions, a blanket of professionalism settling over her. "Bless you, sir. God go with you."

Wally nodded and strode back down the hallway, nurses and orderlies lowering their heads with respect as he passed. Connie's grief following him like a faraway train whistle in the night.

Family Proud of Caring Father-*Bob Schrader was first and foremost a family man. He was proud of his family and they are proud of him. At the time of his death, he and his wife, Connie, had five children. The oldest twins...turned sixteen the day after he died...*

Headline and excerpt, Prince Albert Daily Herald (Tuesday, October 3, 1995)

Chapter Sixteen

```
Friday, October 9, 1970
Prince Albert, Saskatchewan
Schrader House
2230hrs
```

Lynn rested her head on her knees in the backseat of the police car, arms folded around her ears, trying to make sense of what was happening. The rock in her stomach pitched up and back down again, the pain a welcome distraction from the confusion. Pain was real. Pain was manageable.

"Where's my mom?" She didn't bother raising her head; just let the question slide out in a mumble to hang in the air between the two seats.

"She should be home, sweetie. I had a car wait for her at the hospital. I called over to Jed's, his dad brought Barry home."

She felt the car stop and squeezed her dry eyes shut and opened them again. Never one to mince words or sugar coat anything, Wally's announcement that her father was dead had hit her square in the chest, stealing everything from her. No sound came, barely a breath, and she had stared at Wally's face, haggard and apologetic. Jeannette's mother had collapsed into the nearest chair with a cry, Jeannette's father rushing to her side. Jeannette herself had clutched her friend's hand, hugging it to her own chest, tears streaming down her face. Lynn gently extricated her hand without a word, gathered up her coat and followed Wally out to the car, leaving the party guests downstairs without a second thought. Now she sat in the dark outside the house, with Jette drumming his fingers on the steering wheel and Bruce laying on the seat beside her, nose tucked under her bent elbow. She loosened one arm from around her head and put it around Bruce's neck, pressing her head harder into her knees.

"Can I see him?" she whispered.

"He'll be at the hospital just now. Maybe in a few days. I'll take you myself." Wally choked on his last few words.

Lynn slowly raised her head, eyes still bone dry, and sighed. She turned her head to see her four brothers lined up in the big bay window, tallest to smallest, waiting for their sister to come home. The house was lit up; she could see every detail through that window. Nobody could see her in the darkness of the backseat, but she could see her brothers' devastation. She didn't need light to see it. She felt it with every fibre of her soul.

A strangled gasp caught in her throat and she thought she might finally cry. But it didn't come.

"Look at them all. How am I supposed to…what do I…when…" she stuttered, searching for the right words. "What do I do, Wally?" she asked.

The loaded question was met with silence. She heard the door handle pop and Wally got out of the car, then opened her door and held out his hand to her. Hesitating for only a second, she reached out and gripped it like it was the last lifeline on earth. She didn't want to let go. He helped her out of the car, Bruce jumping out after her, gluing himself to her side as they walked slowly up the path.

"You just be Lynn. The person your father is so proud of." He patted the hand that was tucked into the crook of his arm and they stepped onto the porch.

"But I don't know what to say to them. Look at them, they need me." She gestured to the boys, still watching her from the front window. The looks on their faces ranged from pure fear and confusion on the younger three to an indescribable teenage anger on the face of her twin brother. Larry all of a sudden looked very grown up. Her younger brothers looked lost, and she didn't know if she had the strength to help them find their way. How would she find her own way, without her dad to gently guide her along?

Wally had his hand on the doorknob when she stopped him with a tug.

"Will you find out what happened?" She turned to face him, his hard features illuminated by the porch light. He looked tired and on edge. Gripping his thick arm harder, she gave it another tug. "Find out. I want to know what happened to my dad." She stared directly up into his eyes, not wavering. Fully expecting an affirmative response.

Wally's eyes never left hers. "Of course I'll find out. But my first priority was you guys. Now that you're all together safe, Bruce and I'll go back out. We won't stop until we have answers." He lowered his head to hers, resting forehead to forehead, and she braved a tiny hint of a smile for him.

"Thank you." She pulled away first, keeping her face turned away from the window. She took a deep breath, pushed her hair back from her face and straightened her jacket. She wished she had armour to put on, but the only armour she had was the good sense her dad instilled in her.

"My brothers need me."

The door creaked on its hinges when they entered, cutting through the tomb-like silence in the house. It was the quietest the house had ever been. Lynn's arrival seemed to break some kind of spell and the boys rushed at her, swallowing her petite frame in a circle of arms and heads. Terry started crying but the others were as silent as Lynn. She enveloped her brothers in a ring of protection.

They stayed like that for a long time, not at all acting like the energetic, boisterous crew she was used to. It was sobering to see her brothers like this. The uncertainty crashed over her, choking the breath from her. She squeezed them all hard, her arms only going so far, but her heart stretching so much further.

"Do you guys need a snack? Let's go sit." For lack of anything else to do or say, she corralled the boys into the kitchen. She came back to the living room to find her mother laying on the couch, a cloth on her head, the RCMP chaplain sitting on the footstool beside her, holding her hand in quiet prayer. He made the sign of the cross over her mother and Lynn's senses were flooded with…pancakes. Maple syrup and bacon.

Every Sunday, their mother took them to church and their dad stayed behind to make breakfast. *Church is for hatch, match, and dispatch* he would joke as he sent them, scrubbed and dressed in their best, out the door. When they returned home, a giant breakfast always awaited them, perhaps with a few stray officers joining in on the meal and the laughter. She could hear her dad laughing now. That big, booming laugh that made others laugh with him. She would miss his laugh.

Her mother opened her eyes and looked right at her, seemingly not noticing the chaplain at all, even though he still held her hand. Connie held out her other hand. Lynn took a few halting steps forward, knelt beside her mother's soft hip spilling off the side of the couch and accepted the offered hand.

"They'll take care of us. Wally and the boys. They'll take care of us…" Connie's voice was weak and dreamy, her hand limp and chilly.

She hugged her mother and gently released her hand. Connie's eyes fluttered closed again. Stricken by her mother's extreme calm, Lynn turned to the chaplain, "What's wrong?" The chaplain released Connie's other hand and patted Lynn's shoulder with care.

"It's okay, dear. They had to give her a little something to calm her down. A bit of medicine. It's best for her to rest now." The chaplain gently touched her cheek, then bent again in prayer. She stood, coming face to face with Wally.

"Go see to your brothers. She's right, we'll take care of you." Wally stepped past her, intending to give her mother a kiss on the forehead in farewell, so it startled her when her mother's arms suddenly reached out, grabbing Wally around the neck and drawing him close to her face.

Her eyes blazing, she rasped out, "Find him. You find that bastard, Wally." Her eyes fluttered again, but she held fast. "You find him, and you kill him."

Lynn was more surprised by her own lack of reaction than of her mother's sinister order. Wally's eyes went directly to the chaplain, who lowered his head discreetly, eyes closed, lips moving with his prayer.

Wally turned back to stare directly into Connie's eyes. Lynn didn't know if she should stay or go, but she was rooted to the spot, listening to a promise she would carry with her forever.

"I will, Connie," Wally whispered. He dropped to one knee by the couch and reached around his neck to gather up Connie's hands in both of his.

ON SCENE

Between them, their collectively clenched fingers shook with the emotion of his words. "We'll find him. I promise."

Like ticking off a disgusting, morbid checklist, Wally regained his composure on the Schrader porch and set his mind to the next task. He needed to go tell Vallarena Anson that her new husband wasn't going to make it home that night. Or any other night, forever after. He felt like the pied piper of death with Jette waiting for him in the car. Two members in a marked car behind Jette waiting to do their own duty of protecting Vallarena through the night. Behind them stood a civilian car with another RCMP chaplain. All the mice following the piper. He shuddered.

Suddenly the door opened behind him, hitting him in the back.

"Sorry, Wally." Larry winced and slipped out onto the porch around the door, shaking his hair out of his eyes.

"What are you doing?" Wally called out as the boy took the steps down in two long, lanky strides, swinging his jacket on.

"I'm not just sitting here. Lynn has the boys. Mom is…" he shrugged, eyes sliding to the window where they could see Connie asleep on the couch. "Mrs. Anson doesn't have anyone here. I'm going with you."

Wally was certain his look of shock showed clearly on his face.

"Dad would want me to go. She shouldn't be alone."

Scratching at his upper lip, Wally rolled his eyes upward, willing the emotion to stay put and not spill all over this dear boy. He clenched the shoulder of Larry's jacket and nodded, working his jaw back and forth. Bob was always the first one out the door when a colleague was sick or injured. He was always dropping in on the families when members were out of town on a course and the first one to bring flowers and one of Connie's famous coffee cakes when there was a death. Larry was right, Bob really would want someone to go. Wally tried to wipe his face free of everything crashing around in his head, dragging his hand roughly down from forehead to chin.

"Yeah, I know," Larry said. "I feel the same way right now."

Wally stepped off the porch and threw his head back, staring at the few stars he could see through the grey-black clouds. "Okay." He breathed deeply of the night air. "But you'll stay in the car until I come get you."

Larry nodded and walked down the path with Bruce hopping along beside him.

For the first time in his career Wally wished he could discard his chevron patches. To no longer be the leader of men. It was one thing to chase down a suspect in the bush, calling out orders over the radio, but it was another situation altogether to tell wives their husbands were dead. Informing a family you don't know of the loss of a loved one was part of the job he didn't like, nobody did, but it was a necessary duty. When it was a stranger, you could remove yourself emotionally, deal with it, and move on to the investigation. These wives weren't strangers. These men were friends. These children were his. And this night could go to hell, as far as he was concerned.

> *"Wally was a man who just automatically commanded respect. It wasn't that he asked for it, you just respected him for who he was and what he did. You know those British guards? Proper, strait-laced, professional, that was Wally. He just had a presence."*
>
> *Interview with Larry Schrader (2020)*

Chapter Seventeen

Friday, October 9, 1970
Robertson land
An hour and a half after sunset

The well worn soles of his hunting boots made no sound as he walked the barely-there trail he'd been on hundreds…perhaps thousands of times before. How did one know how many times their feet had tread a single trail after so many years of living in one place? He didn't mind the darkness that surrounded him, cloaking him in security, and wondered how the others were fairing. The corner of his mouth twitched a little bit. Not a smile—not in these circumstances—but white men weren't known for their good sense in the bush. At least, not in these parts. He adjusted the rifle strap to rest more comfortably on his shoulder and turned up the collar on his jacket, setting a steady pace northwest. He was almost there.

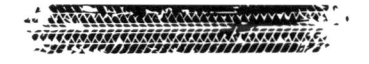

After just two months of wedded bliss, this wasn't the first time Doug was late for dinner and Vallarena knew it wouldn't be the last. She'd been warned a few times by friends of her father's that this life was fraught with ups and downs. She didn't just want to be good at it; she wanted to be great at it.

Trying to suppress her disappointment with understanding and forgiveness, she rechecked her overnight case for the fifth time, and straightened Doug's suitcase on the bed. Aiming for the wonderful efficiency with which her mother ran her household, she had packed him up and left the case open on the bed, ready for any last minute items he might like to add.

"The packing fairy has done it again," she murmured. Her heart warmed to remember her father returning home after work, before a trip, to give her mother a sweet kiss on the apple of her cheek. She always got his things together so they could hit the road the second he walked in the door. She smiled and smoothed the trousers on top; they would just need a quick press before the dance tomorrow night.

Their wedding had been small and filled with love. They didn't even send out invitations; her grandmother just got on the phone and started calling people. She unzipped the garment bag that held the outfit she got married in, anxious to wear it a second time. A beautiful white set with a wide collar and sheer circle design on the sleeves and pants, she never wanted the typical frothy concoction with yards and yards of lace and tulle. She and her sister in law had gone into town to a shop and each picked out something simple but beautiful that they could easily wear again. She hoped she could wear it a thousand times over.

She knew without asking that the wedding dance her mother was preparing was going to be huge, but she was okay with that. She would give her mother this moment and smile gracefully for every photo, because really, she was excited to go home and see her friends and family. Sometimes a fuss was fine, even if it wasn't her usual cup of tea.

She expected keys in the lock, not a knock at the door, and parted the curtain at the front window to glance outside. The porch light clearly illuminated Wally and a chaplain on her doorstep. An ember of fear ignited in her heart, starting a slow burn.

Wally was staring right at her through the curtain and knocked again. She stared back at him, the burn creating a tiny hole in her heart. She pulled the curtain back into place and mechanically put one foot in front of the other, going to the door. She pressed her head against the cool wood for a second

ON SCENE

before opening it, whispering a fervent prayer that Doug was all right. "Bring him home to me, Lord," she said, then cracked open the door.

Wally led the way into the house, looking awkward and out of place without his dog by his side. The chaplain followed him in and nodded respectfully. She ignored the man, flashing an automatic smile at Wally, grasping his arm warmly.

"I'm not used to seeing you without Bruce. Where is he? He's always welcome here." Her smile wavered but she held it in place valiantly.

"Thanks. He's in the car, I didn't think—"

She cut him off with a shaky laugh. "Oh, he won't like that at all. You should—" She tried to turn back to the door, but he stopped her gently. The chaplain stepped forward as well, making her back up. She didn't want the man to touch her. The ember was burning brighter, and the hole had widened.

"Vallarena, we have to talk to you." Wally's hand firmed on her arm.

She cut him off again. "I'm being so rude; I didn't even offer you a cup of coffee. Can I get you something?" She smoothed her hands down the front of her pants and adjusted the matching jacket. Pulling at a thread on her cuff she avoided eye contact with either man. Wally never let go of her arm and stepped closer to her. She raised her eyes barely to the toe of his boots but didn't step away. She watched his boots take another step, completely closing the gap between them. He closed his hands over hers to still them, his grip imploring her to look up.

"I don't need anything. Stop. I have to tell you that Doug was killed tonight."

The gasp that escaped her felt like the last breath she might ever take and she tightened her fingers in Wally's grip. The ember flamed into an inferno, blazing a hole so big she couldn't breathe. A small sob escaped but was not given the opportunity to blossom into full blown hysteria. She clamped her lips closed, eyes drowning and blurring everything in front of her. "How?"

"He and Bob Schrader went out to investigate a complaint. They were both shot and killed on a farm south of MacDowall."

She lost the fight with her face and her mouth dropped open. Shock would have been a welcome, mild reaction compared to the emotions flashing through her.

Kate Kading

"Bob? What about Connie? The kids?" Throwing her remaining composure and propriety out the window, she collapsed into Wally's arms. It wasn't quite a shriek, she still managed to control her voice, but she couldn't stand and the shaky, half hysterical questions tumbled out one after the other.

She felt wild; looking side to side, waiting for Doug to come walking through the door any second. The door remained solid, nobody coming in to save her.

"What about the kids? What about…" her voice was muffled by the cloth of Wally's uniform, the raging fire in her heart threatening to end her.

"Don't worry about them right now. We're here for you," he said.

She buried her face deeper into his chest, sagging against him, focusing on the feeling of him smoothing her hair. This wasn't real. It was a joke. A mean, sick joke that she would surely give her husband hell for. They were always joking, these boys.

"This isn't funny, Wally. You tell Doug to get in here." Her voice got louder, more strangled, and she struggled to breathe. "It's not funny." She gripped Wally's arms, shaking him, screaming about jokes and hell. She yelled Doug's name, and Wally just held on. A solid mast in a violent storm.

She eventually pulled away, looking into his eyes, and the heartache she saw there punched her in the stomach. Her breath whooshed out all at once, the hole in her heart pumping no blood, only pain. It was more than she could bear and she dissolved into wrenching tears, not caring at all that the man who held her was probably more uncomfortable than he had ever been in his whole existence.

Rising up from his chest, she searched Wally's face. "Why? What do I do… how can I…why?"

His jawline was granite, clenched teeth working back and forth. "I don't have a single answer for you, my dear. Not one. For now, call your mama." He smoothed her hair back from her face. "You can leave the rest to us. We won't leave your questions unanswered. Not if it's the last thing we ever do."

```
"When they gave me back his briefcase, it still
had Doug's blood on it."

                        Excerpt of interview with
                        Vallarena (Anson) Blum (2017)
```

Chapter Eighteen

Friday, October 9, 1970
On Scene
2200hrs

The Ident team came in to take fingerprints and go over the abandoned police car after Danny's discovery of…nothing. But he'd had no lofty hopes that the shooter would still be in the vehicle, anyway.

"Now we can get on with things, at least." He was shoulder to shoulder with Joe again. They walked away from the scene, hanging around the perimeter under the guise of awaiting orders, but Danny was too amped up to wait around for the likes of Staff Sergeant Anderson. There was a shooter to find, and you didn't get results sitting around on your ass.

He cast a critical eye over his shoulder. Who would miss him if he just walked away? Officers buzzed around the car like angry bees, with the Staff Sergeant calling out obnoxious orders over a bullhorn.

Without any real direction in mind, they followed the path in the grass made by the tires, coming out to where it met up with the train tracks and the service road. Danny stood in the middle of the tracks looking up into the sky. Huge wet flakes stuck to his eyelashes and he shook his head, looking north up the tracks, his flashlight falling pitifully short in the vast expanse of black night. Turning around, he pointed the flashlight south down the tracks, towards Saskatoon.

"Hey, can you see in the dark?" he asked suddenly.

"Huh?" Greenslade clicked his flashlight on and off, shining it in Danny's face. "Yeah, why?"

"No, I mean without a flashlight. Moon's bright, but obscured. If you wanted to stay hidden out here, you could. Nobody can see in the dark, you need some kind of guide, right?" Danny looked up at the almost full moon.

Greenslade shrugged. "Yeah, I s'pose. Like holding a railing or something?" He propped a boot up on the railroad track, jerked his flashlight down and followed it as far as the beam of light would stretch.

"Yeah," Danny said, "like a railing or something." He walked a few yards down the track and shut his flashlight off. In these parts, the night stretched on for miles with only a few of the better off families bothering with yard lights.

Greenslade turned his flashlight off too, plunging them into enveloping darkness with only the moon, mostly covered by clouds at the moment, trying to shine any light on the area at all. "I bet you could walk from MacDowall nearly to Duck Lake without seeing a single light."

"Bet you could." Danny agreed and grabbed his radio. "Cavello to Mosher." He tapped his foot, agitation growing in his gut. "Come on," he muttered to himself, pressing the button again. "Cavello to Mosher, come in." The radio chattered in and out, and he hoped Mosher heard him and was just waiting for an opening.

"Copy that, Cavello. This is Mosher."

Danny threw his head back in relief. "Greenslade and I are on the train tracks near the service road. We're going to follow them." He let go of the radio button, not knowing if Mosher would agree or not.

"10-4, that's where I'd be if I had to walk in the dark. But send Greenslade back. I need some experience at HQ. Take someone else." Mosher signed off.

"Looks like you're on this trail without me." Joe grabbed Danny's shoulder, shaking it lightly. "Be careful, man."

"Yeah, you too." They walked back through the trees, avoiding the Staff Sergeant. Danny had his eye on the small group that was left. There had to be someone good here who didn't annoy the shit out of him. "Get a car, okay? I'm going to grab someone and we'll need a ride before you head back." Danny grabbed Joe's arm. "Quiet about it, though. I don't need Anderson up my ass."

Greenslade jerked a nod and disappeared.

Relief flooded Danny when he spied Ron Morier helping an Ident member pack up his gear. Morier was out of Rosthern Detachment, about an hour south of Prince Albert, and their detachment areas overlapped. MacDowall was technically in Rosthern's area, but it was on Prince Albert's telephone exchange. Nobody wanted to make a long distance phone call to Rosthern to report something so the officers often passed information back and forth on complaints. He stopped and felt the weight of the 'what ifs' weigh down on him. What if Doug had never taken this complaint in the first place?

He shook it off as quickly as it assaulted him and marched a direct path to Morier. He leaned down to murmur in his ear, "Orders from Mosher. Let's go." Ron's eyes flickered but he didn't hesitate or question. Shaking hands with the Ident member, Ron gathered his own gear—there seemed to be a lot of it—and followed Danny to the car Greenslade had waiting for them.

"Moving in or moving out?" He held the back door of the car open for Ron as he tossed a small pack, canteen, rifle, and extra jacket in before getting in himself.

"You can never be too prepared in the bush. Where you from, anyway? If you knew these parts, you wouldn't be so empty handed." Morier leaned forward, slinging his arms over the seat and resting his chin.

Annoyed, and hoping this wasn't going to be a regular trend tonight, he pushed Ron's arm aside, leaned back in his seat, and laughed without humour. "I can hold my own, greenhorn. Teach you a thing or two."

Ron looked like he was going to shoot back, but Joe interrupted them.

"Someone better tell me where you two are going or I'll drop you off in the middle of the bush to duke it out."

Danny shoved Morier's arm again and turned sideways in the passenger seat.

"If we count back from the time the shots were called in, I figure this guy has about three and a half hours on us. That's assuming he didn't hunker down somewhere for a while." He held his watch under the map light and tapped the face. "It's about thirty kilometres from MacDowall to Duck Lake on that track. If he's headed to Saskatoon, that's the way I'd go. You drop us off south of Duck Lake, and if he comes by that way, we've got him." He pounded a fist into his opposite palm.

Greenslade looked sceptical. "You tell Mosher this?"

Danny shrugged. "Not the exact location. But I figured you could brief him when you get back?" Anticipating an uncomfortable night all the way around, he cranked up the heat and passed his full canteen back to Morier.

With the windows rolled up tight against the melting snow, the air in the cruiser was thick with cigarette smoke. Greenslade blew out a lungful and waved his hand.

"Sure. I'll convince our superior officer that you two thought it was a great idea to go sleep on the train tracks. Excellent." Sarcasm coated his drawl and he grabbed the canteen out of Morier's hand.

Morier gave it over and took a long drag on his cigarette. "Shit, not my idea." On the inhale, he popped a second smoke between his lips, lit it with the red ember from his first, then rolled his window down an inch. "I'm just the backup." He tossed his cigarette butt out the window, rolled it back up and slung his arms over the front seat. Danny pushed him aside.

"It's a good idea. Mosher said so. Just tell him where we are. I know a good spot."

It didn't take long for them to reach the small town of Duck Lake, and sail right past it. He directed Greenslade to a secondary road that crossed the tracks and ordered him to stop.

"This is good, we'll walk from here. Take care." He slammed the car door and waited for Morier to gather his gear.

"You take longer than my mother on a weekend trip." He grabbed Morier's canteen and gun and started walking while the young officer shrugged into his extra jacket, strapped on his pack, and hurried to catch up.

"Where are we going? We can't just stand on the open track all night." Morier looked up and down the track, this stretch not at all like the stretch up at

ON SCENE

MacDowall. There was nothing but gravel and prairie grass here. The trees were several hundred yards away, just a blurred shadow in the moonlight, and the rest of the surrounding area was farm land. Nowhere to stage an ambush at all, should the shooter come their way.

"Nope. We'll have cover. Come on." He kept walking, weak flashlight beam bobbing along ahead of him, glowing cigarette ash the only thing visible by Morier's face.

They walked along for a few minutes, trying not to jump at the night sounds, ears tuned for other signs of life.

"I met Sergeant Schrader once when I had to take files up to Prince Albert. Nice guy." Morier jogged a few steps to catch up. "You know them?"

Danny grunted. Did he know them? The pain in his chest made it hard to swallow. Did you know someone you ate with almost every day? Did you know someone you laughed with, and worked with, nearly every waking hour of your life? "Yeah, you could say that." He was glad for the darkness that hid his face, hid his pain, hid the tears that crept up on him so unexpectedly he didn't know what to do with them. He dashed at his eyes with the back of his hand.

A huge shadow came into view, cutting off the need to say more about Doug and Bob.

"What the hell is that?" Morier pointed his flashlight at the shadow.

Danny roughly cleared the sadness from his throat. "The perfect lookout tower," he said.

The looming off-grey shape was a haystack, set back from the train tracks on the edge of a farmer's field. "If anyone comes past here, we'll be able to see them."

"Yeah, nice. But how're we going to see?" Morier held up his flashlight and made a face. "These don't cover a large area."

Danny shrugged. "True. We'll just have to stay sharp and keep an eye on things. I'm just hoping we got ahead of him." He didn't relish trying to stay awake all night, but he'd do just about anything to be the guy who brought the shooter in.

"Yeah…" Morier wandered closer to him until they were toe to toe and his face brightened in the light of the flashlight. "I have an idea."

Swinging his pack off his back, Morier put it on the ground and stooped down, rummaging. "Here, hold this. And this."

Danny set down their rifles and canteens and held out his hands. Morier piled them with a knife, fishing line, and two cans.

"Hungry?" he asked.

"Sure. But we should go get set up for the night. Not hang around on the tracks." Danny appreciated the offer, but didn't understand the timing.

Morier cranked open the first can with an old military can opener, and handed Danny a camp spoon that folded out of a cover containing a fork and knife as well.

"Just eat it and get out of the way." Morier took the other can from him, popped the top, and unfolded another spoon. He ate the cold stew in three big bites, scraping the can as clean as he could without really seeing the inside. Wiping his sleeve across his mouth, he put the empty can under his arm, motioning him out of the way.

Enjoying his food a little slower, he held the flashlight and watched Morier string fishing line across the track, attaching it to some small bushes and clumps of tall grass on either side. He scooped some rocks up off the track and dropped them into his empty can with an obnoxious rattle, holding it up to Danny's face.

"That's genius." He punched Morier on the arm and finished up what he had left in his can, stooping to grab a handful of rocks.

Attaching a can to each end of their makeshift trip wire, they backed away down the embankment and climbed the tall haystack. Lying on their bellies at the very top, they flattened themselves out of sight, but still had a decent view of the tracks, even if the thin beam of their flashlights only stretched about half way.

"This is it, man. He's going to come this way." Danny tried to sound confident but it was more desperate hope than anything.

ON SCENE

"How do you know? I hope he does, and we're the ones to catch him. But how can you be sure?"

"I'm sure. Because he has the entire RCMP after him, and it's the only way he could get past us in the dark by MacDowall."

Morier grunted and shifted in the hay. "I hope you're right. Put this to bed early. You know, for the families."

Danny sighed, grief and anger mingling in his gut. He reflected on the moment he turned his friend's body over, Mosher shining the light to reveal Doug's staring eyes. He couldn't let the grief take over because the anger was far more useful to him right now. White hot rage kept you warm, it kept you focused, it gave you more fuel when your body would normally give up.

"Oh, we'll put it to bed, all right. We'll find him and he'll never see the light of day, ever again."

Massive Hunt for Farmer Launched-Wilfred Stanley Robertson, 40, a MacDowall area farmer has been charged with the capital murders of Sergeant R. J. Schrader, 41, and Constable D.B. Anson, 30. Robertson is still at large.

Headline and excerpt, Saskatoon StarPhoenix (Saturday, October 10, 1970)

Chapter Nineteen

Friday, October 9, 1970
Prince Albert Detachment
2300hrs

Leaving the Schrader family and Vallarena Anson in the care of the RCMP chaplains and the surveillance teams didn't make Wally feel any better about deserting them. It was a necessary heartache. He couldn't be there to console them and search at the same time. His place was out in the dark forest with Bruce.

Ordering a junior member to man the radio room, Wally stopped in just long enough to get an update. The tight room, crammed with radio gear and telephones, had only four chairs and was usually staffed with several officers at a time, making phone calls and relaying messages to other officers in the field. After the 33, both the radio room and detachment had become a ghost town. It was time to reorganize and put a plan in motion. They needed someone in the radio room if they were going to properly communicate, no matter how badly each of them wanted to be searching.

After a brief exchange on the radio, Wally learned Staff Sergeant Mosher had directed a team to drag a trailer out to MacDowall and set up a small headquarters at the scene. He was impatiently awaiting Wally's return.

"Hurry the hell up. And bring a coffee pot with you." Wally looked around the radio room, spying a table crammed in the corner with an ancient electric percolator on it. Probably once silver, it was now an interesting shade of sludge brown and he didn't even want to know what the inside looked like. Anything that came out of that pot would likely put more hair on your chest, just like Mosher liked it. He tucked the empty pot under his arm, grabbed the can of coffee beside it, a box of sugar cubes, and two chipped, greyish brown cups he was sure used to be white.

Stopping just inside the door, he nodded at the young member, "Don't leave here until a superior officer relieves you. Hear me?" A firm "Yes, sir" followed Wally out the door. He threw the coffee supplies into the cruiser. Jette was still in the driver's seat, smoking cigarettes as fast as he could suck them back if the littered ground outside the driver's window was any indication.

In Wally's estimation, the drive from Prince Albert back to the Robertson place took about nine years. With nine hundred years worth of purgatory in store for him for the promise he'd made Connie. He would gladly take any punishment offered and rot in purgatory forever if it meant finding his friend's killer.

"Look up there." Jette inhaled the last of another cigarette, tossed the butt out the window and slowed down. They were about halfway to MacDowall, the lights of the city far behind them, and came up to a roadblock at a crossroads on the highway. RCMP officers were checking vehicles before letting them continue. Wally eyed the farthest member covering from behind a parked police car, shotgun aimed at the driver of the stopped vehicle. The second member circled the car, checking the occupants and any hiding spots. It was a serious scene. Chances were, locals had never seen anything like this before and weren't likely to ever again.

Jette manoeuvred around the line up of cars, inching his way up the shoulder to the blockade. The officers on the stop waved them through without hesitation, holding up a civilian car to let the cruiser pass. Jette shoulder checked and went to move through when Wally stopped him.

"Hold up, who's that coming up the side?" He strained to turn in his seat and saw a man ambling along the shoulder of the road beside the short line of vehicles. Not many people were out on the highway at this time of night, and none of them should've been on foot.

Jette stopped the car and Wally got out, one hand on his gun, opening the back door for Bruce.

The red of the rotating lights passed ominously across grim faces, over and over again, spotlights sweeping over civilians, catching reactions ranging from simple curiosity to obvious fear as Wally and Bruce slowly stalked down the line.

"Can I help you, sir?" he called out, shining his flashlight directly at the approaching person. "Can I have you get back in your vehicle, please?" The man strolled forward, silent, but not threatening. Bruce kept pace, a low growl vibrating through his side and up Wally's leg where it rubbed against the dog.

"Easy Chief," he murmured under his breath, hand leaning harder on his gun. He slowed his breathing to an even rise and fall, carefully measured to calm him and guarantee true aim.

Bruce ran up to the man and Wally got closer, feeling the pull of relief when he recognized the detachment janitor, Frederick Johnson. He was only required to clean twice a week, but took advantage of the flexible schedule to make sure he visited with every shift in turn. Mr. Johnson always said he didn't mind the drive into the city for the steady work and good conversation with the officers.

"Sergeant Regitnig?" Bruce nosed the man's hand, one paw going up on his knee. "And Bruce, I knew it was you." Mr. Johnson smoothed the fur on Bruce's head a few times with one hand, and rummaged in his baggy overall pocket with the other. Bruce sat expectantly; tail wagging across the ground, kicking up dust and tree debris, and was rewarded with a bite of something.

"Mr. Johnson, you'll spoil my best man." Wally stepped forward to shake his hand, the driver of the car next in line peering over at them with interest. "What brings you out this late?"

"Told you a hundred times to call me Fred, sir. I do the floors over at Mann's Grocery Store in the city. That's a late one. Just got home a bit ago and heard about the trouble." Mr. Johnson shook his head sadly, making Wally cock an eyebrow. Word travelled fast in a small town, but the details of what transpired at the Robertson farm at suppertime had not been released to the public yet.

"Oh yeah? What'd you hear?"

"Shame about them officers. They always had a kind word for me." Head down, shoulders hunched forward, Fred absently petted Bruce.

Wally came closer to gauge any changes in the man's facial expression. "Where'd you hear this?"

Fred paused, staring directly at Wally as if to judge whether he was going to say more. "Well…" he inhaled through his teeth, rubbing the back of his neck, sweeping his eyes away from Wally's gaze. "Folks talk, you know."

"Oh, sure they do. But no, I don't know. Anything you can tell me might be of help, if you're willing?" Wally stepped away to direct a car to move ahead, leaving Fred alone with his decision.

The driver of the car was paying more attention to Wally and Fred's conversation than he was to the line moving ahead of him. Wally noticed the passenger window open a crack. He waved his arm, flashlight directing the car to move along. People listened, and they certainly did talk.

When he came back to Fred and Bruce, it looked as though the man had settled whatever dilemma was plaguing his mind. Wally waited a moment, out of respect, trying to control his raging impatience.

"Did you know my mother was a Robertson?"

The question was posed so casually that Wally didn't register at first. When his mind caught up to the ramifications of what was said, his guard was completely down. It was the last thing he expected Fred to say. He paused to gather his thoughts, wondering how best to proceed, when Fred took a big breath and kept going.

"Stanley Robertson's my first cousin on my mother's side." The wind blew his thin thatch of hair over his forehead and he reached up to push it back. He still looked like he was contemplating the intelligence of revealing this information, but continued nonetheless. "We live right next door to where they are. I know what happened. It's a damn shame, sir. Too many lives lost now, and I don't just mean those officers."

He didn't know who 'they' were but he didn't want to interrupt Fred with questions. "I can't disagree with you, Fred."

He hated the uncertainty of the situation, but there were some certainties in every investigation. Like the fact that someone, somewhere, knew something. The uncertainties laid in whether they would come forward and tell the truth or not. What they said, or didn't say, as the case may be, could make or break an investigation.

"It's not that people agree with what happened, Sergeant. Not a'tall. But he's our friend. Never done nothing bad like this, ever. Folks are going to help him, if he asks." Fred shrugged. "Give him a meal, let him sleep warm for the night. Nothing against you and your fine work." He pushed his hair off his forehead again, looking rather matter of fact, yet apologetic at the same time.

Wally was taken aback by this speech and cleared his throat. "I appreciate your honesty. I won't take it personally, but for the sake of public safety we really do need to find him." Fred was shaking his head in the negative before Wally even finished speaking.

"Nobody's in danger in these here parts, sir. Nope. Nobody." He kept shaking his head, looking down and dragging the toe of his boot back and forth through the dirt. "You don't need to scare these folks with threats and guns." He turned and looked at the dwindling line of cars moving through the eagle eye aim of the member with the shotgun. "You won't find him like this."

"Why do you say that?" Wally narrowed his eyes, hearing something more than a guess in Fred's words.

"You know, Stanley always poked fun at the escapees from the Pen. You boys always seem to catch them on the first or maybe the second day."

Wally nodded. He didn't know what else to do with that statement.

"Me an' Stanley talk lots about what we would do, where we would go. You know, to hide from the police if we were running. Nothin' serious, just two good ol' bushman trying to outdo each other. Been trying to do that since we were kids." Fred got a far off look in his eyes, staring at nothing Wally could see.

ON SCENE

In the course of his career, there were times he wanted to beat the information out of someone if they were jerking him around. But this wasn't one of those times. He needed to get back and let Bruce sniff out the scene. A scent trail never kept. But while Bruce had a nose better than any other Police Service Dog, Wally had a sixth sense when it came to people. Fred Johnson had been a fixture at the detachment for over ten years; before Wally himself had come to Prince Albert. Fred was known as a good worker; a man of good character. With a gaggle of kids to feed, his wife was always in the kitchen and would send the odd banana loaf or batch of cookies to the officers. Wally's sixth sense had never niggled at him around Fred. Trusting that had gotten him this far, so he would hang on to his questions and let Fred tell his story at his own pace.

"Always said he would wait. 'Aw, them boys is stupid' Stanley would say. 'You got to lay low about a week and wait for them to lift the roadblocks. Then you can get out free and clear.' That's what he always said. And I'd agree. Because we both know how to sleep rough. Been taught since we were kids." Fred's mouth compressed and his eyebrows raised, but he didn't say anything else.

"We have the best police trackers in the country here, Fred. We catch the runners because that's what we do."

Fred didn't move but his posture told Wally he thought he was wrong. There was an apology of sorts in the straightening of his back. The settling of his shoulders.

"That may have been the case then, Sergeant, but it's not the case now. Your fancy training isn't going to find him. Not like that."

Fred lifted one hand in a half salute of farewell, thrust both hands deep into the pockets of his overalls, and walked away back down the empty line to his truck, now parked by itself.

Bruce nosed Wally's hand. "Yeah, I know. Let's go." His mind was calculating but he could do that on the road, so he let Bruce lead the way back to the car. Jette was motoring his way through another half pack of cigarettes. He banged on the hood as he rounded the car. "Fire it up, Jette. Let's go."

He shifted uncomfortably in the passenger seat, rubbing at the sharp stubble on his chin. "He's not going to be on the road. Fred said he's a bushman."

He didn't turn to look at Jette, just stared straight ahead as they hit the open highway again. "I'd bet my last dollar he's still on his own land."

"Sleep was not an option that night."

Excerpt of interview with troopmate and friend of Doug Anson (April 2016)

Chapter Twenty

```
Friday, October 9, 1970
On Scene
2330hrs
```

Headquarters wouldn't win any design awards but it was functional enough. Wally didn't care what the makeshift office looked like; he wouldn't be in there for long. He looked around the trailer for a clear spot to set down the dinosaur percolator and can of coffee. A few tables had been set up and already you couldn't see the top of anything. Maps covered every available surface, someone had set up a radio and chairs in one corner, and there were more officers crammed together than Wally even thought possible. They listened intently to Mosher, imposing at the front of the room. It wasn't his size; it was his authority that had taller men look up to him.

Wally stepped back outside the trailer door and leaned heavily against the wall, searching his pockets for a cigarette. Looking up from his lighter, he saw a form strutting towards him and swore under his breath.

Staff Sergeant Anderson got closer, his face appearing more pinched than usual. "It's dark," he snapped. "What are you doing here?" The man never sounded pleasant, and Wally avoided him at the detachment whenever he could.

"Debriefing with Mosher. Then tracking." Wally stood up straighter, enjoying the few inches he had on his superior. Rank was the only thing this man had on him. He took a long drag on his cigarette when Anderson spoke again.

"Don't suppose that mutt could find his own ass in the dark." Anderson sneered at Bruce, who didn't appreciate the comment if his growl was anything to go by.

Wally casually glanced up at the shop light someone had hung on a metal hook beside the trailer door, looked back at Anderson, and exhaled his cloud of smoke directly into the Staff Sergeant's face. "Why don't we turn that light off and see if he can find your ass in the dark?" His low, even tone belied the anger he was holding back, but losing his cool would serve no purpose at all. He had work to do.

Anderson sputtered, waving his hand distastefully in front of his face and brushed invisible dust off the front of his jacket. He had supposedly been directing men in the bush for the last several hours so Wally had no idea how he came out of there without a speck of dirt on him. Even his shoes were still clean.

Anderson glared at him, lip curled in distaste. "That won't be necessary, Sergeant. Carry on." He raised his nose in the air and walked away.

A few steps from the trailer door Anderson tripped over one of the clumps of dirt and rocks that dotted the space and Wally choked on his drag, shoulders shaking in withheld laughter.

"Guess he can't see much in the dark, hey boy?" He flicked his smoke away with a cough and ruffled the fur on Bruce's neck. Mosher had to be almost finished by now.

"You did a great job tonight, men. Nothing more to do here in the dark so I want all of you to rest up. I know you'll have the Schrader and Anson families in your prayers. With the dawn, there's no way Robertson'll be able to hide." Mosher's face hardened and he inhaled sharply through flared nostrils. "We have too many men. Too much dedication. Too much fire power. I'll see everybody back here at 0600." Mosher banged on the table in front of him. "Dismissed."

ON SCENE

The low hum elevated as the officers filed out of the trailer, nodding at Regitnig as they went. He only recognized a few of the faces, but every constable knew hooks when they saw them. The chevron patches on a Sergeant's arm dictated authority, but wouldn't gain automatic respect. Anderson was a clear example of that. Bob Schrader had earned that respect, and even without the higher rank, Doug Anson had earned it too, leading by example as a senior constable. Wally knew his reputation preceded him but he kept that in tight check. He nodded at every single man until he was the last one left in the room with Mosher. He wanted each one of these men to feel appreciated in what they were doing and to thank them in some unspoken way for their efforts.

"Who is this guy, Al?" Wally cleared the maps off one end of the table closest to him and set up the coffee pot. There was no water to be had yet so he couldn't actually make coffee, but busied himself while his mind churned away on the problem at hand.

Mosher rifled through a stack and came up with a few sheets of lined paper scrawled with his handwriting. Patting the desk, he came up with his reading glasses and crammed them onto his nose. Snapping the pages he read, "Wilfred Stanley Robertson, 40, family man. Five foot four, hunter, mostly sells wood for work. That's it so far. Never been in trouble before this." Mosher took off his glasses and threw them down, disgust colouring his face redder than usual.

Wally could often tell how serious a situation was by the colour around Mosher's collar. "Damn it, Al, we have to find him. What's your plan for tonight?"

Mosher smoothed his chestnut moustache thoughtfully. "My plan's the same as yours, I expect. Search every nook and cranny. No way he's out there another day." Mosher sighed, unclipped his tie and undid his top button. "But for tonight, we've got nothing."

A stickler for the tie himself, he knew Al would never do that in front of the other men. Taking a break where they could, they would speak freely here in this room for the few brief moments they had.

"I'm going to go out with Bruce and do another few rounds. We'll stay in the house tonight." He eyed Mosher, gauging his reaction.

Al smirked, moustache twitching. "Yeah, I supposed as much. Just a waste of my time to fight you on it." He rubbed the back of his neck under his loosened shirt collar. "I've set two men in the shed across from the house already and I have Greenslade coming back. Going to keep him on scene tonight. And I made some calls to Shilo." Mosher already had a hand up when Wally snapped to attention with an explosion of breath.

"I don't want to hear it, Regitnig. This investigation is bigger than the both of us. We already have over fifty men out there, a busload of cadets on their way from Regina, and still not enough equipment to cover the ground we need to. The army is bringing in more aircraft, and some secure vehicles for moving men." Mosher lowered his hand, and Wally jumped in.

"But sir, they're loud, and not trained for this type of terrain. We won't be marching in a straight line. Plus, he won't last another day. You said so yourself." Wally stopped his argument when Mosher put his hand up again.

"That's right, and when that happens I'll send them right home. But it's better to be prepared. The army's bringing personnel carriers. The guy on the phone said if I didn't know what it was, just picture a mini tank." Mosher ignored Wally's attempts to further interrupt, raising his voice. "None of our vehicles can get through this bush, you know that. The thing is armoured and can move men faster than we can walk in." Mosher finally relented and waved for Wally to go ahead.

"That's fine, but what about the grids? Do they even know how to move in a search pattern? You know I know my way through this area like the back of Bruce's head. Been staring at both for the last six years." Bruce raised his head at his name, Wally made a stand down hand signal, and Bruce lowered his head back to his front paws.

"I know I don't have to worry about you and ol' Bruce here, slinking through the bush, but I do need to worry about this asshole setting himself up in a tree somewhere pegging off cadets like a carnival game." Mosher paced with his words, throwing his hands up, getting louder and more agitated. "Armed Forces aren't included in the call out, just two personnel carriers, the drivers, a couple of planes and helicopters, and the pilots. Shouldn't be too hard to absorb them into the search plan and get them up to speed. The more force we use, the faster this is resolved." Mosher stopped pacing and clapped him on the shoulder. "Now get out of here. You have a shooter to track, and I have a constable to yell at for shooting up a damn police car."

Wally stopped short, "You what?"

Al scratched at his neck under his collar. "Never mind. When this is all over I'll tell you about it over a beer or three. Remember to check in once in a while." He bent down to scratch Bruce between the ears. "Keep this guy safe, Bruce." The dog barked and jumped up, tail wagging.

"Will do, sir. I made a promise, and I intend to keep it."

"Promise? To who?"

Wally shook his head and went down the wobbly wooden steps. "I'll tell you when we have that beer."

SASK. SUSPECT ASKED TO GIVE HIMSELF UP-*Police used aircraft, helicopters, Canadian Armed Forces personnel carriers, and tracking dogs in a massive search of heavy muskeg-dotted bush near MacDowall."*

Headline and excerpt, Winnipeg Free Press
(Saturday, October 24, 1970)

Chapter Twenty-One

Friday, October 9, 1970
Robertson land
Around 10pm

He hadn't yet found what he was looking for. Hands outstretched, brushing the trees as he passed slowly by them, he might as well have had his eyes closed. He could have, at that. The darkness was thick, enveloping the forest floor, revealing only slices of star shine if he looked straight up through the tops of the surrounding branches. Yet he could still move through the trees, the lay of things set out in his mind, night vision helping him along. He knew the land with an intimacy not many had. That knowledge was still taught through the generations in some families. It was something the Robertsons prided themselves on.

Maybe he would go home for the night. Nobody would be there. The desire was strong but he pushed it aside. He couldn't sleep until he found what he was looking for.

An excellent trapper, sure, but even he couldn't set snares in the dark. A rabbit would be nice, sitting by the warmth of a crackling fire, juice dripping down his chin. He could taste the meat already. He allowed himself the brief reverie, then shook it off. No fire. No succulent rabbit meat. Just one foot in front of the other, until he found his safe place.

ON SCENE

He only heard other people once in his travels, and a single distant shot that made him take pause on the trail. Who were they shooting at? Did they think it was him? He didn't belabour the issue much, simply kept on by the light of the moon. He came upon the base of the hill and his heart lightened. Upwards from here, and not too much farther to go.

The guilt of his actions circled his head like flies and he tried to shoo it away. It wasn't his fault.

There'll be trouble now.

The steep climb took more effort than crossing the flat prairie and the exertion fuelled his anger. Or perhaps it was the other way around. The anger kept him going.

They're gonna come get you.

Surely the police wouldn't have hauled him off for warning another man to stay away from his wife? He hadn't even hit the bastard. He thought about it, of course. A little clip on the ear to remind him to keep to his own business. But he decided not to clip him. Just a warning shot, that was all. But was Ruth right?

You'll go to jail for it.

Those were the words that turned the tide. Now blood was shed and he'd never know what his punishment would have been for warning his cousin to stay away from what did not belong to him. Surely the police would be out for *his* blood now.

An eye for an eye.

Cresting the hill, the silhouette of the lone Jack Pine rose up against the moonlight. With trees surrounding it not half its height, it stood out sharply against the different shades of black and grey in the night sky. A full grown man could barely reach all the way around the trunk, and the tips of the thickly bristled branches nearly swept the ground. Stanley loved to stand under it. The tree was a marvel of nature, a sentinel on this prairie far longer than he'd been alive.

He stood in the solitude and safety, eyes closed, taking a dozen breaths, feeling the fear and uncertainty melt away. He had no plan, but at least he had a safe place to sleep. He emptied his pockets, lining everything up against the base of the tree, set down his rifles, and lowered the ear flaps on his hat, pulling it down over his brow. He zipped his jacket up to his chin, and put his gloves back on. As protected against the cold as his modest gear would allow, he laid down and curled up in a thick layer of pine needles.

Finally, he could sleep.

> "I heard two shots for sure, close together. My wife said, 'Let's get in the car and go.' I could see Stanley's kids coming down the road. I didn't know what to do. I thought whoever was doing the shooting would come down and shoot us too."
>
> *Excerpt of interview with Gordon Robertson, father of accused (1970)*

Chapter Twenty-Two

Friday, October 9, 1970
On Scene
2330hrs

Joe Greenslade had never experienced this kind of uneasiness. Being in the car was fine, but the walk from where he parked in front of the Robertson house over to the side field where the trailer stood was indescribable. Flashlight beam bouncing off misshapen forms, every movement made him look twice, swinging his flashlight wildly from side to side.

Staff Sergeant Mosher said he needed more experienced members at HQ, but that could mean a lot of different things and he wasn't going to know what until he got his orders. He hoped his orders might include an hour or two of sleep. Adrenaline kept you going for a while, but when you came down off that high, plain fear only kept you at a certain level of alert. He marvelled at the intricacies of the body and its defence mechanisms.

Besides the kid who took out the police car mirror, and the sound of the shot itself that echoed miles away, they'd all come up empty handed. Swift and immediate justice was the only thing on Joe's mind. Anything less only enhanced the senseless loss of his buddies.

Coming into the circle of light, he found Jette gearing up just outside the trailer with a sour look on his face.

"What's going on? You headed back to the city?" He took a sip from his canteen and slid down against the wall, taking the lit cigarette Jette offered. The man seemed to keep one perpetually stuck to his face.

"Nope. Double shift. Spent all day at the detachment and all evening on scene and driving Sergeant Regitnig around. Fuck if I ever want that job again." Joe had never seen such sadness in his friend's eyes. "Now I'm on all night roadblock. And don't suggest rotating night shifts to Staff Sergeant Anderson. He'll look at you like you're a damn idiot." Jette yanked on his fur lined hat and shouldered his rifle.

"Shit, Anderson. You hear what happened earlier?" Joe took a long drag on the smoke and gave it back to Jette. The temperature was dropping fast and he crammed his chapped hands down deep into his pockets.

"Just that Mosher lit into a rookie for discharging his firearm. Were you there?" Jette powered through the last of the cigarette, stubbed it out, and lit another all with one hand. The snap of his Zippo lighter so quick and sharp it sounded like he was readying his gun. He checked his pockets and readjusted his jacket.

Joe snorted. "Yeah, we waited around for about an hour, crouched in the fucking freezing grass and mud waiting for Anderson to give some kind of order. Man was the best target I ever saw, hat badge leading the way, buttons reflecting any light that came at him. All he did was walk from one end of the line to the other, yelling at people." He scrubbed at his face and had another drink from his canteen. "Guys were just getting antsy, ya know? We're all surrounding the police car like assholes sitting on our thumbs and this kid pulls off a shot and takes out the passenger side mirror."

Brent's eyebrows shot up. "Really? Hm. Hope it was worth it." He smirked.

"Don't tell Mosher I said this, but it was one hell of a shot."

The trailer door flew open, crashing against the exterior wall and Joe and Brent startled apart.

Mosher stood there with an intense frown and grumbled, "Don't tell Anderson I agree with you, Greenslade. Hell of a shot if the reports are to be believed, but nobody wants to be on the receiving end of me," he thrust a thumb at himself, "so don't repeat it, for fuck's sake." Pointing at them in turn he snapped, "Where're you two supposed to be?"

Joe straightened up, brushing the dirt and leaves off the front of his uniform and quickly put his hat back on. "Just dropped off Cavello and Morier south of Duck Lake on the train tracks, sir. Awaiting your orders."

"I'm headed out to roadblock duty, sir. See you in the morning." Jette readjusted his rifle, picked up his canteen and bag from the ground and disappeared out of the circle of light.

"What the hell, Jette? Whose order is that?" Mosher yelled at Jette's retreating back. "I want you heading back to the city for some sleep in the morning. Don't show your face back here before 1800."

Jette waved over his shoulder.

"Fucking Anderson," Mosher muttered, motioning Joe into the trailer.

Not sure he heard Mosher correctly, he asked, "Sorry, sir?" and stepped into the makeshift office, finding a chair.

"Never mind." Mosher waved him off. "Thanks for coming back. I need you in the shed across from the house."

Joe internally cringed, but an order was an order, and if he really dug into the truth of the matter, he wanted to be in the thick of things when they found this guy.

"10-4, sir. Situation?"

"I've got a cadet and a corporal from North Battleford in there right now. Tell the cadet to get on back to the city and be back here for briefing at 0600."

"Yes, sir." He stood. Spending the night in a shed wasn't the best scenario he could think of, but it certainly wasn't the worst. Cavello and Morier were sleeping on the train tracks. It wasn't a first for any of them. They'd been in plenty of uncomfortable sleeping arrangements during an investigation.

```
"Quit your whining, it's not going to make this go any
faster." Doug shoved Joe's shoulder, shaking a cigarette out
of a crumpled package and grabbing it with his mouth. He felt
the bottom of the package and offered Greenslade his last
```

one. They put their heads together, lighting both with the single flame from Doug's match.

"I'm not whining. This is just shit. There are junior members who could be doing this. Waiting for the dogman, my ass." Standing shoulder to shoulder against an elderly outbuilding well past its prime, they were on orders to guard the scene until one of the dogmasters was available. The possibility of standing in the snow all night loomed like a dark cloud. They'd already been out for several hours with sunset a distant memory.

"Well, we're the ones who chased him in there. You rather let someone else get the collar?" Doug's cigarette tip cast a dim glow around his lower face as he inhaled. Pulling the glowing ember away from himself, he motioned ahead of them, the burning red dot piercing the darkness. "There's no way he got out of there before we set up the perimeter. He's armed. The bush is dense as hell. So...we wait. I just hope we get Regitnig and not Long. He's gotten too many collars since he got here. What a pain in the ass." He liked Henry Long, everyone did, but the kid's crowing could sit right on your last nerve. He was almost too good.

Greenslade agreed with a quiet laugh. "Yeah, don't I know it. Hell of a guy, but not so humble." He chuckled. "Sergeant should knock him down a notch." He stamped his feet against the cold.

Doug did the same. As usual on the prairies, March had been snowy and unforgiving. It never ceased to amaze him the lengths escaped convicts would go to. Backing a private road, the small, thick copse of trees was not even close to the size of one square city block, but it had lots of places to hide that would elude the human eye. Certain their immediate perimeter had penned the suspect in on all sides, and with him and Greenslade covering the opening where the farmer's animals started their path into the trees, the bush was the escapee's only cover.

For now.

ON SCENE

Doug laughed louder around the cigarette and rubbed his gloved hands together. "He did, didn't you hear that? Oh shit, it was great."

Greenslade made a strangled noise. "What? No. How the hell did I miss that?"

"Ah, we all missed it. Regitnig wouldn't humiliate his man in front of any of us. That's not his way." He took another leisurely drag on his smoke and leaned harder into the wall behind him. "All I know is Long took the lead on a chase. Sarge called him back but Long didn't hear him."

Joe snorted. "Didn't hear him or didn't listen?"

"Who knows? The guy was hiding around the corner of a building and grabbed Long around the neck. Had a knife."

Joe let out a low whistle. "Whoa, what happened? Regitnig get him?"

Doug chuckled. "Regitnig planned it. Is that a big enough notch for you?"

"Stay sharp, Greenslade." Mosher's command brought Joe back to the manhunt in front of them. "Let's wrap this up. For Doug and Bob." Mosher reached out and shook Joe's hand in a powerful grip.

"Yes sir," he said again, an edge of vehemence in his voice that didn't even begin to match the storm in his mind.

> "Wally was one of the most dedicated members I have ever known. On every search he didn't quit until he had what we were out for."
>
> Excerpt of interview with (Retired) Staff Sergeant Greenslade (April 2016)

Chapter Twenty-Three

Friday, October 9, 1970
On Scene
2230hrs

The sounds and smells of the night were vastly different than those of the daylight hours. Wally and Bruce moved silently through the trees, listening for prey. Ground search called off for the night, they stayed close to the farm, working the perimeter, trying to pick up a trail. Bruce was slow and methodical, casting to and fro across a five or six foot span as he moved forward. A completely different pace than an active track. When Bruce was hot on a trail there was no back and forth, he was straight as an arrow and ran directly for his mark. There was no mark here in the dark of the forest.

Bruce paused at the hoot of an owl, front leg raised in mid step, head cocked at the sound. The dog growled low in his throat and the owl took flight from a tree a few paces away, the blast of movement startling other night creatures.

"Come on, Chief. Let's call it a night. He's not here." He would've put money on Robertson trying to come back close to his place to hunker down for the night but if he did, Bruce would have known. He patted his leg, beckoning the dog, and turned around to cut a direct path back to the house. With no high paced chase, no imminent danger, Bruce was off leash, free to pace at his leisure and pick up scent where he might. The rain and snow had slowed but what snow did fall had immediately melted, creating a blanket of wetness over the entire forest. Bruce hadn't had a hit all night. Not since finding the abandoned police car.

"Morning will come soon enough. Maybe we'll pick up the trail then. Broken branches, pushed over grass." He patted his leg again, encouraging his partner to let it go, for now. Bruce cast one more look at the path illuminated by Wally's flashlight, looked back and whined.

"No. Come on." He snapped his fingers and was rewarded with an empty space in the trees where his dog used to be.

"Damn it, Bruce." Regretting not leashing his partner sooner, he trudged after him, no patience to deal with Bruce's stubborn streak in the middle of the dark forest, after midnight, on the worst night of his life.

He caught up quickly; Bruce wasn't running, he just stubbornly refused to leave the trail.

The dog looked back and Wally threw up his hands. "There's nothing here, dog. Not a goddamn thing. Do you smell anything? No." His voice gained in volume until he roared his last word at the dark, wet sky. Bruce didn't react.

It was quieter in the forest at night, each sound amplified, but Wally's roar prompted a deeper silence. His shoulders hung forward with his head, an ache radiating from within. The intense silence was broken when something sighed.

Not something.

Some*one*.

Bruce whipped his gaze back down the trail and took off.

Wally crouched and drew his revolver in one movement, waiting for the growling and screaming. He tried to slow his heartbeat, drawing in even breaths. The surge of adrenaline debilitated his logic. He wanted to give chase.

"We've got you now, you son of a bitch," he whispered, staying low, flashlight steady under his weapon, itching for the ruckus that always followed Bruce.

If the dog was the tip of the spear, Wally was the muscle behind the final thrust. But he wasn't so stupid as to go running into the forest with an expert marksman gunning down police officers. He melted into the side of a tree.

With each passing quiet second, his stomach dropped out the bottom of his boots.

There was no ruckus.

The forest was as silent as it ever was on a cold night in October.

His anticipation built like a great grizzly bear rising up on its hind legs. This was it.

He didn't want glory. He wanted justice.

He moved silently, foot by foot, head ducked down, even with his outstretched arms. Foot by agonizing foot he crept, and saw nothing. His muscles screamed but he stayed in position, wondering where his dog was.

He stopped just outside an area too small to be called a clearing. Bruce was frozen in place, about six feet away from a man squatting on the ground, hand outstretched towards the dog. The man wore a tattered tan hunting jacket and matching hat with the ear flaps pulled down against the chill. He was slight, but the hand that stretched out to Bruce was filled with authority. Head bowed a fraction, he didn't move.

"Stop. Police. Show me your hands." The bellowed command came from deep within his chest. He yelled it twice and tracked the man's other hand with his flashlight as it slowly came out from behind his back. The hand was empty.

Bruce should've had him on the ground by now, but he stayed rooted in place.

"Get on your stomach with your hands out." He kept a tight rein on his anger but the order shattered the eerie silence again. "Do it, now."

The man kept his hands out but otherwise didn't move. Something was wrong. Bruce already told him that.

The dog whined and sat without any order to do so. What the hell was he doing?

"Get him." The command cut through the space between them and Wally took two steps forward. Bruce looked from Wally to the man and laid down where he was but kept his head up, ears straight, staying alert.

The man looked up, Wally's beam of light slicing across his features.

ON SCENE

His thick hat was pulled low over his dark brows, the large flaps obscuring the sides of his face. He looked worn but watchful, eyes squinting against the bright light, moving carefully, deliberately.

Wally stared directly into the depth of the man's eyes, etching his features on his memory.

The man was too old to be Stanley Robertson. A life of hard labour spent outdoors aged a person, sure, but there was no hiding the stooped back and arthritic, weathered hands.

His surging adrenaline slowed a notch and he lowered his weapon a fraction, breaking the spell that had settled on them. He was confused as hell but wasn't about to let the man go.

"Get on the ground," he yelled again and Bruce finally stood at the raised command.

The man kept both hands stretched out in front of him and slowly stood up to his full height. Even from more than twenty feet away, Wally could see that he towered over the older man.

The man took a step back and Wally shuffled forward, weapon at the ready. "Stop. Get on the ground now."

The man took another step back. Bruce didn't move and Wally swept his gaze over to the dog. "Get him," he ordered again. When he looked back all he saw was swaying branches.

It was only after the man disappeared that Bruce dove into the bush after him, barking.

Whipping his head left to right, scanning the tops of the trees and the space all around him, Wally expected a bullet to rip through his back. Was this a decoy? An accomplice?

Bruce set up a good racket but Wally didn't think he had the man on the ground. That was a different racket. Revolver up and ready, he followed the noise, zigzagging from tree to tree. Heartbeat erratic in his ears, he didn't bother to try to breathe through it. He let the anger fuel him forward. Anger took you farther than fear.

Bruce's noise led Wally directly to him. He was jogging now to keep up with the dog, shivers crawling up his spine, target heavy on his back.

He stopped short in another small clearing when he came upon his partner, all alone. Bruce cast back and forth, letting out yelps and whines, turning circles like he was lost.

"There's no way…" Wally ran into the trees on the opposite side of the clearing, smashing branches out of his way with both hands, and ran back out again.

The man was a ghost.

MacDowall Shocked by Shootings-*"Robertson 'real quiet type.' Surprise and shock were the reactions Friday night in the tiny community of MacDowall…"*

Headline and excerpt, Prince Albert Daily Herald (Thursday, October 15, 1970)

Chapter Twenty-Four

Saturday, October 10, 1970
On Scene
0030hrs

They weren't far out. It took less than half an hour to cut through the brush and come out of the trees at the edge of the Robertson yard. They were mere feet from where they'd recovered Bob's body. Wally stomped on the bottom line of the rusted barbed wire fence and held the top two lines up for Bruce to walk through. The fence complained mightily when he held the bottom two down and climbed through himself. Had there even been someone there at all? Bruce never barked at the man once.

Why?

"What happened to you? Forgot who calls the shots?" he asked the dog, Bruce cocking his head at him with a quizzical stare.

"Fucking mind tricks," Wally muttered, questioning how real everything had been. It was a real man, wasn't it? Flesh and blood? He'd never seen anyone disappear like that. Evade the dog that fast? Not in his entire career. It wasn't possible.

They skirted a clump of tall weeds and grass growing over an old metal plough surrendering to the earth. Wally swept his flashlight over to the dark spot where the ground was stained black and his heart thudded in his chest. The pain had no name. Bruce started for the spot.

"No. Let's go." He had an urge to kneel at the spot himself but didn't want to feel the cold. It would be colder now than the first time he knelt there. He didn't think that cold would ever leave him. His pants had dried stiff at the knees and scraped against his skin with every step, reminding him.

He turned and started for headquarters, not bothering to check and see if Bruce obeyed. The dog would follow.

Headquarters looked all but deserted. He knew there were friendly eyes on him, even if he couldn't see anyone. He opened the trailer door. Mosher looked exactly as he had when they walked into the detachment that morning. To Wally, their early morning pleasantries and normal routine seemed far away and no longer tangible. Mosher's head popped up from pouring over a map of the area when Wally stepped into the trailer. He had a cup of coffee in his hand, booted foot propped up on his opposite knee, but he noticed with a smile that Al had put his tie back on. It was an odd comfort; he could count on Mosher to be the kind of leader this outfit needed at a time like this.

"Sergeant Regitnig, what's that perimeter look like?" Mosher rested his elbows on his knees, leaning forward.

Wally's answer slipped out of his mouth before his brain caught up. "Looks like shit." He rubbed his face with both hands, feeling heavy and defeated.

Mosher sat straight up, banging his coffee cup down on the table and Wally remembered who he was speaking to.

"Sorry, sir. Perimeter is secure. Permission to take up position inside the house?" He didn't often forget his professionalism. He couldn't remember the last time he said anything out of line or was corrected by a superior officer.

Mosher cut the tension with a definitive knife. "That's what fatigue, grief, and frustration looks like."

Wally shrugged apologetically and pulled a chair up to the table.

Tension easing, they fell into a comfortable silence and Bruce meandered to the corner and flopped down. After a long half growl half groan of canine contentment, he closed his eyes and the trailer fell silent again.

ON SCENE

A shuffling, popping sound made Wally snap his head to the side, listening. "You hear that?"

They tensed, going for their weapons. Straining to listen, it got louder. Pop, pop, pop followed by rustling. One big pop and they hit the floor of the trailer, weapons drawn. Bruce jumped in, barking, while they crawled over to the door. The popping sounded suspiciously like a rifle being loaded; they couldn't take any chances. One behind the other, Mosher taking the lead, they signalled a countdown and threw open the door, guns cocked and aimed at whoever was outside readying a weapon. It was a burst of bravery that met…silence. Wally cursed himself for not searching harder for the ghost-man in the forest.

Nothing stirred outside the trailer but the wind rustling through the trees. Arms still straight and tense, ready to defend themselves, he looked sideways at Mosher, waiting for more.

There it was again. The noise came from behind them this time and they both wheeled around, close to the floor, backs against the doorjamb, aiming at the rear of the trailer.

"Where the hell is that sound coming from?" Mosher ground out. Wally held his position. Bruce was pacing back and forth, barking when the officers raised their guns. Now he quieted, walked away from Wally to the side table, nose in the air. The pop sounded again, making them duck and crouch, but Bruce kept moving forward. His nose ended up an inch from the hot coffee pot, and he woofed.

"Oh for fuck's sake." Wally sat on the floor, forearm going to his head to wipe his drenched brow. "It's the damn coffee percolator."

Mosher's face darkened. "That was…I don't know what that was."

Wally got up, ripped off his Stetson, threw it down on the table, and collapsed into a chair. Mosher re-holstered his gun and set a coffee cup in front of Wally.

"Everyone's on edge. Would you rather it be Robertson loading a rifle right outside the door?" Al grabbed the offending coffee pot, pouring out the thick, black sludge. He was famous at the detachment for harassing the guys who made weak coffee. He'd voiced his preference many times. The spoon standing straight up in his cup was too weak for his taste. "What'd you find out there?" He pulled up to the table, straightening out the maps, and uncapped a felt tip pen with his teeth.

Wally pulled up his own chair and leaned over to inspect the notes on the maps. He warred with the idea of telling Mosher about the man in the forest. It wasn't a ghost, of that he was certain. He hadn't come this far in his career to start blaming questionable situations on things that didn't exist. But he knew the man wasn't Robertson. Was there any point getting Mosher's hopes up for no reason?

"Nothing, sir. Not before dark, not after dark. We'll get a better lay of things with the dawn." Wally sipped at his cooling coffee, made a face and chuckled, toying with the edges of the papers in front of him. "What happened with that shot fired?"

Mosher flipped his hand dismissively. "Another time. Young hotshot mixed with Anderson who doesn't know scene procedure from his own ass."

Wally choked on his coffee and spit, wiping his chin. Mosher frowned and Wally waved him on to continue.

"What's with you and Anderson's ass? Do I even want to know?" Mosher asked dryly.

Wally shook his head, mopping coffee off one sleeve with his other sleeve and said, "No. Not important."

"Ok, then. Where are you headed tomorrow?" Mosher looked at his watch. "…er…today?"

Wally drew a circle around a substantial area northwest of the house.

"So far, five dog teams are here. I gathered what information I could at the radio room. Robertson's going to need a water source. I've heard he's a woodsman. Folks say he could live off the land forever." Mosher looked grim at his words and impatiently motioned for him to go on. "Well, that means water. So I'm going to map out every river, lake, dugout, and rain puddle from here to Prince Albert and split them up between the dogmen." Mosher nodded.

"I stationed someone in the radio room before I left Prince Albert." Wally smacked his forehead. "Oh shit, he's probably still there. I told him not to move until he was relieved by a superior but then forgot to tell anyone else." He winced by way of apology.

Mosher flipped his hand dismissively. "It's fine. Sleeping with your head on the desk in the radio room is a lot more comfortable than pulling double time on roadblock duty like Jette is right now. Or holed up in the shed like Greenslade."

He felt a little less guilty. He was going to have a pretty uncomfortable night himself, hunkered down with Bruce just inside the front door of the Robertson home. He didn't intend to leave the property until they found him. There was a distinct possibility he could come back to the house in the dead of night, thinking nobody would be here. He'd be wrong.

"Yeah, that's true." He scratched at his bristling hair absently, sure his usual neat part was gone. Focus on dress and deportment had understandably blurred. "Did you locate the family?"

Mosher rifled through a stack of files. "Yeah, I sent Rosthern Detachment out to interview some locals right after we cleared the house. Didn't take too long to find them. Robertson's sister Jessie was the one who called it in. She drove down to the gas station to use the phone. Piled Ruth Robertson and all the kids into her truck and took them to a friend's." Mosher frowned as he scanned the paper. "The family will be fine there for tonight, we have officers on surveillance."

Wally's mind connected the dots. Fred's neighbours. He nodded, pressing his fingers into a steeple, resting his lips against them. "Still can't believe there are some folks out here without a phone. Moving them tomorrow?"

Mosher looked resigned. "Yeah, we need to be able to keep track of them. Do some interviews. We'll move them to a hotel in Prince Albert tomorrow."

Wally nodded. Silence stretched between them.

"Sir, I've been—"

"Tell me what you think—"

Their words collided in the air and they stopped with a short chuckle.

"Sorry, sir. Go ahead."

"I'm wondering if we were on the same page already. Tell me what you think of the wife. You read the briefing note?"

"Just the first one that was at the detachment. Do you have anything new?"

"Corporal Waller interviewed the wife but she didn't have much to say. From what I can gather, she opened the front door and Robertson shot Anson right in front of her."

Wally cut off the disgusted grunt that almost escaped him. It wasn't for him to judge or speculate right now. Only cold hard facts would help him.

"Do you think she knew what he was going to do?"

Wally sighed and slouched in his chair. That was something he didn't want to consider. "Depends on what kind of woman she is, I guess," he said. If someone had the power to stop what happened and didn't? It didn't bear consideration. Who would do that?

He stared off at the grimy wall, the vision of Mrs. Robertson opening the door to Anson and just stepping aside so her husband could shoot him. Was there an altercation? Did she try to warn Anson? A big lump formed somewhere around his diaphragm and he pressed on it, bringing his eyes back to Mosher. "Keep Rosthern on those interviews and we'll damn well find out what she knows," Wally said, picking up a sheet from the desk. Large letters across the top proclaimed Robertson a wanted man. The five thousand dollar reward was the biggest he'd ever seen in his career. He whistled through his teeth. Bruce looked up briefly, then rested his head back down.

Mosher nodded, "Yeah, I don't know who authorized that but the C/O is serious."

"They won't be paying out that reward, anyway. We'll find him."

Mosher looked smug. "I know you will." He straightened up. "So what else do you have for me? If you're here…" he pointed to the spot Wally had circled, "then where are we starting? I'll have about forty men at 0600hrs."

Forty just on the ground search. That didn't include air, office support, perimeter security, or roadblocks. That meant they had the better part of one hundred men at their disposal and the thought cut Wally right to the core. Sure, there were orders. But most of these guys, whether they knew Schrader and Anson or not, had come out because one of their own needed them. It was as simple as that.

Wally shifted the maps around and pointed to a line that crossed where the police car was recovered. "Straight across here."

Mosher's mouth drew down slightly. "It sure is a lot of ground, when you see it all laid out like this."

Wally grunted and folded his arms across his chest, sinking his chin into the front of his uniform. "Sure is. But at least we know where we're starting."

"Well, good. We'll lay out the grids for the day search. Shilo will be here, and we have a couple RCMP pilots who flew in from Regina a few hours ago. They'll start at day break. By the time the bus arrived from the south, we had about a hundred officers on scene tonight."

Wally nodded, satisfied that his guess had been correct.

"I'm a long toothed old bastard Wally but I've never seen anything like this. Not in my whole career." Mosher rubbed his head and slugged back the coffee in Wally's abandoned cup.

"I have." Wally was quiet but direct enough to catch Al's undivided attention. "There was one time I headed up a search out in British Columbia. For a little girl. Major Crimes had already pinned it on some loony who got off on killing kids. His file was a mile thick. So they called me and Bruce in as soon as they knew, and we started tracking back in the mountains." He stared at a spot just over Mosher's shoulder, seeing on the bare trailer wall the mountain landscape of the case long past. "For two days we followed a good trail. We went hard but the whole way I felt like something was off." He shifted uncomfortably in his chair, rubbing at his neck, feeling the strain like it was yesterday.

"It itched at me, ya know? The trail was sharp, Bruce never lost it once. After it was all said and done, I knew that's what he wanted. We caught up with them at the end of the second day."

Mosher leaned forward, uncharacteristic sympathy written all over his lined, weathered face.

"Dusk had settled in and I pulled Bruce back when we came up on a little campsite." He paused and closed his eyes. A crackling fire, obnoxiously cheery, inside a tidy ring of rocks, with other domestic camping items scattered around. He remembered the war raging within him, readying himself for battle as he took in the cozy mountain scene. It was all backwards.

Feeling Mosher's impatience, he opened his eyes. "This guy was sitting in front of a fire with the little girl in his lap. I remember she had pigtails in her hair and he had a fist wrapped around one of them."

It was Mosher's turn to close his eyes. Lowering his head, he sighed heavily. The sigh of a man who'd seen things that couldn't be unseen. Wally nodded, knowing. They'd both been on the highway to hell and come out the other side, only to ready themselves to travel it again.

"She was whimpering but not hysterical, the little trooper. He had a long hunting knife held to her throat." Wally drew another breath and Mosher swore under his.

"Shit, Wally. You never told me this before. I know this case. She was still alive when you got there." Mosher looked incredulous, rubbing a spot on his forehead.

"Yeah. He wanted us to find him. Waited for us to arrive then killed that little girl right in front of me." Al's face crumpled and he balled his fists as Wally went on. "Bruce was new. Went ballistic. Nearly tore the guy's throat out. I left him to it but the guy slashed Bruce and broke free. Came at me."

Mosher had pulled his weapon more than once. There was no need for Wally to explain what happened next. That didn't stop him from continuing. Perhaps getting it off his chest could help put these particular ghosts to rest. "I put a single shot in his forehead. Dropped him like a stone." He lowered his head, finding even less satisfaction in the retelling of it than he had when he'd fired the gun. He'd never told the details to anyone. Not even Dolores.

"Finding Bob tonight, out there, all by himself with his blood soaking into my pants, I was trying to figure it out."

Mosher sat back, face screwed up in question. "Trying to figure what out?"

Wally choked on a sigh. "Which one hurt more."

ON SCENE

Murder Suspect Evades Police Net-*RCMP said the officers were shot at without warning and their hand guns and cruiser taken. It is possible that Robertson is warmly dressed and has a .22-calibre rifle. Temperatures in the area have been in the low 20s at night…*

Headline and excerpt, Saskatoon StarPhoenix
(Tuesday, October 13, 1970)

Chapter Twenty-Five

```
Saturday, October 10, 1970
On Scene
0450hrs
```

The night was an excruciating pain in the ass.

Wally spent four hours pretending to rest, but the ache of loss, the pain of regret, and the slow burning, angry desire to jump to action had him shifting every minute or two. Bruce's pacing on the rough wood floor didn't help. The dog stopped to nose the dried blood spatter on every pass of the door where Anson was shot. Even in the pitch dark Wally knew the blood was still there. It would always be there, soaked into the wood, staining it dark brown. No amount of scrubbing would remove the stains. Only the regular wear and tear of little hands on the jamb, doors slamming, book bags banging against it, and the hard use of a big family would ever fade the spots. He hated the thought of it. He wanted to rip the door clean off its hinges and burn it in the yard.

They say it's darkest right before the dawn. He didn't know who the hell 'they' were, but they were right. The sun wouldn't rise until after seven at this time of year, and squinting down at his watch illuminated by his heavy metal flashlight, he saw it was not quite five. He should have known. Dolores fondly called this his prowling hour. It was best in the summer when the sun was breaking the horizon and the birds were singing, but even in the depths of winter in Saskatchewan he never slept far past his prowling hour.

He missed her. They'd gone more than twenty-four hours without speaking on countless occasions. He didn't often get to call home when he was tracking someone and she understood. But just then, he had an inexplicable pull towards a phone. Towards his wife.

"Greenslade?" He'd cracked the kitchen window an inch to better hear outside, and raised himself up off the floor to look out, calling low across the dirt yard. Joe was looking out the door of the shed.

"I heard you walk across the floor. It's okay." Joe raised his gun in salute and closed the shed door.

Taking that as the go ahead, Bruce bolted ahead of Wally out the door and off the porch, heading into the trees to do what a dog does in the morning. Tugging at the zipper of his uniform pants, he thought he'd best follow suit.

The office trailer was deserted, and for once Wally was thankful for Mosher's absence. He was glad Al was getting some sleep or just pretending to, like he did. He whistled for Bruce, opened the back door of the car, and took a deep breath of the frosty air, blowing out a cloud of warmth. The haze floated around his face for a second, then disappeared into the chill.

The drive into MacDowall took all of three minutes. The pitch blackness seeming to give an inch as Wally started to see the outlines of the trees against the sky. But he wouldn't go so far as to say the sun was thinking of rising yet.

A single light shining outside the service station attached to Fran's Café cast a yellow glow over the thick, icy fog that still hung close to the ground. There were no vehicles parked outside the place, but movement caught Wally's eye in the big window. He slowed the car to a roll, pulling around the side of the building.

Normally a gentle ring over the din of customers, at this hour the bell above the door broke the silence like a jackhammer. Wally paused in the entrance, not wanting to scare whoever was there.

"You're the tracker. Was wondering when I was going to meet you." A woman in her forties with short brown curls peeked out from around a wall and immediately disappeared again. "I've got the coffee on."

Wally cleared his throat and stepped up to the counter.

"Thank you, but it's sure not me with the nose. Is my dog allowed...?" Uncomfortable with talking to the empty space behind the counter, he trailed off and tried to lean around the wall.

The woman popped out again and he got a better look at her. Tidy appearance with her short hair, she was younger than him but had eyes as wise as they came. They creased warmly at the corners when she smiled. She looked like she knew things. Dolores called that an 'old soul.' Her diminutive body was wrapped in a white apron and she carried a bowl full of dough nearly bigger than she was.

"He's welcome if he stays off my counters. That goes for your gun, too." Keen dark brown eyes stared directly at him as she set a cup of coffee down. She put the bowl on the counter beside it and started kneading the dough with impressive authority.

"Yes, ma'am. Bruce is a gentleman. I don't make a habit of taking my gun off in public." A smirk pulled at the corner of his mouth and he buried it in the coffee cup. He took a sip and meant to put the cup down and go use the phone, but the wonderful flavour immediately pulled him back. He took a second sip and couldn't stop the blissful sigh that escaped him.

Her eyes twinkled with pleasure, satisfaction radiating from her welcoming face. "Yes sir. That's the reason I'm open at this hour. I swear I get more customers for early breakfast than I get the whole rest of the day. It's the coffee." She stopped beating the dough in the bowl and winked, swiping a hand across her apron front and thrusting it out in front of her. "Fran." She nodded once at the single syllable that spoke volumes about her personality.

"Sergeant Walter Regitnig." He grasped the hard, work worn hand in his own, enveloping the whole thing. Fran didn't give an inch. Her handshake was as firm and no nonsense as she was. He lifted his chin to his left where Bruce had made himself comfortable. "My partner, Bruce." He removed his hat and set it on the counter, straddling the metal stool.

Fran nodded again and went back to her dough, eyes staying firm on Wally.

"Terrible shame what went on," she said, hands slowing in the bowl.

The sadness that crept into her sparkling eyes hit Wally where it hurt. So many were affected by something started by three people. He gave his head a shake. One person. This was all started by the decisions of one person.

She shivered slightly and went back to kneading, "A few of you stopped for a bite late last night. We were ordered to lock everything up, but I couldn't keep folks out. They didn't take too kindly to the officers." Her gaze never wavered from his while her hands continued their work.

"Yes ma'am. I'm sorry for your trouble," he murmured, keeping at his cup, both to be polite and drink it up before it got cold, but mostly because it was the best damn coffee he'd had since being at home with his wife. Even then, it wasn't the coffee that was better at home, it was the company. "Everything smoothed over, I hope?"

"No, everything didn't smooth over." The sharp voice cracked like a whip from the back corner of the restaurant and made Wally stand and draw his weapon in one fluid movement. Bruce's barking drowned out the rest of whatever the man in the back had to say. Wally ordered the dog quiet but stood at the ready.

"You hush, Roy. I don't need trouble." Fran waved a finger in his general direction and Wally eased her with a raised hand and re-holstered his gun. The man looked older, dishevelled, and drawn. Biggest thing about him was his voice. He was no physical threat.

The man, Roy, was leaning on the back doorjamb—for how long, Wally didn't know. He slid a side eye at Bruce. Why hadn't the dog alerted him when the man came in? A lot of these locals moved silently through the bush, apparently that applied to restaurants as well.

"We don't need you out here. You'll never find 'im." Roy turned around and spat out the back door.

"My dog thinks otherwise. If he's still in the area, we'll find him." Wally eased his stance, but didn't sit down.

Roy let out a short, abrasive laugh that set Bruce to snarling. "You won't find 'im cause you're lookin' the cop way. Call off that mutt or I'll shoot 'im."

The empty threat didn't bother Wally, but the first statement hung on him like a persistent monkey, wrapping around his head and not letting go. *The cop way.*

"Try it. See what happens," Wally ground out, staring the man down.

Fran stood frozen during this exchange, dough forgotten on the counter, hands clenched at her middle against her apron. She looked like she might speak, but nothing was said. The silence stretched between them, crackling on a gaze that nobody would break.

Roy, for all his bravado, had the good sense to eventually shuffle under Wally's scrutiny, pulling at his collar and backing up a step. His body language was more uncertain than threatening. Wally wasn't going to waste any more time on him. Draining the remnants of his coffee, he dropped a few quarters on the counter and nodded his thanks to Fran. She relaxed her shoulders and started kneading her dough again, but kept glancing up every few seconds. Wally wouldn't be so stupid as to turn his back on the man, so he sidestepped over to the phone, one eye on the back door, and one eye on Bruce.

"Stand down," he murmured, and Bruce sat, whining up at him. Wally leaned against the wall beside the pay phone, giving himself a good view of the entire restaurant and the back door as the dime jingled down into the phone and he dialled.

"Did I wake you, my dear?" he asked, her soft breathing the only indication she was on the line. Dolores didn't need to say hello, she would know full well who it was at this hour.

"Of course not. It's your prowling hour." Her voice was husky and held the softness of sleep.

Wally chuckled. "That it is. How're things up there?"

Dolores sighed and he heard her stretch. "As good as can be expected. I went over and stayed with Connie until the children were asleep." The catch in her voice slammed into Wally, her sadness weakening his emotions.

Clearing his throat, he kept his voice down but his eyes sharp. Roy hadn't moved from the doorway, but he certainly didn't need to hear what Wally had to say to his wife. Or that he had a wife at all.

"I'm sorry I'm not there," he said, pausing at her dismissive murmur.

ON SCENE

"I miss you, too. But you need to be exactly where you are."

He grunted. "I miss waking up to your blonde hair in my face."

It was Dolores's turn to grunt. "My hair hasn't been blonde in a few years. I'm afraid last night gave me a few more grey hairs."

"Impossible. You look exactly the same as the day we met."

"I hope your eyesight is better in the field. I'm sending food down with day shift."

"Thank you, Love. Hug Connie and Vallarena for me, okay?"

"Every hour. Keep yourself safe. Bring him in."

"You know I will."

There was a soft, familiar sound as his wife kissed the receiver and the line went dead.

She always managed to fill him up before he had to go back out.

He stepped away from the phone, put his hat on and tugged at the brim in farewell.

"Thank you for the excellent coffee, Fran. If you have any trouble at all," he eyed Roy, squinting hard at the man like he could control his actions with a simple stare, "I'm only a phone call away."

"Thank you, Sergeant, but I can handle my own. You just handle yours, all right?"

"Yes, ma'am." There was nothing else he could say. He snapped his fingers at Bruce and they left, door chiming behind them.

RCMP Killer Still Elusive-*The slayings touched off one of the most intensive manhunts in the province's history. Every available man in the Prince Albert subdivision was immediately thrown into the hunt..."*

Headline and excerpt, Regina Leader Post
(Tuesday, October 13, 1970)

Chapter Twenty-Six

Saturday, October 10, 1970
On Scene
0630hrs

HQ was just starting to come alive and Wally jumped back in, commanding cadets and dog teams, showing them the water locations he'd highlighted for Mosher the previous night. The lack of incident overnight, and lack of a bed, didn't alter his focus in the least.

The morning muster was organized chaos, and Mosher's words rang in his ears. "They were one of us, Doug and Bob. Our men. Our family. Our friends. We won't take this lightly. And we sure as hell won't give up any more of our men in this search. He's out there; armed and dangerous. Protect each other, watch your backs, and for the love of God, come home safely. We'll find him, gentlemen. I don't have to remind any of you what's at stake here."

The briefing broke up shortly after that, searchers scattering to different areas, day shift roadblock members heading out to relieve the night shift. Everyone knew their job.

Wally packaged his grief up nice and tight and tried to push it way down deep into his boot where it belonged. Letting his emotions surface when he talked to his wife was fine, but this day had no room for tears. He marvelled at Mosher's ability to inspire greatness in his men when he knew Al was fighting his own feelings about this case. Even Wally himself felt a renewed energy, with an improved outlook on catching this killer. Not that he ever doubted their collective ability, but things seemed bleakest in the dark of the night when there were no leads to be found. The sun was thin but persistent, and he knew that with the dawn, new information would come to light.

He readied himself for a long search day, watering Bruce while trying to drink another cup of coffee. It was nearly unpalatable compared to Fran's.

Bruce's ears perked and he jerked his head around, staring out at the sky above the treeline. Wally's eyes automatically followed, but all he saw was dull grey haze with the sunrise trying to break through in places. A few geese honked their departure of the area before winter settled in.

"Dad, look! It's like they're announcing the beginning of winter." Garry dropped his fishing reel into his lap and pointed at the long V formation of birds flying directly over the boat.

Wally lurched forward and snatched up the reel before something under the water grabbed Garry's bait and took his whole rod for a swim. "Watch it, buddy. Or you'll be announcing the end of your fishing day." Barry and Terry laughed at that, but Wally saw them settle an extra firm hand on their own rods. Bob chuckled, carefully tying Larry's line to secure his favourite lure. He was always the last to cast when they took the boys out in the boat. Between snacks, tying lures, and making sure the twins didn't up end their little brother into the lake, he and Wally always had their hands full.

Gazing up at the sky, Bob watched Larry land a perfect cast over Barry's head and grinned. "Oh, I don't know about announcing winter. I always thought it sounded like they were yelling at us 'Run! Run! Get out while you can.'." The boys laughed uproariously at this, and started telling their best deep snow stories. After a few September fishing trips with nothing but Jackfish biting, they would be in the depths of a brutal Saskatchewan winter before they could say Canada Goose.

Mere weeks had passed since that day. Wally startled at his shortness of breath, caught in ragged gasps at the thought that those fishing trips would never happen again. Still looking up, but seeing nothing but blurry sky, he steeled himself against the panic. Those trips *would* happen again. He'd make sure of it. He'd make damn sure the Schrader kids were taken care of.

When he focused his eyes again the geese had disappeared, and the thumping of helicopter blades replaced their winter warning. Shading his eyes and squinting for a better look, he saw the military helicopter clear the farthest trees. Even after all his years as a dogman, he still marvelled at how fast Bruce picked up on these things. How quick he was. How astute. His ears were better than all the officers combined.

The helicopter had drifted closer during Wally's marvelling. Officers were forced to shout at each other over the noise. The Huey cleared the treeline closest to headquarters and he quickly realized they had every intention of landing in the field directly behind the trailer.

The door to the trailer burst open and he heard the squawk of the radio. "Alpha Kilo One Niner to base, requesting permission to land behind HQ, as ordered." Officers darted this way and that, the more experienced members making sure the new guys weren't near the landing zone. Wally smirked when he saw a young officer grabbed by the collar and yanked away. He'd been staring up in awe, body pelted with debris, as the copter hovered well above the site waiting for clearance.

"Base to Alpha Kilo One Niner, copy that, you are cleared to land." Mosher's voice carried through the open door. Confident the office was well manned, Wally approached the landing zone, covering his head with his arms, leaning into the churning wind, Bruce pressing in behind his legs. They waited for the huge machine to touch down, and the engine to cut and die. Slowly, the tornado of debris lessened, and he ducked forward to throw open the pilot's door.

"Regitnig." He thrust out his hand and caught one hell of a grip with a pilot who looked about his own age.

"Captain Freedman. Load me up, sir."

He appreciated the immediacy of this pilot and wasted no time, calling over Henry and Ace.

ON SCENE

"You got a second?" he yelled at Long, who nodded. "Okay, go get another dogman, make sure he has a second, and get back here on the double. You're out with the first chopper."

Long pumped a fist, followed by a cocky grin. "Of course we're first. You need the best out there." He took off before Wally could put him in his place. A little confidence wasn't a bad thing but Henry Long was fast on his way to another good setting-down.

Bruce barked at the treeline again and Wally saw the second Huey on approach. He directed Henry and the other team onto the landed chopper and banged on the pilot's door, giving him a thumbs up. He ran to take cover by the trailer as the blades came to life and whipped debris at anyone standing too close.

The second Huey landed without incident and took off with another two dog teams. Wally was satisfied the farthest corners of the search area would be well covered by lunch.

Each dogman had a second, someone to carry maps and supplies, check directions, and help out. With teams in from out of province, not many knew the local officers, but it didn't make a difference; an RCMP officer was an RCMP officer, no matter what province you hailed from. Wally took no time in plucking officers from the ranks, grilling them on whether or not they could keep up the gruelling pace, pairing them up with the dogmasters, and sending them on their way. The dogmasters could all run behind their canine partners for miles and miles without resting, and their seconds couldn't slow them down.

He ended up with Constable Friesen, who initially swore he was fit and active, lifted weights, and enjoyed being outside. What he failed to mention was that he was the loudest, clumsiest cadet in the history of the Force.

It being first thing in the morning, and subjected to Mosher's coffee with no real food, Wally thought he was just being impatient and critical the first time Constable Friesen tripped over the underbrush, dropping his maps and canteen. Wally stopped short and called Bruce to halt, waiting for the Constable to gather himself.

"Sorry, sir. It'll just take me a minute here…" In a comedy of errors, Friesen picked up his maps, dropped his canteen, picked up his canteen and dropped his maps. Wally had to turn around and close his eyes or risk losing his temper before the sun had even fully come up.

"Sure, Friesen, take your time. We've got all day."

Friesen looked confused. "Really?" Apparently, the man couldn't think and walk at the same time because he stopped dead to ask the question.

Wally glared at the constable, which hurried him considerably, and they continued in the direction Regitnig had set for them. "No, not really. Now move your ass. You're supposed to be able to keep up with the dog." Wally set off at a jog, letting out some leash and giving Bruce his head.

Not ten more minutes into the trek, he couldn't hear himself think for all the thrashing going on behind him. He let out a growling grunt and wheeled around on the constable.

"Haven't you ever walked through the bush before? Quiet your feet, man." He searched Friesen's face for any bit of remorse and found only a blank stare that confirmed what he already suspected.

"Uh, no sir. This is my first time. From Ontario." He grinned and thrust a thumb at himself. "Graduating Depot next week. This is my first time north of Saskatoon."

Wally wanted to smack himself in the head. The value of a dogman was his ability to move quickly and silently but with this bumbling troll trailing along behind him they might as well announce their arrival to Robertson on a megaphone, flying a big flag above their heads. There was nothing he could do about it now; he needed to clear the next area on his map before lunch. Come noon he would hustle Friesen back to base faster than the cadet could drop a map.

"Look, you walk like this. Ease your foot down; don't just drop it into the leaves. You need to be quiet." Wally tried not to roll his eyes. Friesen nodded and dropped his map again.

"Okay, Sergeant. Will do. I've just never been—" he started chattering again and Wally held up a hand.

ON SCENE

"Friesen, you ever been shot at?" He almost felt bad watching the blood drain completely from the cadet's face.

Friesen's Adam's apple bobbed convulsively. "No, sir."

Wally raised his eyes to the tops of the trees and stared a circle around them. "If you don't shut it, you will be." They weren't exactly out in the open, but this was Robertson's territory. Wally rolled his shoulders, shaking off the feeling of eyes on the back of his neck. He hardened his glare at Friesen, wondering why he had to explain any of this.

Friesen zipped his fingers across his pursed lips, nodding vigorously. Wally sighed deeply from his chest, feeling the weight there. This kid didn't have a clue. He supposed ignorance really would be bliss.

The entire morning was accompanied by Friesen's constant thrashing and dropping things, saying sorry, then saying sorry for speaking. By the time they circled the deserted, stagnant water hole and got back to headquarters, Wally was shocked he hadn't buried the body in a nice remote spot. He was quite proud of himself for that, and for not giving up and leaving Friesen out in the bush by himself, even though the back of his head throbbed as if Robertson had stared a hole in it.

When they got back to headquarters just after 1300hrs, there were officers darting every which way. A few dogmen had come back in for new coordinates, and Wally scanned the faces for a familiar one. He saw Ace before he located Long, giving the dog a good rough pat on both sides.

"How are you, buddy? Find anything good out there?" Paws up on his shoulders, Wally stretched his face back, avoiding Ace's enthusiastic tongue. Long turned away from the group he was speaking to.

"Sergeant Regitnig. How are ya, Bruce?" Henry roughhoused with Bruce a minute, then tossed both dogs a piece of something from his pocket. "Going to send me out anywhere difficult? I'm ready for another round."

"Well it's lucky I found you. You have a second for the afternoon?" Wally glanced over his shoulder to make sure Friesen was still there.

Long shook his head. "Just lost my second to the air search crew. They needed another pair of eyes. Who've you got for me?"

"Constable Friesen, meet Constable Long. You'll be his second for the afternoon." Wally pointed a finger in Long's face. "Make sure you don't lose him. He comes back all in one piece."

"Wait, what?" Long sounded a little bit confused and a lot worried.

Wally whistled at Bruce and snatched his map from Friesen with a snicker. It'd be good for the cocky little shit to have to practice some patience today. If Bob and Doug were here, they'd heartily support the action. It hadn't even been twenty-four hours and Wally missed them both with a pain that stabbed him in the gut every time he thought about them.

He grabbed two brown bag lunches piled on a table outside the trailer. He imagined Dolores had rallied some of the ladies at the church or something. He didn't know how she did it, but food always magically appeared when he was on a case. Peering in the bag he saw peanut butter and purple jelly oozing out of some haphazard waxed paper. Bless the ladies and their PB and J. Anything would taste like heaven after the night he had.

He walked into the bush on the far west side of the house, map in one hand, sandwich in the other, perusing the area. Bruce had his nose to the ground but was taking his time about it. The map wasn't amazing, but there was an area he hadn't been out to yet that might have a water source. He headed out that way to see for himself what it looked like, and whether it had been searched by anyone else yet. Some genius—he was sure it was Staff Sergeant Anderson—had come up with the idea of laying down toilet paper when an area was searched to let other officers know it had been cleared. It was wet and cold last night, and the toilet paper was only one-ply, so the idea had been quickly set aside but not before most of the immediate area looked like a gang of high school boys had a spit ball fight. Wally had bigger things to worry about than ill-conceived ideas. He dragged his boots along the rough forest floor, scraping the clumping white bits off as he went.

They stalked through the bush at a good pace, Wally putting himself in the shoes of the shooter. He imagined the location of the abandoned police car, the location of the house, and his current location, all three making a triangle in his mind. Logic told him he needed to go out farther.

ON SCENE

"Where would I go, boy? What would I do, if I was him?" Bruce stopped and looked back, ears perked up as high as they could go. "You'd answer me, if you could."

There wasn't a case in the last decade Wally hadn't discussed with Bob.

```
"Damn inmates. We spend more time chasing escapees than we
spend putting them behind bars sometimes." Schrader pounded a
fist on his desk and threw the file away from him.

"What the hell are you complaining about? You don't have
to leave the desk. It's me and Bruce slogging through the
swamp." Wally shot him a disgusted look and picked up the
file. "This one has some hunting experience. So, what would
you do, mister big time hunter?"

Bob leaned back in his chair, a satisfied smile replacing the
frustration. "Well, I don't know about that, but I did bag a
good one last season. It's all about high ground, my friend.
There isn't much of it here, but if you can get up on a rise
and look down, you'll bag yourself a good one every time. And
if you have good cover, you can see anything coming at you."
```

Wally stopped walking, hearing Bob's words echo through his head. High ground. He shoved the rest of the sandwich into his mouth with the heel of his hand and wiped it on his pants, looking around for a spot to open up the map. Spying a nice wide fallen log, he unfolded the map, smoothing the wrinkles out to get a good view of the area. Bruce jumped up, resting his front paws on Wally's leg.

"Cop way, my ass. We'll find him our way." He pointed to where they were with his left forefinger and with his right, traced over all the wavy dotted lines denoting rises and valleys in the area.

There wasn't much that could be considered high ground anywhere near the Robertson property. His eyes carefully went back over the area again, but nothing new jumped out at him.

"Where's the property line here?" he murmured, gently sliding Bruce's chin over to reveal the very top northwest corner of the Robertson land where he wasn't sure they'd done any tracking yet. It wasn't much, but the lines and dots told him that area did, indeed, have a valley. And where there was a valley, there had to be higher ground.

He stabbed at the corner, causing Bruce to jerk his head up and woof. "That's it. There's the high ground, Bob." Wally gathered up his map and slung his canteen over his shoulder.

"Let's go, Bruce. Something's there." Bruce barked and jumped down, dashing ahead a few yards, then turned around to wait for Wally.

"Go, I'll catch up. Hurry up or it'll be pitch black on the way back in." Wally looked up and surveyed the afternoon sun. The land was vast; Robertson owned a substantial chunk of wild bush, excellent for hunting.

He had no idea how long it would take him to walk out there, but he was going to find out.

There was a nice bit of sunshine to ease the cold from Stanley's bones. He stood up and stretched under the tree, then stopped and closed his eyes. He released his breath and held it, quieting his body so he could listen without interruption. He heard some bird song, but nothing else. Peering out between the branches into the valley below, movement drew his attention to the water and he squinted hard trying to make it out. Just a fox out for an early morning drink. Nothing human out this far yet. The birds would quiet if someone approached.

He gathered up his weapons and used a loose branch to brush away any evidence in the pine needles of a body lying down for the night. He had to move around to stay warm; if they came across his safe spot, he didn't want anything left behind. Perhaps he could secure some food now that the light of a new day was shining on his face.

ON SCENE

Police Search on Foot-*Using the Robertson farm...as a base, the armed searchers are being sent into the bush in five groups, each under a unit commander and each group using a tracking dog."*

*Headline and excerpt, Regina Leader Post
(Thursday, October 15, 1970)*

Chapter Twenty-Seven

Saturday, October 10, 1970
On Scene
1900hrs

Hours of traipsing back and forth through the dense bush, lower branches grabbing at his legs and slowing his progress put Wally in a decently foul mood by the time he got within sight of the area he sought. Looking up at the tops of the trees, he saw a lone Jack Pine off in the distance, swaying gently in the fall breeze. Judging by the distance they still had to travel to get there, the thing was huge. Wally cursed under his breath and called Bruce back.

They hadn't caught any scent at all, Bruce tracking back and forth, forging ahead quite a ways, letting his human counterpart deal with the branches that grabbed at his coat and pants.

"Bruce." Wally whistled, waiting for the dog to realize there was no more forward today. Staring at the top of the Jack Pine, he shifted his vision to the sun, barely visible now above the treeline. If they didn't turn back now, they would be out in the pitch dark again. Wally and Bruce had tracked in the dark many times, but it was a wise officer who knew when he was out too far, and it was too cold to sleep rough tonight. Hypothermia wasn't something he wanted to wrestle with.

But even the threat of hypothermia couldn't get that tree off his mind. Bruce ran back, leaning into Wally's leg as he stopped long enough to fold his map into a neat square around the spot. He marked where he was, and how far he had yet to go, looking for solid natural land markers, and gauging the position of the sun.

"We'll get a ride out here tomorrow, Chief. This is where we start." He stabbed the map with his forefinger. Sixth sense nagging at him, he reluctantly turned to go, knowing if they double timed it, they may make it back safely enough by moonlight.

The entire afternoon had been nearly as uneventful as the previous night, unless you counted meeting Corporal Perkins at lunch. He smirked as he jogged alongside Bruce. Perkins drove one of the army's personnel vehicles which Wally had to admit was much safer and more efficient at moving men through the bush than walking in on foot. Today proved that outright. If he'd not been so damn stubborn and hitched a ride with Perkins, he may have cleared the area around the Jack Pine and been back in time to grab a bite and have a chat with shift change. The thing was made of solid metal, had six wheels on it and resembled a mini tank. It wasn't fast, but mowed over everything in its path, keeping the officers inside safe from outside gunfire should their shooter happen to pop out from wherever he was hiding.

Corporal Perkins was from somewhere in England, a thick accent punctuating the fact that he said fuck about every second word, no matter who he was talking to or what he was explaining. The man arrived on the huge Hercules army plane sometime before dawn and by early afternoon, when Wally dumped the burden of Constable Friesen on Henry, the cadets were calling Perkins 'Corporal Fuck-Fuck'. At first, Wally tried to put a stern kybosh on the ridiculous—though well-earned—nickname, but it was going to be a lost cause. Besides, Perkins wasn't part of his outfit. Hopefully the search would end quickly, and he'd go back to his army unit in Manitoba before they got any formal complaints about him. A quick end to this search; it's what Wally prayed for hourly. *Just let us find him.*

Now as the sun started to dip below the horizon, he jogged straight through, only stopping twice to check the map. Walking grid was a lot different than jogging as the crow flew. When they got close to the Robertson house, they need only look up. Outside headquarters a couple fires burned for warmth and were easy to spot if you still had enough daylight to see the smoke above the trees. It was getting dark fast, but the run had gotten them back in good time and he saw the tendrils of smoke curling up over the bare poplar branches.

Shift change was done and everyone on night duties had dispersed to roadblocks or hunkered down at their posts for the night. There were a few officers hanging around the fire pits, probably waiting on rides back to the city, but other than that, things were quiet. He dumped his stuff beside the trailer and shuffled up to one of the fire pits, exchanging tired but polite nods with the other members. He tried to relax his mind, breathing deeply, taking in the silence. It was short lived.

Mosher's voice carried through the trailer door. "You spent your whole first day crashing through every fence in the area." He didn't sound overly happy with whoever he was yelling at.

There was a pause and Wally elbowed the member next to him. "When there's a pause after Mosher yells, it's someone trying to explain their way out of it. He hates that." Anticipating some kind of explosion, Wally didn't move when the door to the trailer flew open, crashing against the wall and making the rest of the group jump out of their skins. An officer stumbled down the step and Mosher's voice followed him out.

"I don't give a goddamn what you do in Manitoba. We're the Royal Canadian Mounted Police and this is F Division. You do it my way, or no way." Mosher appeared at the door, pointing at the officer who saluted him smartly.

"Yes, sir. So fucking sorry, sir," the military man said, causing some hilarity with the RCMP officers beside the trailer. Mosher winced and roared.

Wally smirked and whispered to the officer next to him. "I don't think there were any words in that." The other officer shook his head and sidled closer to the fire.

"Damn it, Perkins. Get out of my sight. Quit running through fences. Just keep the men from getting shot." Perkins saluted again, spun on his heel, and marched away. Mosher leaned heavily on the door frame, looking like he was about to suffer from cardiac arrest.

"It's okay, Al. I doubt anyone listens to Perkins." Wally walked over and smacked Mosher on the back, turning to the rest of the members hanging around outside the trailer. "You all get back to the city and get some sleep."

He closed the door firmly on his order, blocking out the responsibilities of the day.

Mosher sat, still looking like he needed a hospital. "That damn guy is messing with my blood pressure, Wally. He's only been here one day. One goddamn day. I have farmers from here clear down to Rosthern calling me up already, threatening to send us bills for their fences."

"I don't want to say 'I told you so' but…" Wally ducked the stapler that flew at his head and hit the far wall. Bruce started barking like a lunatic and went to retrieve the offending piece of metal.

Mosher cracked the knuckles of his left hand, arthritis bending his first two fingers. "You cheeky son of a bitch, don't start with me. I suppose I'll take a few broken fences if he's keeping our guys from getting killed in the woods." Bruce padded over and put the stapler in Mosher's hand. "Don't you start with me, either. Go lie down over there." Mosher dropped the stapler on the table, wiped the dog slobber off on his pants, and pulled some maps closer to him. The corner of his moustache ticked with annoyance. "Enough of this shit. Where were you today?" He pushed one particularly colourful map at Wally.

He lifted pages until a marker rolled out from under them. Uncapping it, he circled the watering hole he cleared earlier that morning with Friesen and shuddered at the memory. He wondered how Long had made out, and if Friesen was wandering out in the woods all alone as they spoke. Wally snorted.

"Nothing about this is funny, Regitnig." Mosher growled. He ripped the pen out of Wally's hand and circled a spot, labelling it 'DDD'.

"Sorry. Just wondering how Long and Ace did today."

"You know exactly how he did, so stop being an asshole." Al pointed a stern finger at him, but Wally could see he was trying hard not to give in to the smile that pulled at his moustache. "I'm fucking shocked Long didn't kill Friesen and dump him in that slough he cleared this afternoon. Quit screwing with the kid, he'll lose his temper and I don't need that kind of paperwork." His moustache twitched again. Mosher was a hardass, but he appreciated the razzing just as much as the next guy. A little hilarity didn't need to feel like a betrayal to Bob and Doug if it was something they would've appreciated themselves.

"Yes, sir." Wally turned the map towards him. "What's 'DDD'? I marked that exact spot." He pointed at the circle Mosher made on the master map.

"Darby's Dirty Dozen. We have them going out in teams of twelve and these guys named themselves after the Corporal heading up their unit. I don't give a crap what they name themselves, as long as they all come back in one piece. We expanded the search to thirty square kilometres today, and these guys went a hell of a long ways out." Mosher stabbed at the circled spot with his pen.

"You mean they cleared that area? Right here, exactly?" Wally finely outlined the wavy lines and dots where his Jack Pine tree was. He stopped at the ridiculous possessiveness of that. His. It wasn't his but he wasn't going to ignore whatever it was that told him to check that spot.

Mosher nodded absently. "Yeah, that's the spot. Bit of water there, some high ground. They went over about mid morning, I think." He rummaged around on the desk, overturning files and loose papers until he found what he was looking for. "Yeah, it was 1030hrs today. Perkins gave them a ride out there. Fucking Perkins."

Wally's mind was so occupied dissecting the fact that someone else had searched the area he was so certain about, that he didn't register Mosher's dig at Perkins. He supposed he should be glad the area was searched in a timely manner, but there was a grain of disappointment that he didn't do it himself. And that it came up empty. "There was nothing there? They searched it thoroughly?"

"I wasn't out there holding their hands, but they damn well better have done their jobs." Mosher squinted at Wally. "Why?"

Wally slouched in his chair. "Nah, it's nothing. I just had a feeling about that spot."

"Well you and your feeling can get your ass back to town and sleep. Then your feeling can clear this spot tomorrow morning." Mosher outlined a small box east of the highway in the complete opposite direction of the tree.

ON SCENE

Wally grunted and flipped his hand. "Sure." He readjusted in his chair trying not to sound anxious. "This dirty dozen, they a trustworthy lot? Any experience there?" He had no chance of sounding nonchalant with the length of time he'd worked with Mosher.

"Wally, you and Bruce aren't a two man team handling everything on your own. You have to rely on the rest of us, too. What's eating you?"

"Nothing. Never mind. I was just…sure. But if it's clear, it's clear." He stood abruptly, and Bruce scrambled to his feet. "You need me to take anything back to the city? You should go get some sleep, too."

Mosher scrubbed at his face, making his eyebrow hairs stand up in all directions. He was always so combed and polished it rattled Wally to see his superior's haggard appearance. Mosher stretched and said, "Nah, you don't have to take anything with you. I'm heading back right away. I'll go check on the night surveillance teams first." Al reached out to shake Wally's hand.

"I'll look in on Connie and Vallarena when I get back." Wally glanced at his watch, it wasn't even 2200hrs yet. Nobody had been sleeping much, so he had no doubt he'd find them awake— probably staring into their coffee cups at the Schraders' kitchen table.

If you didn't carry a gun, there wasn't much else to do these days.

Hunt for Slayer of Mounties Continues-*The lower front panel of the front door window is splotched with dried blood, a grim reminder to the double murder which took place here. More exposed to possible rifle fire are the team of dog handlers…*

Headline and excerpt, Regina Leader Post (Wednesday, October 14, 1970)

Chapter Twenty-Eight

Saturday, October 10, 1970
Schrader House
2230hrs

The door to the Schrader home was opened by a sweet, familiar face and the pinched feeling Wally had melted into relief.

"Shirley, I can't tell you how happy I am to see you." He scooped her up in a gigantic hug, the kind of hug the wives complained about, with a laugh, because they got squished into all the painful equipment on the duty belt. Lifting Shirley's feet clear off the floor, he tightened the hug until she let out a little gasp.

"Good to see you too, Wally." She touched his cheek when he set her down. "I'm so very sorry for your loss."

He cleared his throat, looking everywhere but Shirley's eyes. It had been well over a year since Des Cunnin transferred out to Ottawa, but he and his wife Shirley still had a special place at Prince Albert Detachment. Dear, long-time friends of the Schraders, they had overlapped at a couple of posts over the years and always caused a stir when the two families went anywhere together. Ten kids in two families caused some talk. And usually a bit of chaos, too.

"It's your loss too, Shirley. Yours, and Des's. Is he here?" He stepped into the house, an uncomfortable shiver going up his spine at how quiet it was. He didn't think he would ever get used to that.

ON SCENE

"No, Des stayed back. Someone had to keep the home fires burning."

"Your kids set the house on fire again?" Wally quipped without thinking, and Shirley laughed and patted his chest. They stopped and stared at each other, and he felt the clench of guilt for laughing and joking.

Shirley scolded him, "Don't do that, Wally. Don't feel bad. Bob wouldn't like how quiet this house is. I didn't like how quiet our house got when Des and I told our five, and I know Bob would hate how this is affecting his kids. It's okay to joke and laugh. In fact, I insist on it." She took Wally by the arm and led him into the living room where Connie was reclined on the couch. Lynn was curled up in an armchair in the corner, eyes like wide, deep pools. She wasn't missing a thing and was too young to bear the burden of it.

"Ladies." He took off his hat, clenching it between his arm and his side, and came up to take Connie's offered hand. He knelt beside her.

"Did you find him?" she whispered, pulling him close to her.

"Not yet, sweetie, but we will," Wally whispered back fervently. Connie let go of Wally's hand and closed her eyes. Tears coursed down her cheeks, re-wetting salty tracks that had dried white. He wished he had better news for her. He wanted nothing more than to be the person who brought justice to these families. For them. For himself. But especially for Bob and Doug.

He straightened to feel someone hug him from behind, and he turned to embrace Vallarena. They stood still in that hug for a long time; he didn't know how to let her go. He let her choose when the time was right and when she did, she offered, like always, "Can I get you something to eat? There's no shortage." She fiddled with a wad of tissues.

"Did you call your mama? I thought you were going to Pierceland." He was interrupted by a brisk voice behind him.

"Of course she called her mama; Pierceland came to her. I'll make sure they all eat and sleep a bit." Mrs. Sharp came in from the kitchen, wiping her hands on a dish towel and shook Wally's hand.

"It's really good to see you again, ma'am. Thank you for being here…when I can't be." He held on to her soft hand a moment longer, bowing his head and closing his eyes. "Thank you."

"Nonsense, Walter. You have work to do. Now come in, I've got a pot roast heating. I don't know who brought it, but it smells wonderful and you probably haven't eaten all day." She guided him into the kitchen and he saw his breath of fresh air. His wife put her hands on his cheeks, deep blue eyes searching his. They hadn't lost their sparkle, not in more than twenty years of marriage. She drew him close for a quick kiss and he breathed in her scent, settling his hands on hers.

"Thank you," he whispered, tension easing from his shoulders.

"Of course," Dolores whispered back, leading him to the table. The scraping of chairs and the creak of the oven door brought the boys wandering into the kitchen. Not their usual boisterous selves but they couldn't suppress their natural, youthful curiosity.

"Hey, Wally. Did you find the guy who shot our dad?" Barry always had a way of getting right to the point. The boy leaned against Wally, a casual elbow on his shoulder, and looked him dead in the eyes when he asked. Wally didn't break the eye contact but rolled his shoulders, trying to settle the weight of responsibility.

"Not yet, buddy. But we will." He was starting to feel like a broken record.

"Where's Bruce?" Terry asked, snatching a cookie off a tray only to have it smoothly confiscated by Shirley.

"Bruce is in the car. He's tired and will surely forget his manners. I didn't want him begging supper off of me." The boys smirked. "How about you all get a plate and eat with me so I'm not lonely? Then I'm sure Shirley will let you have a cookie before bed. You should be asleep already." He pulled out a chair for Terry.

"Can't sleep, Wally. We got to stay up real late last night, too."

Wally's heart tore another inch at the matter of fact statement. He leaned over and tousled Terry's dark blond hair, making the boy's freckled nose wrinkle up with pleasure. "I know, Sport. It's going to be a rough week, right? But we'll look out for each other."

Vallarena and her mother gently directed the children to their seats with a steaming plate in front of each of them. Lynn quietly stepped inside the door, leaning against the jamb but refused a plate of food. Wally winked at her and she gave him a small smile. He mouthed 'Happy Birthday' and she shrugged, pointing to a half eaten cake on a stand.

All four boys dug in with Wally, and Dolores sighed with contentment. "There. This is the way it should be. They just needed you to eat with them, Wally." She tried to smile wider, a single tear pooling under her right eye. Wally raised his fork in a silent salute. He couldn't bear her tears and was glad his mouth was full.

"Reminds me of Bob and Des, drinking beer on the deck this summer," Shirley said, a catch in her throat. She tried to clear it, wavering on her inhale. "They had this running joke that neither one of them should drink alone, so when one opened a new bottle, the other one had to as well. Went like that all week." Her face softened at the memory.

"That was the best trip ever," Garry said succinctly, mopping gravy up off his plate with a bun.

"Yeah, I liked Niagara Falls the best," Terry said around a mouthful. "And when Dad played catch with us all the time."

Shirley put her arm around Terry, gathering him up into a motherly hug. "It really was the best trip. I'm so thankful you came out to visit us. It's all my kids can talk about, even after two months."

"I liked the changing of the guard in Ottawa," Lynn said quietly, warming to the conversation. "Remember when Dad tried to get a picture of us all and that guy dropped the camera?" She let out a giggle and put a hand over her mouth.

"It's okay, honey. It was pretty funny. But he didn't exactly drop it." Shirley laughed.

```
"All right everyone, come on. Barry, leave your brother
alone. Larry, grab Terry for me. Now stand together. We'll
get someone to take our photo. Both families!" Bob looked
around and caught the eye of another tourist. "Mind taking
our picture?" The man seemed amenable to the idea and took
the camera, waiting for the group to sort themselves out.
```

"Okay, everyone say cheese," Bob yelled. The fourteen of them all yelled cheese, the children somewhat louder than necessary, and that made the adults grin harder. The camera clicked, and the group immediately broke apart with kids rolling on the grass, laughing and shouting.

The man who took the photo smiled and stepped forward to hand the camera back to Bob, but was caught up by several boys roughhousing on the slight hill, flailing and rolling. A random limb caught the man's leg and took him down into the pile, the camera flying out of his hands and landing on the concrete path with a crash. Even the children froze with a gasp.

"Good thing it was our last day in Ottawa because that was the last photo we got on that trip." Everyone in the kitchen looked up to see Connie lingering in the doorway, a far off look in her teary eyes. "The camera was destroyed beyond repair, but the film came out fine." She leaned over to the side of the refrigerator and released a magnet clip, passing the infamous photo around.

There were some sighs and soft laughs as everyone took a look. When it came to her, Lynn stared at it, hugged it to her, and gently clipped it back to the fridge magnet.

"Okay, guys. Let's get to bed and let mom and the ladies talk to Wally." Groans from the younger boys, but appreciative looks from the women followed Lynn and Larry out the kitchen door as they herded their brothers ahead of them. They all took a cookie and a kiss on the head from Shirley, even Larry who was so much taller than Shirley that she grabbed his shoulders and pulled him down to her. Standing on tip toe, she kissed his cheek and patted it. He flushed at the attention and crammed the cookie into his mouth, swinging the door shut behind him.

Suddenly, there was silence again. Vallarena and her mother poured some coffee, and Shirley came over to hug Connie. Dolores settled herself beside Wally, a warm, gentle hand grasping his forearm.

"I'm so glad you came to visit," Shirley said again, her face taking on a serious shadow, tightening her hold on her best friend. "Remember when Bob stopped the car after you guys pulled out?"

ON SCENE

Connie frowned slightly, struggling to recall, and then lit with remembrance.

Shirley wiped at her eyes and took a long breath. "I never told you what happened. It didn't seem important at the time."

"Have a safe drive. Love you. Be good!" Shirley kissed as many cheeks as she could reach in the mob of hugging children. The Cunnin children would miss their friends dreadfully, even though they'd been in Ottawa over a year already. Letters flew across the provinces frequently and they were already counting the days until they saw each other again.

The Schrader kids piled into the station wagon, arguing over who would get the spacious rear spot, and Bob grinned.

"So it begins," he shouted at the sky, shaking Des's hand and patting him on the back. "Good to see you, buddy. Don't be a stranger." The women hugged long and hard, then the families separated and the Cunnins stood arm in arm watching the station wagon pull away.

The kids lost interest quickly, disappearing into the house, but Shirley and Des kept waving, not intending to stop until the car and camper were out of sight. Half a block down, the car screeched to a halt and the driver door flew open.

"Uh-oh." Des groaned. "Either someone forgot something or Garry has to go to the bathroom again." Bob got out of the car alone and jogged back to the Cunnins, throwing his arms around Des, engulfing his friend in a huge bear hug. The two men pounded each other on the back.

"I'm afraid I'll never see you again, Desi."

In the retelling of the moment, Shirley couldn't hold herself in check. A hiccup escaped her and she held Connie to her chest so hard she shook.

"And so it was." Shirley rocked back and forth, rubbing Connie's back, letting her grief and regret for all that was lost flood into her friend's hair.

"Bob was Des's best bud and Connie was Godmother to our middle daughter. We are dining out

Kate Kading

on memories in our life right now, but the Schraders fill many pages. Bob, Connie, and the children motored to us in Ottawa the summer of '70, putting up their trailer in our side yard. What an immense store of memories does that evoke."

Interview with Shirley Cunnin (April 2016)

Chapter Twenty-Nine

Saturday, October 10, 1970
Northwest corner of the Robertson property
Just after sunset

The second night settled around him, less comforting than the first.

Now the twilight brought uncertainty instead of safety, and his breath came up short at the prospect of having to make a better plan than just walking all day. It had been a good thing he took the time to erase his presence from the area that morning. Stooping to cup his hand in the small pond, he had splashed his face, had a sip, and dunked his canteen in. Expecting only the sound of the bubbles rising from the canteen, the rumble of an engine had startled him beyond comprehension.

It wasn't difficult to elude the heavily armed men who meticulously combed the area. He simply walked away, farther northwest onto his uncle's property. But he wasn't interested in this game of cat and mouse.

As the sun set on his first full day of being a hunted man, he wondered what came next, and made his way back to his sanctuary. His feet were heavy, but he tried not to drag them and leave a trail that was easy to follow. The wet leaves were excellent cover; no scent and no footprints to be had.

He ducked under the tree, relieved his shoulder of the heavy burden of two rifles, sat down and looked directly into the eyes of his father.

"Son," his father said quietly, gripping Stanley's forearm. He felt such sadness in the embrace.

He lowered his head to his father's arm. "I'm sorry," he gasped out. He felt a hand press into the back of his head.

"I know."

Stanley shook his head, raising his eyes to Gordon's. "I didn't mean to. Ruth—" His insides churned just uttering his wife's name. The burning gorge rose halfway up his throat, but there wasn't much of anything in his stomach to vomit up. It had been a long time since his last meal.

Gordon raised his hand and pulled off the oversized tan hunting cap. He silenced him with a wave of his cap. "None of that matters. You know what needs to be done."

Panic welled up inside Stanley. His heart beat faster and sweat broke out on his forehead, despite the chill of the night. He wiped his damp hands on the length of his thighs and drew a ragged breath.

"I know."

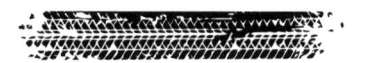

"This is such bullshit." Brent Jette took a long final drag on his cigarette, threw it down and crushed it under his boot, grinding it viciously into the gravel. Blowing a long stream of smoke behind him, he paced the length of the police car, trying to stay awake. Night shift roadblock duty wasn't as fun as it sounded. His mouth quirked at his own joke and he cast a look at his partner for the night. A young member from Tisdale, he was efficient enough, good at his job, and didn't need direction, but the man was also quieter than the proverbial church mouse. Well into the second night of mostly silent pacing, he found himself longing for the annoying—but entertaining—banter of his co-workers at Prince Albert. Things were not going to be the same without Doug's stories. He lowered his head just long enough to get his grief under control.

ON SCENE

For the officers, things changed constantly. You transferred all the time, moving around the province to fill gaps wherever needed. But there were a few constants in the Force; a few things you could count on. One of them was family, both at home and at work. Your detachment family intertwined with your blood relatives to the point where you didn't know where one ended and the other began. The pain was debilitating if he focused on it. The loss of his Force brothers was more painful than anything he'd ever experienced before, and he was certain everyone at the detachment felt the same. Brothers of the heart. Now their hearts were broken.

Brent saw headlights miles down the road, and paced impatiently until the vehicle was close enough to stop. Hand resting on the butt of the sidearm holstered at his hip, he held a hand out for the truck to pull over. Without a word, Constable Church Mouse cocked his shotgun, resting it across the hood of the police car.

He approached carefully, shining his flashlight past the driver into the passenger seat. "Good evening, sir. Have anyone else with you tonight?" He went over the inside of the truck with a glance, sweeping his flashlight beam into the back.

"Just me and old Sprocket," the driver drawled, yawning.

Before he got a good look, he had a face full of snarling dog and his heart seized in his chest.

"Shit." He jumped and drew his gun, lowering it fast when he saw it was just a mixed-breed farm dog making himself heard.

"Sorry about that. Sprocket, knock it off." The dog responded immediately to his master's voice, lying down in the bed of the truck. Brent was thankful nothing was blocking his view and he could get them on their way. No tool boxes, no blankets, and nowhere to hide.

"Where you coming from?" He asked curtly, staying a good distance away from Sprocket, coming in closer to the driver's window. The faint smell of alcohol reached him and he took another step forward.

"Just had some hands of cards at my brother's place." The driver flexed his hands on the steering wheel and stared straight forward.

"How many beers did you have with your cards? Or is that a bit of home brew I smell?" he asked.

The man's head snapped toward him in shock. "No sir, not me," the man spluttered, shaking his head.

Brent stopped him. "Look, no use lying to us," he said, and came right up to the window to take a good whiff, shining the flashlight in the man's face to watch his pupils shrink immediately. He flicked the flashlight back and forth over the man's eyes, but his dilation seemed normal. The smell was faint, and there were no empties on the floor of the truck. Just a rifle across the back of the seat, like every other farmer in the area.

"Just two beers with supper."

Brent squinted at him, flicking his flashlight around some more and then, satisfied, he nodded. "All right then."

The man sagged in relief, shoulders relaxing. Guilty men didn't relax; he took that as a good sign.

"You can carry on." His curt order was met with a quick nod from the driver and he pulled away, gravel kicking up behind the truck as it gained speed. Brent jumped again when Sprocket let loose with some obnoxious barking in farewell.

A snicker from behind him grated on his nerves. "Shut up," he growled, glaring over his shoulder. The other constable shrugged, unsuccessfully trying to wipe the smirk off his face.

Brent leaned against the front of the car, eyes closed, listening to the departing truck for quite some time. Well after midnight, there wasn't much to hear. The odd owl hooted, but they hadn't averaged more than a car an hour since they took up the spot just after seven. Slow traffic and nothing to find, anywhere.

He finally lost the sound of the truck and concentrated on the night that surrounded him. In the middle of summer there would be a cacophony of bugs and frogs, but October on the prairies was different. The cold never bothered him, but it did silence the wildlife. No crickets sang, no bullfrogs croaked. It was just quiet. He found it unnerving.

ON SCENE

One good thing about Constable Church Mouse was that a man could be alone with his thoughts. He went over the events of yesterday, over and over again, to see where they went wrong. To find the pivotal moment where someone, somewhere, could have made a different choice, causing the whole chain of events to change. He chafed at his lack of information. He'd find Sergeant Regitnig in the morning and insist on knowing what his commanding officers knew.

Mulling the case with his eyes closed made him startle that much harder when he heard the gunshot.

"What the hell?" The cigarette fell from his mouth and he fumbled with it, trying to brush it off his front before it burned a hole in his uniform.

He stormed a few yards up the road, glaring at his partner.

"Did you hear that? That was a gunshot, for sure. I'd bet my spurs on it." He pointed at the other officer with certainty.

"Maybe your card player's night hunting. You see a spotlight in his truck?"

Brent shook his head. "No, but he could've had something under the seat. I should've checked. Coming back from cards at 3 a.m.? Who does that?" He had his own answer directly after the words escaped him. The officers did that all the time.

"I do that with my family at Christmas. All night poker." Constable Church Mouse was sure getting chatty all of a sudden. Annoyed, Brent went back to the car and leaned in, grabbing the radio.

"Alpha six-one-eight to base." There had been very little radio chatter between midnight and two, and for the last hour they hadn't heard a peep out of anybody. He hoped someone was still alert enough to answer him.

"Alpha six-one-eight to base," he repeated impatiently, clamping a new cigarette between his lips and lighting it.

"Come back Alpha six-one-eight," a far off voice answered, too thin to recognize who it was. Probably a corporal relegated to overnight duty in the radio room.

"We're on Canon road east of MacDowall and just heard a gunshot. Can you confirm, over." The pause was so long he thought he'd have to repeat himself, but then the voice came back.

"Negative Alpha six-one-eight, no gunshots reported. Probably a backfiring vehicle." He rolled his eyes skyward and muttered, "Yeah, right. Traffic is crazy out here," before pressing the button on his radio again.

"You sure about that? Anyone else on this channel hear a gunshot?" A couple negatives rang out and he threw down the mic.

"You heard it, right?" he yelled out the open door. His counterpart slowly shrugged and nodded haltingly. "Well, did you or didn't you? For fuck's sake, that was a gunshot." He picked up the mic again. "Alpha six-one-eight to base, be advised of gunfire, my location at oh three hundred, over."

Whoever was on the radio had to be new, he noted, as the responses took way longer than normal. The radio man was addressing a superior somewhere, he just didn't know who. Then the voice sighed in frustration and cursed right over the radio, forgetting to sigh and swear first, and then press the button. Common rookie mistake. It made Brent laugh but didn't relieve his intense frustration.

"Noted, Alpha six-one-eight. But you're to stay at your post."

Brent threw the radio down and got out of the car, stomping down the gravel road muttering to himself. It wasn't a car backfiring. Was his card player a poacher? His mind raced, body refusing to keep still, and he quickened his pace up and down the road.

Where did it come from? Who pulled off that shot?

> "I have known Wilfred Stanley Robertson all my life. Stanley and I were the best of friends. He didn't even seem mad when he fired the shot at me. You couldn't tell when Stanley was mad. He wouldn't show it."
>
> Excerpt of interview with "Don Nelson" regarding the initial altercation (October 1970)

Chapter Thirty

Monday, October 12, 1970
Highway 11, Southbound
0645hrs

Monday morning was clear and cold, frost blanketing every surface like the fine white sheet that covered a body after a murder.

Over the weekend, a lot had happened and yet nothing had happened at all. Wally was humbled by the dedication of the members, like Cavello and Morier who'd taken it upon themselves to patrol the train tracks at night. They had trouble hiding their disappointment that they hadn't caught so much as a tiptoe from the shooter despite jumping at every night noise. Wally didn't think Greenslade had gotten more than a few hours sleep since Friday because he hadn't seen him leave the scene. Brent Jette wouldn't let any of them forget about the alleged shot he heard. Out of all the men Wally was trying to keep tabs on, that particular happening devilled him the most. He didn't doubt Jette's hearing in the least. If the man said it was a gunshot, it was. But the fact still remained that nobody else had heard it and they didn't know where it came from. Another hotshot bored on roadblock duty? If it was, nobody was copping to it.

Mind still in the thick of the details, he took the turn into MacDowall and pulled into the parking lot of the café. Henry Long now knew every bit of water within a thirty kilometre radius of the farm, and wasn't about to give up. He wondered if he could send Long back out to double up on certain areas that were already searched without the young constable kicking up a stink. The Jack Pine swayed in Wally's memory.

He pushed open the door to Fran's, surprised that she would be open on Thanksgiving Monday. Bruce pushed in ahead of him, going straight to the water bowl Fran put out after that first morning Wally walked into the restaurant. He was making a habit of dropping in morning and evening, introducing himself to people, and keeping his ears open. He'd never given over to listening to the gossip on coffee row, but his run in with Roy had him wondering what others were saying. This investigation didn't involve some random stranger. Stanley Robertson was a trusted friend to many in the area, and Wally didn't doubt someone was helping him somewhere.

His coffee shop trips were in direct conflict with his staunch belief in police procedure but the stats were undeniable. Whether it was a suspect or a missing child, they were always found close to home. He hated to admit it, but Robertson was still in the area. He could almost guarantee that someone in the café knew exactly where he was hiding. So he veered from his procedure…and he listened.

Conversation came to an abrupt halt when Wally strolled from the door to the back booth. Heads turned, eyes followed, hands went up to mouths, and the whispers started.

Fran came bustling down the aisle with her coffee pot and a clean cup, setting it down and greeting him a little louder than necessary.

"Sure nice to see you, Sergeant Regitnig. Can't thank y'all enough for your kindness fixing my back door yesterday. Can I get you anything else?" Her extra chipper speech made him cock an eyebrow at her.

In a low voice he said, "Fran, it's fine. I can handle the talk. Coffee is great. Don't worry about me." Her dark brows came together with concern and she nodded, patting his arm.

Bruce finished draining the water bowl and came to sprawl himself on Wally's feet under the table.

ON SCENE

"You comfy, Chief?" He looked under the table and felt the rumble of Bruce's groan. He sat back, sipping his coffee in mock contentment, all eyes still on him. But it was okay. He just had to wait it out.

After a ridiculously drawn out quarter hour, the buzz in the café started to pick back up. People either forgot he was there, or just got more comfortable with their gossip partner and thought Wally couldn't hear them. Either which way, the talk started up again and all he had to do was listen. Not his favourite method of investigating, but in the field you learned to use what was available to you.

"Did you hear they've been through Mr. Wall's house three times? Only picking on him cause he's Stanley's uncle. If they want to suspect all his kin, that's pert near half the town."

"Went through my yard twice now. I know who and what's on my own land, I told 'em. Shoot, Stanley's probably holed up in his own cellar."

"I was out half the night yesterday, helping John round up his cattle. Them army boys knocked the fence down and there was cattle everywhere. Joanna called over to say they were in her yard making a mess, and so we went over to help."

"Had some young buck out knocking on doors all over town to tell us to lock up and stay inside. I tell ya, it's *them* who needs to keep their heads down. Stanley's not going to shoot any of us."

"Nope. Hopefully he'll shoot more of them, if they don't shoot him first."

The café went silent. People fidgeted, only reminded there was a police officer among them when he was directly mentioned. Wally didn't doubt they were right. What's to stop Robertson from shooting more of them? He knew none of his men had gotten Robertson. That's not something you kept to yourself.

One older man in overalls and a green cap leaned back in his booth to look at Wally.

"No need to shush, folks. I ain't scared to say the truth. Any one of you would help Stanley, if he came knocking. He wouldn't hurt any of us and you know it." His voice got louder with his speech, a building rumble of agreement backing him up. "They probably will end up shooting Stanley anyway."

The man adjusted his hat and settled back into his seat. "That's the truth of the matter."

Wally didn't break eye contact with the man, and moved his foot so Bruce would get off of it. It was the people who didn't say anything that knew the most.

He stood, put his Stetson on, taking care with the angle and pulling it low over his eyes. He dropped a few dollar bills onto the table.

"Fran, their coffee is all on me this morning."

He'd already carefully surveyed the half dozen people in the café, and there was nobody withholding anything. Just a bunch of windbags with a whole lot of bluster.

Wally snapped his fingers at Bruce, who stopped sniffing along the wall and came to sit at his side. "The truth of the matter is your friend is charged with two capital murders. We *will* find him."

He touched the edge of his hat to Fran on his way out, boots assaulting the tile floor in the thick silence of the café.

Robertson Eludes Police Net... - *Robertson has eluded searchers since last Friday evening and police believe he is alive in the dense bush near his farmhouse three and a half miles south west of MacDowall which is 25 miles southwest of Prince Albert.*

Headline and excerpt, Prince Albert Daily Herald (Saturday, October 17, 1970)

Chapter Thirty-One

Wednesday, October 14, 1970
Anson Residence
0900hrs

It was too soon. Only five days after learning her husband was dead, Vallarena was expected to polish up her pearls and bury him in a regimental funeral in Regina. Too many strangers would hug her. Too many people would offer awkward condolences she didn't need. Not for lack of care or sympathy, it was just that she could feel their relief that it wasn't their husband. The men would pat her back and she'd try not to get tears on their uniform shoulder.

The entire week had gone by in a blur, her autopilot taking over for the things she had to deal with, her parents taking care of the rest. They were already gone, heading down to Regina in their own car so they could pick up her brother on the way.

Sitting on the couch in the dark blue dress her friend Joan picked out for her, she waited for her driver. Staring at the wall was the safest thing she could do; she'd been doing it a lot lately.

Her body jerked at the sharp rap at the door. Would she ever relax again? In the last few days it had been nothing but chaplains, officers, and a steady stream of casseroles from the ladies' group at the church. If she ate another bite she would likely vomit her grief all over the new carpet in the living room. Even looking at the carpet made her weepy. Doug had taken so much pride in having her pick out exactly what she wanted.

Pulling her eyes away from the floor, she stared at her lap, fingers toying with her gold wedding band, still shiny and new. Her mother's was worn to a dull sheen, the beauty of it no less than the day Vallarena's father put it on her mother's finger. It had become a part of her, and the shine now reflected in her eyes rather than the ring itself. She mourned her own opportunity to wear her wedding ring for so long it became a part of her.

Another sharp knock made her shake off the dreams that would not be and stand reluctantly, smoothing the front of her dress, hands reaching up to pat her hair. She forgot she should answer the door when someone knocked on it.

Her impatient visitor got a third series of knocks half way completed before she wrenched open the door.

"Yes, I'm ready. Let me get my purse." She went to turn away, but noticed there was no regular car in the drive, just a marked police car. Her gaze flickered up to the officer's face.

"Can I help you?" she spit out her question harshly. After the parade that had gone through her house this week, she just wanted a few minutes of peace.

"Mrs. D. B. Anson?" An unknown officer in full uniform addressed her formally. She was on her guard immediately, observing his straight hat and tie, perfectly aligned buttons, and newly shined boots. Two chevrons on his sleeve told her he was a corporal, and one look at his face told her he meant business. He was accompanied by a constable, less crisp in his dress and much younger, gripping some flattened boxes, eyes shifting back and forth. She didn't have to guess too hard to know that he didn't want to be there.

"I…was." She choked on that statement, gulping back her tears. There was no way she would cry in front of men she didn't know.

The corporal stepped past her into the house without being invited, thrusting a paper into her hands. "We've been ordered to gather Constable Anson's effects, ma'am. We won't be long, if you'll direct us to his trunk?" The anxious looking constable stayed on the front step, gaze bouncing between her and his corporal.

ON SCENE

"Excuse me? You what? Can't this wait? I'm on my way out." She read the few brief lines in the letter in her hand "…collection of any and all items belonging to the Royal Canadian Mounted Police…" Her eyes started to swim and she blinked rapidly to stay them. No tears. She needed to be strong.

"Uniforms, paperwork, anything that belongs to the Force, ma'am. Where's Constable Anson's service trunk? This won't take long," the officer repeated, walking into the living room and looking around. Vallarena followed him, slowly gathering her strength about her. She gripped the door, head down, grief coming to a boiling point and turning into lava hot anger.

"I don't understand. Anything in this house belongs to me." She blew her breath out, willing this horrible situation to be a dream. For Doug to come strolling through the door and fix things like he always did. She had never been a wilting flower, the daughter of a Conservation Officer knew how to handle herself around law enforcement, but marrying Doug had been wonderful. A beautiful partnership that promised to give both of them the freedom to be themselves. She appreciated the way he took charge. He knew full well she was capable, but it was nice to have him take care of things sometimes. Now she had to deal with this on her own. He wouldn't swagger through the door, demanding to know who was who and what was what, with his quiet but commanding air of confidence.

"It's not yours anymore, ma'am. Just direct us to the trunk, please." The officer waited pointedly, staring at her, unblinking. She pointed to the bedroom and he spun smartly on his heel, calling to the other officer.

Numbly, she followed, dazed at why they would be interested in what Doug had in his trunk.

The two officers lost no time in dismantling the neat order of the trunk at the foot of their bed. She'd never looked very closely to see what he kept in the bottom, but the top was filled with useful items, precisely organized in Doug's way. Extra buttons and patches, tie pins, belts neatly coiled.

The corporal grabbed things from the top tray and tossed them into the first box. Something caught Vallarena's eye in the waterfall of odds and ends.

Shrieking with indignation, she ran into the bedroom and shoved the larger man aside. She grabbed wildly inside the box to rescue what little of sentimental value she could hold on to.

"This does not-," she bit off the word, breath hissing through her clenched teeth, "belong to the Force." Clutching Doug's father's pocket watch to her chest, breath coming hard, she glared at the corporal, her face flaming hot. She had no more words in that second but hoped her ferocious stare was enough to stay him. The corporal didn't move, but did seem to soften an ounce.

"Please, ma'am. Can you just take Constable Anson's personal items out for us? It would save you the hassle of having them mailed back to you after everything's catalogued." He was still all business, but she saw a flicker of pity in his eyes. "We're just trying to do our jobs, ma'am."

Still hugging the watch, her head dropped and she felt a tear make its way down her cheek. She was tired of crying. So very tired. The effort it took to hold her head up was too much right now. Gathering every grain of strength she had left, she put the watch on the dresser and walked purposefully over to Doug's trunk. Kneeling down, she took care to neatly pleat her dress under her legs. She stared at the top tray, not knowing where to start, then something drew her attention. With gentle fingers, she picked up a dried flower that had once been a corsage, the ribbon and pin still attached. She turned the brown, crinkled carnation over in her hands, marvelling at the sentimentality of her husband. They'd met a couple years before, in her parents' kitchen. The Conservation officers in the Pierceland area often invited nearby RCMP officers for coffee at odd hours, when shifts or complaints overlapped. It was late, and Vallarena had just come in from a dance, flushed and happy. Her father introduced her to Doug and she chatted with him for a long while, sipping at some tea but not really tasting it. Ten years her senior, Doug Anson captivated her with his charming smile and life experience. She always said she would never marry a law enforcement officer, likely would never marry at all. She dreamed of a big ranch with horses but without even knowing it, Doug had changed that. He'd admired her corsage and she'd jokingly taken it off her lapel and pinned it to his uniform that night. Two years later, here it was in his trunk.

ON SCENE

She set it aside and, shoulders shaking with unshed tears, quickened her search, rifling frantically through the top tray. If every personal item in here was going to do this to her, she hoped her speed would at least delay the coming tide.

The cuff links he wore with his suit, a silk tie, two photo books, and a stack of pressed handkerchiefs went into the pile on the dresser. A framed photo of his parents was nestled in between some notebooks and she snatched it up, pressing it to her chest. Doug's father had died in the service when Doug was a baby. This was the only decent photo he had of him. She stood up, setting the studio portrait up on the dresser, and turned back to remove the tray and look in the bottom of the trunk. His riding crop and pieces of his serge were neatly lined up in the bottom with his shoe polish and rags, along with some other random items he used to keep his kit in top condition. The only other thing she saw that she wanted was Doug's personal file. He'd shown it to her when they moved into their new house, flipping through the pages and laughing at some of the things he had recorded over his thirty years of life and decade of policing.

"It's just a hodge podge of stuff. Report cards and awards, my enrolment papers—did you know I had to apply three separate times because they thought my chest measurement was too small?" He shook his head and kept leafing through the pages. "They finally accepted me after I beefed up a bit." He flexed his biceps comically and Vallarena laughed, grabbing his arm.

"Puny," she declared, letting out a whoop of delight when he scooped her up in his arms and spun her around.

"Watch yourself, Mrs. Anson. You'll get into trouble." He set her back down in her chair and caressed her cheek. Another paper caught his eye and his face sobered.

"Some records from when I got into that car accident." He shuffled the papers, some typed and some handwritten. "And letters my family wrote me when I was in the hospital." She reached over and traced a scar, barely visible, from his temple to the bottom of his chin.

"You can't even tell." She leaned in and rained a line of soft kisses down the length of it.

Doug made a noise in his throat but smiled. "I can tell. Every day I run my razor over that spot. One hundred and sixty-seven stitches will do that." He rubbed at the raised line on his cheek. Almost invisible most days, his scars stood out white against his tanned skin if he got cold or over exerted himself. The only time in the last few years anyone had noticed his scars at all was last winter when he went through the ice saving some kids on the river. That, and the time he helped Bob move his new refrigerator into the house. Overexertion, indeed. He thought his eyeballs were going to pop out of their sockets that day.

Doug shook himself and held another paper out to her. "Here's my release form from the hospital. Best day of my life."

She gave him a little frown. "The very best day?" Her frown melted immediately when he gathered her up in a hug and kissed her.

"Okay, it was the best day right up until August 8, 1970. How about that?" She smiled at him, adoring the way his eyes danced when they talked like this, all alone with nobody demanding his attention or rigid professionalism.

"That's right. Oh, I love this photo." Her eyes drifted back to the file and she plucked a photo of them on horseback in a field near her parents' home. "This was a good day, too."

Doug chuckled. "And here's the bill of sale for that old girl. She's a great trail horse." He turned over a few more pages and closed the file. "Funny how your whole life can be summed up in a file folder."

"Ma'am? Are you through?"

She jumped a mile at the deep male voice and snapped the file shut, hugging it to herself and turning her tear streaked face away from the officer.

"Yes, I'm done. You can take the rest, if you must." She scooped up a hanky and pressed it to her eyes.

"I'll need the file as well, ma'am." The officer held out his hand. She shook her head absently.

"No need. This is Doug's personal file. There's nothing of interest in here for you." She locked her arms around the file and started for the bedroom door. She was stopped by a steely voice.

"That'll have to be for the RCMP to decide. We'll go through it and return any personal items in due course." The officer tried to pull the thick file out of her grasp but she didn't give in.

Panic welled up inside her and suddenly the file was a lifeline; the last thing she had to hold on to. She was well and truly losing her husband.

"No. This doesn't belong to you." She pulled on the folder, some smaller papers exploding from it and fluttering to the ground. It felt like an anvil had settled right on the middle of her chest and she couldn't control the rise in her voice. "You can't have this," she said through clenched teeth, giving a desperate yank. The file momentarily freed, a few more pages fluttering to the floor. She gripped the heavy folder in one arm, dropping to the floor to frantically gather up the lost pages, and shove them back under the front cover.

"Ma'am, don't make this harder than it already is." The officer looked haggard and held out his hand.

She wished she had some kind of weapon to smack him across his face. "Stop calling me ma'am," she shrieked, throat constricting with the violence of her scream, body convulsing with the depth of her despair.

The officer startled, looking like he was going to give up, but then he set his jaw and lurched forward, getting his hands on the file and pulling back, dragging Vallarena with him. Losing herself in the devastating emotion of the battle, she swore that she was not going to let them win. In a situation she had no control over, no say whatsoever, where her entire world had come crashing down, she would have this one victory. Surprising herself, she conjured strength she never knew she had, wrenching the file out of the officer's grip, and running out of the bedroom. Stopping in the kitchen to grab Doug's extra lighter, she stormed out the back door like a woman possessed.

"If I can't have this, neither can you," she bellowed, eyes wide, grief and anger blinding her.

The officer came out the back door and skidded to a stop before her. Holding the file in one hand, the weight of it bending over, exposing the corners of dozens of pieces of paper, she clicked the lighter under the edge.

"Ma'am, this isn't necessary." The officer put out a hand to stop her, but she would not be deterred. She didn't know why this set her off, but she was done. They weren't going to take anything else away from her.

The dry paper caught easily and the flames flickered up to her wrist almost immediately. She adjusted her grip on the file, lighting the other end, turning it this way and that, watching the flames catch and dance.

The officers just stood there, looking dumbfounded. She was sure they would've tried to stomp the flames out had she not still been holding on to the file as it burned. She finally had to let it go, dropping it onto the concrete patio, pages separating and fuelling the flames.

The fire ate the written history of Doug's life and accomplishments, and she just watched it all go up in smoke. She still held on to the memories. They couldn't take those away from her.

By the time she heard the doorbell there was quite a campfire going, but she turned her back on it, and the officers, and stalked back into the house with as much dignity as she could manage. Stopping at the hallway mirror, she smoothed her hair, pinned the black lace in place, carefully re-applied her lipstick, and tucked the silver tube into her purse. She opened the door to Wally Regitnig standing on the step in full RCMP regalia with his hat in his hand. He held out his arm to her, gesturing to the long black car in the driveway.

"Are you ready?" he murmured gently.

"No," she whispered, anguish flowing from the single word. "I'm not ready for any of this."

Wally's eyes welled and his face hardened. He took her hand and tucked it firmly into the crook of his arm, walking her down the steps. He started to help her into the back of the car, but she stopped him, turning back to the two officers coming out of the house with boxes in their arms.

"I hope you put that fire out, gentlemen. I have to go bury my husband."

ON SCENE

RCMP Officers' Burial in Regina—*A full military service will be held from the RCMP chapel with Archbishop G.F.C. Jackson officiating.*

Headline and excerpt, Prince Albert Daily Herald
(Tuesday October 13, 1970)

Chapter Thirty-Two

Wednesday, October 14, 1970
Highway 11 Southbound
0930hrs

The funeral procession was unlike anything Lynn had ever seen, even on television. Two hearses bearing the bodies of her father and Doug led the way, black and shiny. They had Canadian flags in the windows. Behind those were marked police cars, roof lights flashing. The families came next in long black cars. Garry and Barry rode with Wally and Dolores, at Wally's insistence, climbing into the car after Mrs. Anson and their mother. Lynn could hear the boys' hushed exclamations on the other side of the tinted glass and she tapped on it.

"Be good," she said, trying to see inside but was hustled into the next car. Terry wanted to ride with their grandparents, so Lynn and Larry went with him and they were soon on their way through the city.

The procession was long; ten cars that she could see, but she knew there were more. They stopped for nothing and nobody, slowly making their way through each city intersection. People were scattered along the route here and there waving flags, and some saluted. She didn't know how to feel, couldn't cry, and didn't want any of this. The day couldn't end soon enough.

ON SCENE

The highway was no different than the city. They didn't stop for anything, and she saw officers at each crossroad, blocking traffic. Many officers raised their hands in greeting. She waved back.

"They can't see you." Larry pointed to the tinted glass. He didn't laugh at her but she felt the heat rise in her cheeks and sat on her hands.

They drove for miles in silence. She wished someone would talk. It didn't matter about what. Even Terry was silent, holding Grandma's hand. Lynn had never seen her brother sit still for such a long time. Larry picked at a thread on his cuff.

The convoy approached Rosthern and slowed. There were half a dozen police cars lining the highway, lights and sirens going, with all the officers standing in lines on both sides, saluting. Grandma's breath caught and she reached into her sleeve for a tissue.

An hour after that, they proceeded through Saskatoon at the same sedate pace and sped up as they approached the highway south to Regina. She'd never seen so many police cars in her life, each stationed at cross roads through the cities, on the highway, and at every major intersection.

It was perhaps because of that efficiency that everyone in the car reacted so strongly when they felt the procession slow down. She lifted her head to look through the front windshield at the other cars. Far ahead, she could see that the lead cars were pulling over.

"What's going on up there?" the driver murmured, probably to no one in particular but Lynn promptly answered him.

"Garry has to go to the bathroom."

Larry snorted and nodded. "Yeah, I bet. I'm surprised we got this far already."

Larry and Terry stretched to see over the officers in the front seat and sure enough, they heard Wally's voice call out over the radio.

"Be advised, procession is halted. We need a bathroom break in car three." Lynn smiled and watched every car pull over, front and back. Then Wally got out of the car in front of them, and held the door open. Garry hopped out and ran down the ditch, disappearing behind some shrubs.

Lynn could hear her father's booming laughter, enveloping her like a warm hug.

The procession was a long and sombre affair.

Barry and Garry hadn't been to Regina in years, and had never witnessed a regimental funeral, much less one to bury their own father. Wally's hand shook with the thought and he clenched his fist, pushing the knuckles into the side of his thigh to stop the ridiculous tell. He covertly surveyed the others in the car. If anyone took note of his weakness, they had the grace not to mention it.

They had come through the city smoothly enough, stopping a ways from Depot to organize the march.

A highly decorated Sergeant directed the order of the procession in front of them as they awaited their spot in line. Sixteen members took up position to flank the hearses, eight on each side.

Every breath Wally took weighed him down until his chest felt like it was hovering somewhere around his spurs.

Resembling a ghost coming out of the shadows, a horse in full RCMP tack with no rider walked past their stopped car. A second followed behind and Wally blinked. He gave his head a shake, looking back at the ethereal forms. War horses ready for battle with no riders to guide them through the chaos. The symbolic gesture wasn't something he would ever get used to seeing. He'd led the horse for other regimental funerals, but seeing it from this perspective was so damned uncomfortable the high collar of his serge jacket tightened around his neck.

"What's that?" Barry asked.

Voice thick on his first attempt, Wally stuck two fingers into the neck of his uniform and pulled down. He tried again. "That's called a charger. Those are your dad's boots." His voice failed him altogether.

Connie muffled her cry with a hanky thrust into her hand by Dolores.

ON SCENE

Garry asked, "What's it for?" His breath caught on the question. He seemed so small, even though, at fourteen, both boys were taller than their mother.

Wally coughed and looked at the opposite window, gathering his armour that so far hadn't failed him.

"The riderless horse symbolizes our lost comrade in arms. The backwards boots in the stirrups show how death is the opposite of life," he said, no more ready to look the boys in the eyes as he was before, but he put on a brave face and turned to them again. He let the corner of his mouth rise. "There's going to be a lot of stuff that you don't understand today. Just know it's all for your dad and Doug."

Connie came undone, leaning heavily on Dolores. She'd refused any kind of calming drug and Wally started to wonder at the wisdom of allowing that.

Admiration for his wife outshone the darkness in his soul for a fleeting moment. Like a steadfast rock, she took care of everyone. He watched as she surreptitiously slipped each of the boys some Scotch mints from her purse.

When she leaned back he softly touched her elbow. She didn't take her eyes away from Vallarena, but her mouth twitched in acknowledgement. There was no way he could get through this day of hell without her.

The stabbing discomfort reached an unmanageable level. Leaning forward he asked the driver, "Why aren't we moving?" The question came out sharper than he intended. Dolores always told him he never knew what to do with feelings beyond hungry, tired, and angry. He'd laughed it off until today. What did you do with feelings that smashed your soul and made you want to torch an entire forest just to find one man?

The driver eased his hand up like he didn't want to make any sudden movements and said, "It's all right, Sergeant. This is our muster point. The Drill Sergeant will show us into the procession." His eyes slid nervously to the side in the rear view mirror.

"Thank you, Corporal. Carry on." He felt heat in his cheeks and rolled his shoulders, trying to settle them in his snug jacket.

Dolores patted his leg and gave him a look he was used to. "It'll be fine, dear," she said softly. "You let that young man do his job. Your turn is coming."

201

He nodded curtly, making the overflow from one eye splash onto his jacket. Appalled, he cleared his throat hard and dashed his sleeve across his face, gold patches scratching his cheek.

This was a job he didn't want.

For Bob and Doug, he would carry this discomposure that topped much of what he'd dealt with in his long career. He had to do his duty by them.

The hearses rolled into position behind the chargers and the entire line moved forward over a slight rise in the road to allow the cars behind room to manoeuvre.

Hundreds of RCMP officers in red serge lined the road on the other side of the rise, waiting for the command to fall in. It was an imposing sight. Wally's stomach lurched and he reached up to put a hand over the medals on his chest, pressing hard, the edges digging into his hand.

"What are they giving you a medal for? I'm the one who pulled him out of the car." Bob slugged Wally on the shoulder with a laugh.

"You want it? You can have it. They're making me go to a ceremony." Wally crumpled the official looking letterhead and threw it into the nearest garbage. Bob promptly went after it.

"No siree. You're going. You're going to dust yourself off, get yourself to Regina, and let your wife dress up and be proud of you."

"Nah. Like you said, you're the one who pulled him out of the car."

"Yeah, well, you're the one who carried him to safety. Then came back for me," Bob said, voice deepening at the last. "I don't know how I got caught on that wreckage but if it wasn't for you, Connie would be raising two kids by herself."

Wally tried to shrug it off, but Bob wasn't having that. He grabbed Wally's raised shoulder and pressed it down, pounding on it firmly until his friend relaxed.

ON SCENE

"We'll all go, how about that? We'll get Connie's folks in to watch the twins. The women will love the night out. I can laugh and point while you're on stage accepting the medal, if it'll make you feel better," Bob said, his eyes glinting with the outburst of laughter Wally knew was bubbling close to the surface.

"Yes, it would make me feel better. We have to do this stuff together," Wally said, sighing with resignation and smoothing the letter Bob handed back to him.

Two days later, the officer they pulled from the burning police car died in hospital. Wally pressed the medal harder. He'd accepted it quietly the week after in the Assistant Commissioner's office, on the same day he and Bob marched in the regimental funeral. Wally had carried the man's Stetson.

A keening broke through his sadness, low at first, but gaining in momentum. The bagpipes were joined by the thump of drums in a plaintive song that jarred the heart and wound its way around every honourable memory Wally had of his best friend.

A Corporal and a Sergeant marched past his window and fell into step behind the hearses, each reverently carrying a Stetson hat. He didn't regret taking the time to handpick each officer who participated in the final march. The men carrying the ceremonial items did so with the highest amount of respect for their friends. It was a small gift Wally gave them, for purely personal reasons. This last march—the final farewell—would be how the sea of men at Depot Division remembered Bob Schrader and Doug Anson. They didn't know them like Wally did. He felt a crushing obligation to imprint his friends on not only their memories, but on the memories of every officer that came after them.

Their car pulled forward at the direction of the Sergeant, a corps of officers in front of them and one behind, silently protecting the cars carrying the family members.

Not a boot was out of step.

Wally's armour failed him completely for the first time in his career. Dolores discreetly pressed a tissue into the crook of his elbow, squeezing his arm.

Better to right himself in the car than go to pieces in front of the men, he thought, wiping his eyes and blowing his nose viciously into the tissue.

Barry jumped at the honk, a truly shocked look on his face. "It's okay, Wally. We're here," he said. His naturally heartfelt statement had Wally blowing a second time and reaching for the two other tissues Vallarena and Connie held out to him. He gave his eyes another good hard wipe and nodded.

"That you are, my boy. That you are. I'm here, too."

"Me, too," Dolores whispered. Connie held onto her, a low sobbing coming from deep inside her. Vallarena turned toward the window and her breath caught.

Civilians, bundled up against the cold, lined the street half a dozen deep for nearly a mile before the main gate. Some of the children waved little Canadian flags. An elderly gentleman held a trembling salute a few steps away from the crowd. The urge to salute back was strong but Wally knew the man couldn't see him. He pressed his stiff hand into the seat.

"Are they all here for Dad?" Garry breathed out, face pressed against the side window.

"No, dummy. They're here for Doug, too," Barry retorted. Wally laid a gentle hand on the boy's arm and shook his head.

Barry poked his brother's leg with the toe of his polished shoe and mouthed "sorry" at him. They braved tenuous smiles at each other and turned back to look out the window.

Wally still held Barry's arm. "They're all here for both of them, because of the outstanding men they were. They're here for you, too. And for your mother. And Mrs. Anson." Wally nodded at the ladies in turn, sorry to see their tears flow harder. All the uniformed members marched ahead of the cars now, at the Drill Sergeant's order, to line up row upon row, surrounding the area where the casket bearers would gather.

The cars rolled through the main gates, and Connie and Vallarena gasped. Dolores reached over and took both their hands.

ON SCENE

Flags flew at half mast at every building and the sea of red serge officers blanketing the grounds saluted in unison as the cars passed them and stopped near the parade square.

For the space of two breaths, there was no movement.

The honour guard was ordered into position, the pipes and drums reaching a crescendo. Gold buttons glinting in the sun, polished leather shining smartly against the red of the serge, boots stomping the pavement in time to the thunderous drumbeats, they moved as one body around the perimeter of the parade square, where vehicles were never allowed to drive.

Marching two by two, the pipes died down as the guard approached the cenotaph, and the men on the outside saluted sharply. Wally himself had done so a hundred times or more in his career, and it still made his chest burn.

"What are they carrying?" Barry asked, sidling up closer to his brother to see better.

"Those long things with the flags on the end are called lances. Some of the officers will have swords, and rifles too, when we go out to the cemetery." Wally cleared his throat.

The guard came to rest as ordered, their final steps punctuated by the last drumbeats. The pipes died down. You could hear a pin drop in the parade square.

The Drill Sergeant broke the silence, directing the casket bearers forward.

"I have to go now but I'll see you inside the chapel. Be good to your mother, and take care of Mrs. Anson, okay?" He hugged Barry and Garry, gave Dolores a meaningful look, and got out of the car.

Aware of no one but the men in front of him, he strode to the hearses with a confidence he didn't feel.

"All right, gentlemen. Eight and eight," he murmured, almost to himself as more orders were called out by the Drill Sergeant, directing the drummers and pipers around the square. The pipes picked up again and the sound carried the grief of every person in attendance. The casket bearers shuffled into line, shoulder to shoulder, readying themselves to bear the weight of not only their friends but of the hundreds of eyes upon them.

"Thank you for being here." He looked each of them in the eye for a moment, men he'd worked with, bled with, and grieved with. Greenslade and Jette led the bearer party for Schrader. Cavello and Long lead for Anson. Wally gave each a sharp nod in turn, settling last on Henry Long. His young face matched the colour of the overcast sky, sweat standing out on his cheeks even in the cool breeze.

Wally came closer. It wasn't sweat. He barely recognized the man before him—far from the grinning, cocky kid he worked with every day. Long's devastation crumpled Wally's spirit, if it could get any lower, and his face prickled fiercely trying to put all his armour back in place.

Wally looked at Cavello, a silent plea passing between them, and the officer acknowledged, putting a gloved hand on Henry's shoulder, squeezing hard. He wouldn't proceed until he was sure Henry could handle it. Cavello squeezed again, the strength of the grip shaking his forearm and Henry raised his head nodding resolutely.

Coughing roughly, Wally nodded back and opened the back doors of the first hearse.

Nothing moved forward without his go ahead, so he stayed where he was with one hand on Bob's casket, the fabric of the flag smooth under his glove. His chest heaved with his next breath and he bit down on the inside of his cheek until he tasted blood. He'd be goddamned if he'd let his best friend down now.

"Gentlemen, if you would." His order was low but firm and he stepped aside. Greenslade and Jette reached in and smoothly pulled Schrader's casket out of the hearse as Cavello and Long pulled Anson's out. On Wally's command, both were boosted up onto the waiting shoulders of all the casket bearers. Jette sniffed and coughed, covering a ragged breath. Wally paused, a hand resting on the front of each casket, giving the men all a moment to settle.

Coughs and throat clearing unsuccessfully covered stifled sobs. He took a moment himself then reassured them, "Not until you're ready, gentlemen."

Closing his eyes, he prayed for strength, and for the protection of the families.

"There are no words to describe how thankful I am to have—" his throat caught. He pushed out, on a strangled breath, "—to have known you both."

ON SCENE

He finally pulled himself away.

A single piper broke from the ranks to march in slow order across the parade square. Wally followed the even cadence of the music, casket bearers behind him. Without turning around, he ordered the rest of the processional to fall into step behind them. Even through his grief, and the grief of the members surrounding him, he felt pride in what they were doing.

They came up the steps to the chapel and he held the door to allow the casket bearers to proceed, one behind the other. Back ramrod straight, chest as high as he could hold it, he executed his sharpest salute as the caskets passed him. The skirl of the pipes bounced off the high, arched ceiling of the beautiful old chapel. Laying members to rest since the days of the North West Mounted Police, nearly a century later it never ceased to leave him in breathless awe.

He held the door open, waiting until the caskets were set on their stands and the Stetsons placed on top of the Canadian flags. Something released inside him; his part of the funeral was over. It wasn't relief or thankfulness. He couldn't rightly put his finger on what the feeling was. Just an overwhelming sense of finality.

With that uncertain definition hanging over his head, he turned to watch mourners filter out of their vehicles, mix with the red-coated officers, and file in to say their final goodbyes.

Wally stayed at the door of the chapel; he simply had nowhere else to be just then. The families and officers from Prince Albert Detachment looked to him to lead. A far bigger role than he anticipated today. Worse, they looked to him for comfort he felt woefully inadequate to provide.

He didn't notice Lynn right away, hanging back with Dolores at the bottom of the steps, waiting for everyone else to go into the chapel. He was worried about her; to the best of his knowledge she hadn't cried yet, and that scared the hell out of him. He started to take note when people recognized Lynn and stopped for an embrace. Wally felt for her, watching the slight grimace grow broader with each well wisher.

But ever gracious, she held the manners instilled in her by her parents. After at least a dozen, Wally's heart bled for the poor thing as Dolores couldn't see Lynn's face; but he could. An insistent need to help her took over. Exchanging a look with his wife over the head of the man he shook hands with, Dolores nodded and gently pulled Lynn to her, smoothly cutting off another well-meaning mother hen. Dolores shook the woman's hand, her warm smile firmly in place as she gestured to Wally at the top of the stairs. The woman looked over, nodded, and the couple moved on, much to Lynn's relief.

The line eased, and still she stuck to the bottom of the stairs, fidgeting with a button on her wool coat. Wally waited for her to approach in her own time, if that was what she wanted. He'd discussed with Dolores the possibility of any one of the children needing to leave the service.

Understandably, Lynn's distress was blended with a confusion that he wasn't used to seeing on the confident young girl's face. He watched her out of the corner of his eye while he shook hands with some officers and their wives before turning to guide them into the capable hands of another usher.

A tiny voice behind him made him look up. She was there, looking so grown up in her dark blue dress, matching jacket, and pearl necklace, brown hair curling at her shoulders. Hands at her mouth, Wally couldn't understand what she was saying.

"What's that, honey?" He leaned in closer, reaching out to her.

She threw herself into Wally's arms, burying her face into his shoulder, going limp against him. Hanging on fiercely, he pressed his cheek against her head and felt the vibration of muffled words against him.

"Hm?" he asked, pulling away just enough to press his ear closer.

"I want my daddy," she whimpered.

"I know you do. I know," he whispered, tightening his arm around her. He reached out for Dolores with his other arm, silent tears coursing down her face. She'd breached the limits of her armour, too.

The three of them walked up the centre aisle as one, Lynn's devastated tears drowned out by the murmurs and sobs of others, the shuffle of boots, and the beginning notes of the organ.

The grief in the chapel was palpable. But what stirred in his gut, more violently than any grief or rage over what he could not change, was the guilt.

He'd failed them. Failed them all.

Because he hadn't found Robertson.

ON SCENE

Sask. Suspect Asked To Give Himself Up-*The RCMP Thursday asked murder suspect Wilfred Stanley Robertson to give himself up. He was charged with two counts of capital murder after Sgt. R.J. Schrader, 41, and Constable D.B. Anson, 30, were fatally wounded while investigating a family dispute in the MacDowall area. "He will be given every consideration and it goes without saying that his rights will be fully protected."*

Headline and excerpt, Winnipeg Free Press (Saturday, October 24, 1970)

Chapter Thirty-Three

Friday, October 16, 1970
Robertson Land
Dawn

Not able to use his rifle, hunting had been pretty sparse the past week and his stomach complained mightily. He'd caught the odd rabbit with snares, but it wasn't enough. Looking up at the vast grey gloom of the morning sky, he felt a sense of urgency that always came at this time of year. An innate need to prepare. He should be farther north hunting big game right now, so the freezer would be full come winter. But that was not to be. It was only mid month, but you could feel the big snow coming. When it did, maybe they would all go home. He'd have a harder time covering his tracks in deep snow. He needed them all to leave.

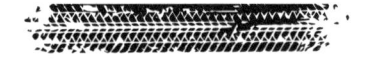

The small clearing behind the headquarters trailer had served as their briefing area since day one. Lumpy, uneven ground with tufts of prairie grasses growing in clumps dotted the area, but it was big enough for a few dozen men to gather, and was protected on one side from the brisk northern winds that blew through even the warmest coat. The clearing wasn't as glamorous as the long, heavily scratched table at the detachment with squeaky wooden

ON SCENE

chairs, a single window, and the smell of cigarettes and stale coffee in the air, but it served its purpose. The officers all stood, even though Staff Sergeant Anderson had proposed they bring in enough chairs for everyone, "to at least behave like civilized men."

Wally had taken the lead from Mosher, keeping silent and pretending the man hadn't spoken at all. Dragging fifty chairs out to the bush wasn't an idea that deserved attention.

Mosher dismissed the briefing sharply, and after a second of hesitation, added gruffly, "Be safe out there."

He'd never seen Mosher like this. The past week had taken its toll on everyone Wally talked to, but Al looked especially on edge. Leading the investigation, and coming up empty day after day chipped away at a man. But what was grating harder on the commanding officer was dealing with the daily problems that came along with having nearly one hundred men searching practically on top of one another, and trying to get along with another military entity with their own set of rules. They had discussed it on more than one occasion.

"I believe I told you I wanted a moment of time." Anderson's voice interrupted Mosher's dismissal, ringing out over the murmur of officers.

Wally locked eyes with Mosher, a million questions flying silently between them. Mosher's eyes were clear. *For fuck's sake, now what?*

Wally made the face he usually made when Dolores asked who ate all the ice cream. *I have no idea, but this isn't going to go well.*

"Yes, of course, Staff Sergeant Anderson. The floor is yours." Mosher gestured to the lines of men that formed back up after Anderson's interruption.

Parting the middle of the gathering like the Red Sea, Anderson strode up the middle between the men, looking slowly left then right, hands gripping the lapels of his jacket. He approached the command table and did an about face, shuffling to the side. Disgusted, Wally kept his physical tells in check. He knew Anderson moved to the side so he could see Mosher when he said whatever it was he had to say. Wally couldn't stop his grimace at the imagined smell of Anderson's ego.

Kate Kading

What a peacock.

"I believe we should focus our attention on the river. Yesterday, I had a constable drive a patrol boat up and down the water that borders the Robertson property, so as to draw fire and reveal the suspect's location." Anderson smoothed his lapels and looked smugly at Wally before continuing.

All Wally saw was red.

"You did *what?*"

Shouts went up through the ranks as Wally came straight through them to his target. Bruce started barking, weaving between legs, trying to stick near his master.

With Wally's grip, Anderson's feet left the ground, toes dangling uselessly in the dirt, hands slapping at the fists that balled the uniform around his neck, choking off his airway.

"You did what with one of my men?" He shook as he lowered his arms to bring Anderson's bulging face closer to his. Drops of spit hit him as he squeezed the man's neck harder.

Trolling up and down the river, the banks high around you, knowing there was a sharpshooter out there with your number? His insides churned.

No.

Even with his decades of experience, he shrunk at the thought of doing that. Just floating along, waiting for your brains to paint the side of the boat? That fear stayed with you for a lifetime.

What kind of person ordered someone to do that?

This kind of person.

His disgust boiled over watching the man's indignant gaze flick from side to side, his panic becoming a tangible thing.

"You cowardly bastard," Wally whispered each measured word square into Anderson's face. "I'm going to make sure you never—" he was cut off by Mosher who didn't have to say a word. Wally's eyes darted around the clearing. Every member there knew who was in control. It wasn't Wally. Or Anderson.

Mosher's iron grip on Wally's arm brought some reason back to the front of his mind and he eased his hold on Anderson. The man collapsed to the ground in an exaggerated gasping heap, but immediately scrambled back to his feet. He straightened his uniform with one hand, smoothing his lapel convulsively, pointing an accusing finger at Wally who quieted Bruce but didn't move.

"I insist—" Anderson started, but stopped abruptly when he saw Mosher close his eyes and slowly shake his head.

Mosher didn't take his hand off Wally's arm but motioned Anderson closer. He hadn't gathered his wits about him enough to disobey. Their heads were so close together Wally could smell the fear on Anderson's breath.

Mosher made his statement in a low, sinister rumble. "Not. One. Word. You'll both walk away. Be wary of whom you order into danger, Staff Sergeant," his eyes narrowed at Anderson, "or it's the last order you'll ever give."

Anderson narrowed his eyes back at Mosher. His nostrils flared, and he huffed, "This isn't over." He spun around and stomped off, back stiff, fists balled up at his sides.

Mosher took a step back from Wally and bellowed, "Dismissed."

Officers broke away from the neat standing lines, glancing at each other. Some low murmurs of discussion reached Wally, but most were gathering their gear in a direct manner.

They would pair with the same partners, use the same maps, cross off where they'd been, highlight where they were going. Nothing new. Except seeing their superiors go at each other. That, sure as shit, was new.

Wally set all thoughts of Anderson aside and squinted at the horizon where the sun was thinking about winking at the overnight moon. Starting briefing just before daybreak, there was enough pre-dawn light to function, and it gave the teams time to get out to their starting points. *They even had enough time to witness the scuffle without being late.* He cringed at his brief loss of control, however well deserved.

Not that their vigilance had reaped any rewards. Some false sightings, a ton of potential leads that ended up dry, and a bunch of officers tromping through the forest, chasing after every wisp of campfire smoke they spied in the distance. Some pulled their weapons at every snapped branch they heard. Quite a few still thought Robertson was in the area, laying low, just biding his time.

The last officer trickled away, hurrying to catch up with his team, leaving Mosher gripping the sides of the table, staring down at a detailed topographical map. Wally approached and adjusted the top map so he could see it better. Bruce jumped up to the table, resting his front paws gently on the edge, ears up, ready for the briefing.

"Who was it?" Wally didn't need to pre-empt that with any sort of explanation.

"Ron Morier from Rosthern Detachment. He'll be okay. Tough as nails, that kid. I paired him back up with Cavello and told him if anyone orders him different to call me." Mosher's succinct response didn't fool Wally one bit. The air was thick between them, and he knew he owed his superior something.

"Sorry." He cleared his throat and adjusted his duty belt. "Out of line." He flicked the snap on his holster. Mosher nodded. That was it.

Jabbing a finger at a tiny smudge of a water source, Wally found the beginning of a smile. "Constable Long's been getting a bit too cocky with his map and compass, said he wanted a bigger challenge, so I had the helicopter drop him and Ace off in the middle of nowhere and ordered him to clear this... lake. Dugout? Shit, it looks more like someone spit on the map." That got a twitch of Mosher's moustache, so Wally surged forward with his story. "I thought for sure I had him; maybe teach him a lesson to not be so damned full of himself. But, nope. Son of a bitch found it, cleared it, and was back before dark with a shit eatin' grin on his face." Mosher gave a small chuckle and Wally cocked an eyebrow. "We'll have to come up with something better to do to him." He ended the story by picking up a felt tip pen from the pile on the table, outlined the scrubby area Long and Ace had cleared and with a disgusted grunt, tinged with pride he would never admit to, he put an x through the spot.

"Go throw him in the river so he'll be ready to pull out that damned army carrier next time it gets stuck. Corporal Fuck-Fuck was at it again yesterday. Hung up right on the side of the riverbank like a jackass. Hasn't he ever been through terrain rougher than a straight road?" Mosher posed the question directly but Wally had no answer for him. "Took most of the day to get it out, and held up two of my teams. With all the shit that idiot has broken, the fences he's mowed down, and the people he's pissed off, I'm starting to think he's been more of a liability than an asset." Mosher took an angry swipe at a Styrofoam coffee cup sitting on the edge of the table, sending it flying. A few drops of cold coffee landed on the maps in front of him and he wiped at them with his sleeve. Bruce jumped at the outburst and ran to the cup, chasing it another few feet with the wind, picked it up, and returned it to the table. He jumped back up with his front paws, depositing the cup beside Mosher's hand.

"Yeah, well, do what you have to do, sir. We can handle ourselves." Wally stood rigidly, arms clasped behind his back.

Mosher stared at him, hard. "I already know that, Regitnig. Gave the orders yesterday for them to pack up and head home. The Hercules should be taking off any minute." He looked at his watch and let out a sigh of relief. "And I sent most of the cadets back to Depot yesterday."

Wally couldn't hide his surprise. "Sorry, sir. I've been a little out of touch. Greenslade and I have been out every day, sun up to sundown."

Mosher nodded, crossing his arms over his chest and pinning Wally with a piercing look. "You think I don't keep track of you two? I know where you are, most of the time."

"He's a good man, that Greenslade. Efficient, quiet in the bush, and he keeps up. All I can ask. Except—" Wally cut himself off, internally cursing, hoping Mosher didn't notice, but of course he wasn't so lucky.

Al picked up on it right away; a dog with a bone. "Except what? You know something I don't?"

Wally fidgeted with the snap on his holster again and looked around, avoiding eye contact.

Mosher leaned closer and motioned Wally in. Sometimes the silent orders were the loudest of all.

He broke his rigid stance and stepped forward. "It's not that I know something you don't, sir. It's just—" he broke off, not sure how belligerent Mosher would allow him to be just then.

"Speak freely, Sergeant. I don't have time to lolly-gag." Still leaning on the map table, Mosher gave him a look that made him certain he really could speak freely.

"We've got nothing, sir. A handful of false sightings, and a hundred officers searching the area with nothing to show for it." Wally's forceful whisper exploded from him, trying to keep his frustration between the two of them. "Give me a broken branch. A hair. A footprint. Anything. You give me one microscopic piece of Robertson, and Bruce and I'll find him." Bruce barked once, staring right back at Al like he knew all the answers.

"It's not a sprint, Wally. Not with this guy. He could live in these woods indefinitely, you know that. Hell, it's been reported in the newspapers enough that everyone knows it." Mosher shook a stack of wrinkled newsprint and threw it back down. "We just have to wait for that one slip up that leads us right to him." He flipped the map over, looking at the grid drawn on the back.

Wally started shaking his head in Al's first few words. In for a penny, in for a pound. If he was going to be written up for insubordination he might as well be all in. "But there's nothing. Not one piece of evidence that he's been moving around the area at all. And there isn't going to be anything. He's hunkered down somewhere. All we need for him to pop his head out of his hidey-hole is a little bit of quiet." He stopped talking, feeling out of words and curious to see how his superior was going to take this information.

A stiff wind lifted the edge of the map and Mosher slammed it down, glaring at Wally with a half closed eye. Al looked tired, but Wally well remembered his vast knowledge. He considered every angle before giving a definitive answer in anything he did.

"You've never been wrong, Regitnig. Annoying as all hell, but never wrong." Mosher rubbed at his forehead so hard the skin shifted from side to side. Wally suspected he wouldn't be successful if he was trying to rub away doubt or fear. He immediately pushed the latter out of his mind. He'd never known Al Mosher to have any fear.

Bruce nimbly hopped down from his resting spot at the table and walked around to nose his way under Mosher's free hand. Mosher grunted but didn't take his hand away.

Movement at the treeline gave Wally pause, his eyes drifting over Mosher's shoulder to the far side of the clearing.

The area wasn't huge, but it was big enough to blur a clear view of a person walking slowly toward them, keeping to the edge of the trees.

Wally squinted, the fuzzy form becoming clearer with each step. The man had a rifle slung over his shoulder and wore a thick green hunting jacket with a plaid cap. He squinted harder.

Finally.

A shout went up on the other side of the clearing where the officers on duty in the yard had set themselves up. Each one was armed with a .308 and not a single one would miss.

The sky closed in on Wally, his vision narrowing. He needed to take Robertson alive.

He had to find out why.

Twelve rifles clicking their safety off at the same time was deafening.

He upended the table in his single-minded bid to get there first, maps and papers raining down on Mosher who had just turned around.

There was no question in Wally's mind.

They're going to shoot him.

"Get him," he ordered Bruce under his breath, breaking into a run. Louder, over the flurry of Bruce taking off across the field he bellowed, "Hold your fire."

He'd never screamed orders like this before, desperation strangling him.

"Don't shoot. Stand down." His last order rasping and raw, he waved his arms over his head as he ran towards Robertson.

Bruce hit the man first, hard in the mid section, knocking him flat on his back. He locked his teeth on an arm, his whole body on top of the fugitive. The noise was all-consuming. His vision narrowed further until all he could see was the target and he wanted a part of it. A part of the satisfaction of getting his hands on the man.

He didn't want to speculate why Robertson decided to turn himself in. He'd ask those questions later. In a dead run, with the most wanted man in the country in his sights, he wasn't bent on logic. He'd find out why after.

He toppled onto the growling mass of his partner, throwing an arm around Robertson's neck. He rolled and tried to haul the man to his feet, not caring that the action probably cut off his air. With Bruce pulling down, they were too heavy for Wally to just stand up. Grabbing his wrist, he bent his forearm and squeezed tighter, leaning into the hold, struggling to his knees. Bruce pulled harder, shaking the man's arm. Wally fought to keep up his hold on Robertson's neck. Nothing could make him let go.

"Out, Bruce." Wally yelled over Bruce's grunting and growling. "Goddamn it, I've got him."

"You hear that, you son of a bitch?" he rasped in Robertson's ear, "I've got you."

From his position on his knees with the substantially smaller man crushed between him and the dog, he pushed forward and laid on Robertson and Bruce. The dog finally let go, backing out from under the pile. Wally flattened himself on Robertson, arm still pressing around his neck.

He blinked hard.

It was the most difficult thing he'd ever done, not tensing the muscles of his forearm harder and harder to feel the life slowly drain away from this murderer. He was commissioned to uphold the laws of the land, to Maintain the Right, but what about the unspoken laws of men? The laws of brotherhood and revenge? The promise to never let this happen again.

The deep boom of Mosher's voice knocked on the inside of Wally's skull, somewhere towards the back. He wanted to ignore it but it was there, constant as a distant church bell. He felt pressure on his back and strained his neck forward against the arm there. The voice became clearer, close to his ear.

"You got him. Let go."

ON SCENE

Wally didn't relent. Bruce's barking muddled the voices. Who was crying? It wasn't him. Was it in his head? Robertson didn't strike him as an emotional man.

He didn't have to open his eyes to know they were surrounded. Orders shouted, men yelling back, none of it mattered.

Wally squeezed.

The grip on his own neck tightened in reflex.

Dark spots floated at the edge of his vision, swirling around, making the voices echo.

"Ok," he gasped. He tried to nod.

The hold instantly lessened but didn't let go altogether. He turned his head and felt Al's moustache against his face.

"You good?" Mosher asked. "I'm letting go. Do this right."

"Yeah."

The tension released all at once and his vision came back into focus. The black dots disappeared as fast as they came, and he was true to his word. He slipped his arm out from around Robertson and quieted Bruce. When the barking stopped, the crying was the only thing he could hear. His heart pounded so hard his head throbbed with it.

Wally grabbed Robertson's shoulder and rolled him face up, both hands holding him down by the chest, ready to replace them with a knee if he had to.

The red, snot-smeared face of a young man cut through Wally's reality. He didn't even look old enough to shave.

"What in holy hell? Who's that?" Mosher's question did nothing to still the confusion. Wally staggered back, reaching for the ground.

The kid put his hands up over his head, mumbling and sobbing.

Wally put his head in his hands, elbows on his knees. "What did he say?"

Mosher gently pulled the boy's arms away from his face.

"It's Henderson," the boy cried, "Henderson! For God sake." He folded his arms back over his eyes and wailed, "Please tell him to stop."

There was an uncomfortable silence broken by a dozen rifles being lowered. Men shuffled back and dispersed at Mosher's order.

"You want to get yourself shot?" Mosher yelled directly down at the officer who winced harder, arms still up around his head. "What the fuck are you doing dressed like the suspect, stalking around the premises?"

Wally didn't know how to deal with the tidal wave of anger crashing around inside him. Anger and horror. He'd nearly…no. He didn't want to think about it. Didn't want to think about what he'd almost done to this kid. This kid who wasn't Robertson. He'd experienced too many disappointments in the past week. Goddamn it all to hell, they needed a win.

Wally grabbed the sleeve of the young officer's thick hunting jacket and tugged him to his feet.

"S-sorry," the boy stuttered.

Wally shook his head. This kid was apologizing to him? Crushing disappointment was warring with the deepest sense of regret he thought he'd ever experienced in his life. He'd never made a mistake like this and didn't deserve this boy's apology. "No, I'm sorry. Henderson, was it?" He lowered his head to Henderson's, grabbing him around the back of the neck and pulling him closer. "I'm so sorry."

The boy hiccupped on a ragged breath.

Mosher gripped them by the shoulders and nobody moved for a precious moment.

Henderson let both arms drop to his sides and Wally noticed a wad of papers clenched in one fist. "What's that?" He nodded his head towards the wad and in the calmer break in conversation, Bruce barked. Henderson jumped a country mile and Wally shot out an arm to steady him. Maybe a couple of easier questions first.

"Where are you supposed to be, cadet?" He dusted the kid off and pried the papers out of his frozen fingers.

ON SCENE

"Not a cadet," Henderson said between shaky gasps. "Posted to North Battleford. Running messages from the Telex." The boy eyed Bruce while trying to stand at attention. He listed to one side and Wally absently reached out to right him again while studying the crumpled papers.

Henderson gasped and doubled over, hands on his knees, still trying to catch his breath. "Ordered to put that in Staff Sergeant Mosher's hands, on the double."

"Next time, don't come walking onto my crime scene dressed like the suspect, carrying a rifle. The dogs don't like it."

Henderson raised his eyes to Wally's and winced. "The dogs. Right."

Mosher dismissed the young officer with a wave.

Henderson cast a leery glance back over his shoulder and Bruce barked. The kid jumped again and sprinted away.

"Good Lord, you thought—"

Mosher's look of sadness was more than Wally could take and he held up his hand. "Yeah. Yeah, I thought. Hell, I'm sorry Al." Adrenaline still making things a little blurry around the edges, Wally felt the heat creeping up his neck and his insides shook. He noted the signs of shock without much concern. It would pass. But the regret wasn't likely to go away.

Mosher let out a burst of breath. "Hell, I know you are. We're fine." He gestured to the papers.

Remembering what he held, Wally waved the Telex messages. "You're not going to like this." He smoothed the stack of papers over his thigh, shuffling them back into order. "A kid died."

Mosher's eyes snapped open wide and he grabbed the papers out of Wally's outstretched hand. "What the hell? How? Who?" He silently read through each message, some of the type barely discernible after its trip from the office clenched in Constable Henderson's sweaty fist.

Lips moving, he murmured the odd time with a particularly useful bit of information. Mosher stopped flipping through the pages, abruptly turned around and stomped across the clearing to the office.

Wally and Bruce followed, double time, standing back when they reached the door as Mosher ordered everyone out.

"Wherever you're supposed to be, get there. Now." The officers made for the door, grabbing maps, coats, and rifles. Mosher wasn't in the mood for negotiations and the officers clearly saw that.

He spread the messages out on the desk, rubbing his smooth chin. He'd obviously stolen some time to shower and shave. Something Wally thought he should make time for sometime soon. He self consciously scrubbed at his two day stubble. With Greenslade as his second he could cover more ground and he'd only been going back to the city to sleep every other night. Dolores had been leaving food in the fridge for them, and the couch was made up fresh in anticipation of Greenslade's return. She was a good woman, and Wally never felt worthy of her gentle, understanding spirit.

Going through the papers one by one, Mosher studied the details. "A bunch of teenagers escaped from that boys' home in Regina, stole a car and tore up the highway towards Saskatoon. Broke through the roadblocks at Craik and Hanley, and kept on going. Christ." Mosher groaned, hand going through his hair. "Left a path of injuries and wrecked cars. A corporal was ordered to shoot out the tires right before Saskatoon. Driver lost control and rolled." He blew out all his air, stretching his arms over his head.

Wally whistled low, "Terrible. You think any of them jumped the gun and thought it was Robertson?" The possibility hung heavy in the air between them. The weight of mistake crushed the breath from Wally's chest.

Al shook his head, shuffling the Telex messages again for the appropriate page. "No. That's the reason for the Telex. From what there is here, it looks like they knew it was the boys all along. But that's not going to matter to the press." He slammed his fist down on the table. "That's not all. They originally thought he died from injuries sustained in the rollover, but when the coroner arrived he confirmed a gunshot wound." Mosher swore under his breath.

Wally shook his head sadly. Wasn't there enough death in the province for the week? For a bloody lifetime?

"Vehicle swerved, bullet ricocheted through the driver's door." Mosher looked on the back of the Telex pages. "That's it. Nothing more."

ON SCENE

Wally closed his eyes but didn't get a chance to speak anymore on the subject. The door to the trailer banged open and one of the helicopter pilots stuck his head in, yelling for Mosher. Bruce barked like mad until Wally told him to stand down.

"I'm not deaf, what is it?" Mosher yelled back, stepping out of the trailer to address the pilot.

The door slammed shut and Wally was left alone with his regret and fatigue. He slumped into a chair, elbows on the table, head in his hands. He had to take advantage and let his guard down for just a moment. It would fortify him for the next round.

How long can I do this?

This game of cat and mouse where he didn't exactly know who was the hunter, and who the hunted. His worry for the men under him plagued the few thoughts not occupied with maps and search grids. And there was still the corner of his mind reserved only for his family. His home life seemed very far away when he was in the middle of the woods trying to get into the head of a murderer.

As long as it takes.

"This is it, man. Last day." Mosher banged back into the trailer and threw a clipboard down on the table with his announcement. "Like you said yourself, it's been over a week with nothing and the head ups have called a halt to the big operation. North Battleford, Tisdale, Blaine Lake, Spiritwood—they all have to go home. Shoot, even the newspapers have lost interest." His boots thumped hard as he paced, punctuating the news.

Wally didn't move but his spirit rose a notch. "So it's us, then. Prince Albert and Rosthern." It wasn't a question.

Al crossed his arms over his chest and nodded in time with his slow, thumping pace. "Air search and army are called off. Regular duty only. We're on our own from here on out."

Wally sat long enough for his resolve to harden like granite. No matter. It was what he wanted, anyway. All they needed was a little bit of quiet.

He stood up and let out a sharp whistle. Bruce jumped up and ran to the door.

Kate Kading

"They can call off whoever they want. We're going to find him, Al."

> "I hunted only once with him years ago because I am no hunter but he is a hunter and knows this reserve here like the back of his hand. I don't ever recall him saying he didn't like cops or game wardens. I can't remember him ever disliking anyone. I don't think Stanley had an enemy in the world."

Excerpt from an interview with a neighbour of Robertson (1970)

Chapter Thirty-Four

```
Friday, December 25, 1970
On Scene
1600hrs
```

Christmas day he should have been tucked up with Dolores in front of a roaring fire watching the kids open presents, laughing, and drinking homemade egg nog. Instead, he was staring at the back of Greenslade's muskrat hat trying to decide if it was bird shit or food stuck to the fur.

The winter stretched before them like a fresh piece of paper. The first heavy snow that stayed came in late November, blanketing everything in new beginnings. The animals slept, but Wally and Joe persevered.

On the one hand, the snow helped. Tracking footprints in deep snow was a lot easier than tracking through frozen mud. But on the other hand, it made getting around that much harder. Driving the police cars into some areas became impossible. A couple of members from Rosthern detachment brought out snowmobiles enabling them to get into out-of-the-way areas. People called in sightings of smoke on a regular basis, sending the officers out to remote hunting cabins. Wally was thankful for the help and comforted by the rev of the engines when they went out to check on leads; he felt like maybe he and Joe weren't alone in this business.

It was ridiculous for them to feel alone though; his logical mind knew they weren't. There were officers stretched across four provinces still investigating this case, working it every day. Robertson had been on the most wanted list since day one, and the $5000 reward remained. The wanted poster papered the country west of Winnipeg to the British Columbia coast. Hundreds of man hours still went into the investigation but it never felt like enough.

When you were the only two humans, and one canine, on a very large section of land quieted by a heavy winter, you felt very much alone in the world.

"What's stuck to your hat?" Wally couldn't help himself. He needed a distraction from the misery of hiking through the snow in minus thirty with the wind coming directly at their faces. Christmas was supposed to be a time of renewal and celebration. All this day was doing was reminding him of how much they'd lost.

"What? Oh, that." Joe grabbed the hat off his head and looked at what Wally pointed to. He took a swipe at it with his finger and licked it. Wally gagged and Joe laughed. "It's icing. When the call came in at the detachment about the wood smoke out here Cavello threw a Christmas cookie at me for the road. His aim was off."

"Oh, good. I thought it was bird shit." Wally chuckled and caught himself. "Doesn't seem right, does it? Eating Christmas cookies and laughing when they aren't here anymore." He stopped walking and they leaned against the surrounding trees. Bruce came back around and sat between Wally's legs. He sighed heavily and the dog whined.

Greenslade put his hat back on. "It's not right at all. What do you think they'd do in our place?" He opened his coat, digging into the inside pocket.

"Dunno. Be at home with their families, I hope."

Greenslade snorted. "Like hell they would be." He held out a piece of paper and Wally took it from him.

It wasn't paper; it was a photograph. One of the women must have snapped it on a card night because they were all there. Cavello had a hand to his hair while talking to Jette. Greenslade and Long looked like they were arguing over a card. Anson was smirking right at the camera, and Bob had his arm around Wally, their heads together, deep in conversation. Wally breathed in as deeply as he could, the air biting his lungs.

ON SCENE

He let out the breath all at once. "You're right. They'd be out here. Doesn't make it better though."

"Nope." Greenslade always had a way with words.

Wally nodded. Not quite ready to hand the photo back. "What were you doing when the call came in?"

"Day shift with Cavello. I figured with no family here I might as well let someone else have the day." Greenslade shrugged and lit a cigarette, still leaning on the tree. "What were you doing? Kids come home?"

"Oh yeah, both of them. I was just about to give Dolores her gift. Ended up leaving it on the hall table as I walked out the door."

"She's great, Sarge. She'll understand. What'd you get her?"

Wally hesitated. There was no reason to keep it from Joe but he felt shy about it and couldn't explain why. It wasn't an extravagant necklace by a long shot but he didn't know if the young member would quite understand.

"Dolores always says every Force Wife needs a good string of pearls. She says it's classy." He rubbed the back of his neck. "Well, hers weren't real and had been glued a few times. I don't know what made me buy them now but…" he trailed off and grabbed at his hat, rolling it up in his hands. "I just thought maybe she'd like some real ones. Sort of fitting that I got called out before I could give them to her."

"Fitting? How come?"

"I think it just struck me how good a woman she is with me out here all the time. And she never says boo about it, just that we should find him for Vallarena and Connie." He slapped his hat on his leg a few times to loosen the ice and snow. "She'll think it's an extravagance she doesn't need but if she opens the box while I'm gone maybe she'll keep the necklace." He laughed. "God knows she deserves it."

Greenslade stubbed out his cigarette. "Might be nice for one of these sightings to amount to something sometime. Make it worth being away from her. Don't know about you, Sarge, but I'm getting tired of chasing smoke."

Wally's chest was ready to cave in with the depth of his agreement. A tip came in and they were off and running, only to find nothing at all. If they had concrete evidence of Robertson lurking around it might just take away some of his guilt. Maybe. "It'd be a good Christmas gift for the kids, I'll tell you that. And for Connie and Vallarena."

Greenslade lit another cigarette. "Yup. I'm glad I got them all a little something. It's the most Christmas shopping I've ever done, besides helping my mom shop for my brothers and sisters." He coloured a bit around the collar and Wally let a smile curve one corner of his mouth. He didn't dare let it go farther lest he lose control. The tears had been sneaking up on him, from time to time, catching him off guard and making it harder to control his face. Greenslade wasn't the only member at the detachment who had gotten the families a "little something." It busted up Wally's insides completely when he heard the men had been buying gifts in the days leading up to what would be a devastating Christmas for all of them.

He cleared his throat and thumped the back of Joe's coat with his huge leather mitt. "Okay, enough of this. Let's get back."

Joe swiped his sleeve across his eyes, cleared his throat, and spat against the base of the tree. "Yup. We'll be back by dark if we hurry."

By February, the cold changed as it did on the prairies. Their eyebrows and lashes caked thick with ice. Boots squeaked in the snow, and the sound grated on their nerves. The weather was starting to get to them and they wondered if Robertson was holed up in someone's house. Or had been eaten by a bear.

"Investigation has moved farther west. Did you read the report?" Wally asked Joe, stopping to consult his map. He looked up again, shielding his eyes from the bright sun to catch the tendrils of smoke curling up from the tree tops in the distance.

"Yeah, that uncle of Robertson's is going to wish he never left Saskatchewan." Greenslade chuckled. "He swore the move out there had nothing to do with Stanley. Got really mad when members started tailing him. Did you know one of the guys on that surveillance detail was a troopmate of Doug's?"

Wally shook his head. "No, I didn't know. But I'm not surprised. Small world."

ON SCENE

Trying to clear yet another report of smoke spotted "in the distance", they came up on a hunting cabin, splitting up to approach from opposite sides. Every time they did this, Wally's blood pressure normalized faster than the last time. Thinking back to the first few they did in the early days of the search, he realized how normal this had become for them and he reflected on that. The heart pounding fear of being shot in the back eased and had been replaced with a single-minded need for justice.

Circling around the back of the cabin, he ordered Bruce into position, waiting for Greenslade to signal him. If there was a rear door or window, they left Bruce back there while they stormed the front. It always made for a nice surprise if someone tried to slip out. So far, Bruce had only been needed once. A smoke sighting was called in, and they sped out on the double, using access roads and farm yards to get to the cabin as quickly as possible. They stormed the front door to find a partially clothed female screaming hysterically, then they heard a howling fight out back. After the situation was brought under control and Wally called Bruce off, they learned that the boyfriend of the screaming female thought the door was being kicked in by her father, and had flung himself out the back window only to be set upon by wolves. Or, at least, that's how the boy described it. Wally thought Bruce rather liked the comparison.

So no matter what, they sent Bruce to watch the back and that's where he was now. Waiting in the snow for someone to fling themselves out a window.

Greenslade's voice rang out over the radio, "Uh, Sarge, you need to see this." There was no urgency at all, and Wally thought he detected a note of laughter, but hurried around the side with his gun drawn, nonetheless.

He came up to the front porch to see Greenslade with a piece of paper in his hand, shoulders shaking with snorting laughter.

Wally snatched it away from him. "What's this?" he asked, looking at the paper. In large block letters it read 'NOT STANLEY'. He looked at Greenslade. "Are you kidding me?"

Greenslade slapped his knee and laughed harder. "Nope. It was nailed right here to the door." Weapons ready, they still followed precise protocol on entering the cabin but, sure enough, found a trapper inside enjoying a cup of coffee with a pot of stew bubbling on the fire. Smelled like rabbit.

They ended up staying for a bite to eat and some good conversation, because what else could they do in a situation like that?

The cold weather may have chased them inside more days than he cared for, but it didn't mean Wally intended to stop searching. Through the bitterly cold winter months, he made a habit of showing up at Fran's Café in the wee hours of morning coffee time. No matter the cool local attitude towards police, Fran was always kind and helpful, asking after Dolores and letting Wally know if she heard anything new or unusual.

Sometimes there were hecklers who yelled things at Wally. "Give up. You'll never find him," and "When are you going to pay me back for my broken fence?" were two favourites. But it was the quiet ones you wanted. Sometimes they appreciated a listening ear.

Wally just enjoyed the smell of baking cinnamon buns that seemed to wrap around his head and stay with him all day. He sipped the coffee that Fran swore she didn't add anything to but had a hint of cinnamon in the aftertaste. It was rich and dark but lacked the bitter kick that tended to take your breath away at other diners.

Bruce sprawled out across Wally's boots under the table. Something he never did at the office, but seemed to enjoy at Fran's.

It was in some of the quiet moments that Wally learned of Mrs. Robertson's extracurricular activities and he started piecing together what could have happened that night. Ruth had been interviewed a couple of times but it was apparent she wouldn't be a reliable witness. Wally had discarded the idea of interviewing her yet again; there wasn't any point. She didn't know anything of value when it came to locating Stanley.

Other days there were more officers in the café than locals, but Fran didn't seem to mind. They'd started fuelling up the police cars in MacDowall, and came out for lunch on a weekly basis, bringing more money into the small business than she would normally see during her slowest months of the year.

As per usual in the province, March went in like a lion, and came out like a bigger lion. On one of Wally's visits, a blizzard was blowing through and it was just Fran, Wally, and Bruce in the restaurant.

"Sergeant Regitnig, do you mind if I ask you a question?" Fran topped up his coffee cup, and picked up her cleaning rag, wiping the long counter over and over again as was her habit.

"Fran, call me Wally. We've gone over this." He smiled and sipped his coffee again, sighing with deep appreciation.

"Have you looked in the mirror lately? Been home to see your wife?" Her soft brown eyes regarded Wally with concern.

"Don't worry, Fran. I'm home every night. Been that way for months," he said, waving a hand dismissively.

Fran shook her head. "You're tired. I can see it in your sunken cheeks." She stilled her hand on the cleaning rag.

"Nah, I just haven't eaten enough of your delicious cooking lately." Her wise eyes told him she wasn't fooled.

"If you look like this going home to your wife every night, sleeping in your bed, and eating a decent meal here every morning, do you really think Stanley is still alive out there?" She left her cloth on the counter and walked over to the window. "Even in a hunting cabin with food and wood for a fire, it's a rough go from February until spring." She wrapped her arms around herself against the chill that gusted in around the window seal.

"I was going to ask you the very same question. Seems the locals know more than me."

She shook her head definitively. "I'd have heard if someone had him."

Wally nodded, staring out at the whipping wind and thick snowflakes that seemed to be blowing straight sideways rather than falling down from the sky. "Yeah, he's still out there," he said, before draining his coffee and fishing some dollar bills out of his pocket. "I can feel it in my bones."

Kate Kading

"Possible sighting of Stanley Robertson—(Name Redacted) reports that during the 'cold snap' in February he was working in the bush and heard a shot from a 'big rifle'. He stated that it sounded like it came from between the two entrances to the North Cabin Road. He walked back into the woods and saw human tracks as if one man had been walking in the bush alone. He didn't pursue it further at the time other than to mention it to two other bush workers nearby. They stated that they heard it too but suggested it was someone shooting a deer. He didn't report same to the police because he was afraid we would catch one of the locals for a Game Act Offence and he didn't want to Squeal. This was reported now only when he noticed the P.C. driving through the Forest Preserve."

Excerpt of statement taken by Corporal R.H. Waller regarding a sighting of Robertson (Feb 1971)

Chapter Thirty-Five

Saturday, May 1, 1971

Prince Albert Detachment

0900hrs

Spring was never gradual in the Northern Boreal Forest around Prince Albert. One minute it was snowing, the next minute the sun was shining and there were crocuses blooming. There was no halfway. Wally waited, bloody impatient, for as long as he could.

On the first of May the day dawned bright and clear, and he knew the roads would start drying up nicely. He'd been monitoring them for weeks.

Coming in the back door of the detachment, he and Bruce took the stairs two at a time and stomped across the length of the floor to Mosher's office. Throwing open the door without knocking, Wally shouted, "See the sun? Ground search is back on." He banged on the door jamb a few times, just to make sure Al heard him, and pounded right back down the stairs and out the door. It was time to find a killer.

The winter had given over without much of a fight, and game was easier to come by. Walking the trap line had become much easier, avoiding detection even easier yet. The soles of his boots would need replacing soon. Too many miles, too much wet terrain, too much steady pacing of this land he loved. He could feel the damp seeping in through his wool socks, mended many times over. Ignoring it, he stood still, taking in the beauty before him.

The low hanging moon blended subtly with the predawn sky, showing just a tinge of silver against the lavender expanse behind it. It was light out, he could see the outlines of the trees, but the sun hadn't yet broken the horizon, lending a haziness to the sky that touched the trees and faded into the earth. It didn't last long. A bare breath of time where everything around him felt ethereal. In the next breath, the first sharp rays of sunlight shot out from the tops of the gently rolling hills, hitting the new buds on the trees and burning off the lavender haze as if it had never really existed at all.

He blinked, and the magic of the moon was a mere memory, fading into a non-descript grey that would hang, forgotten, overwhelmed by the rising sun. The lavender was no more. His ethereal world vanished, replaced by a world where so many men existed having never breathlessly admired a predawn moon.

The moment over, practicality won out, as it must. There was work to be done.

Keeping to the treeline, he skirted an open area where the army had mowed down a bunch of young saplings with one of their machines. This had once been a prime hunting spot at this time of day, with the deer coming to nibble at the young trees and paw the ground in search of the first greens of spring. But that was no more. The noise, the exhaust, the men, the dogs—they'd chased most of the big game away from the area in the fall when he should have bagged at least a couple deer to see the family fed through winter. He shrugged off that disappointment; there was no way he could have gone about his regular hunt with the search on. Even if the army hadn't come through and trampled everything, you couldn't fire a weapon within ten miles of anywhere without calling in the cavalry. He pursed his lips firmly. He could do without calling in the cavalry.

ON SCENE

He stopped walking again, listening to the chirps from the trees. The birds were active; that was a good sign. As long as he heard them, there was nobody else around. It was nice to hear them again. He sat on a protruding log and sipped from his battered canteen.

The thick of the winter had been fairly quiet, with just a few officers on snow machines to elude every now and again, but last week's fine weather brought renewed activity. Tracks in the melting snow and new mud that froze overnight were harder to find, and the searchers didn't bother to hide their tracks at all. He could see where they'd been. A dog was running with his handler, taking up the hunt once more. Even from his precarious positions, skittering about the woods when he caught glimpses of the officer, he could see this was a man to be respected. He'd found the handler more than once, lined him up in the sight of his rifle, watching him as he tracked, but he never pulled the trigger. He had no other intent than to observe and learn.

He knew it'd be that same officer who'd taken up the search again last week. The man with the gold arrows on his sleeve. The same man he saw almost every day he ventured out, before the bitterly cold weather set in. One day, he might know his name.

Stowing his canteen away, he set off again, angling to the North East to check his farthest trap line. It had been his most successful through the winter, catching the odd rabbit to keep him fed. He never required much, but some bigger game would be a luxury with this warm weather.

Turning his face as he walked, he caught the warm breeze on his cheek, rejoicing in the turning of the season. Life was easier when the snow melted. Maybe it would lighten his heart, as well.

The soft lump at the first snare surprised him as he came over the slight slope. A nice hare to start off the morning was a good way to buoy his spirits for the day ahead. He pulled out a rough sack, put the rabbit in it, and tied it to his belt. He stopped for a moment to thank the Creator for the abundance he was shown.

If the first hare surprised him, the second and third were a pure and pleasant shock. His belt was getting heavy, but he still walked the remainder of the trap line. He looked up at the tantalizing smoke curling above the trees. This line always took him within smelling distance of town.

He weighed his odds. He didn't need three rabbits. He knew Fran would buy one or two off him, and the money would be good. He wondered who would be in the café this early in the morning. Perhaps it was worth the risk. He didn't want to cause any trouble, though.

The walk wasn't overly far for someone used to many miles at a time, and when he cleared the trees, he saw what he was hoping he would never see again. A police car was sitting in front of Fran's Café, serene in the morning light.

Was it the possibility of meeting the dog handler again that had his heart pounding? Or was it just time to walk in there, sit down, and enjoy a good cup of coffee before whatever was going to happen, happened? Of their own volition, his feet moved, one after the other, towards the café. The rabbits swung heavily from his belt, their distinct tang touching his nostrils.

Stepping through the front door, the delicate jingle of the bell turned all heads as it did in every small town café. A couple of people paused, their forks in mid air, mouths hanging open. He heard a gasp and the clatter of a cup on a table, but didn't look up. The first person he made eye contact with was Fran. He held the sack up to her and she nodded without hesitation, motioning him to the end of the counter like she had dozens of times before. He set the sack on the brown paper she spread out, and looking neither right nor left, walked to the back of the café and sat down. The worn vinyl was the softest thing he'd sat on in months; a welcome respite, and he nodded his thanks when Fran put a steaming cup of coffee in front of him. Tendrils curling up around his face, he wrapped his hands around the white mug, savouring the feeling of normal for the moment. Eyes closed, he took a sip of the strong coffee. Fran's coffee was the best. Even better with a piece of pie, but he hadn't had that luxury in a good long while.

At least a dozen pairs of eyes followed him when he'd walked past the half full restaurant to the back. Now they all turned, staring, lips moving behind hands. The officer must have been paying for fuel on the other side because just then, he stepped into the restaurant area. Hands at his belt, dog at his side, he stood for a moment surveying the place, and to his credit didn't even startle when his eyes settled on the back table. He was thinner than he had

ON SCENE

been back in October, but was no less imposing. Without hesitation, hurry, or concern, the officer walked directly to the back of the café.

Their eyes locked.

"I know who you are," the officer said.

Despite the hard go of the winter, he was clean cut, pressed, and well put together. He was wearing a tie. It struck him as contrary to the job the officer did, pushing through dense bush looking for people. He'd never worn a tie in his life.

They broke eye contact, and he saw the officer had mud on his boots, but who didn't at this time of year? There was a name tag pinned to his wool jacket that read 'W.J.O. Regitnig' and the early morning light caught his gold buttons. He wondered what the W stood for.

"I suspect so." His voice was scratchy from lack of use and he took another sip of coffee.

To his utter surprise, the officer sat down across from him and looked him square in the eye.

"I'm still looking for your son."

He glanced back down at his coffee cup, tracing the rim with a dirty finger and wondered when the officer had figured out who he was. The first night they came across each other in the woods he knew the officer thought he was Stanley. The dog whined beside him and Gordon put out the back of his hand for the animal to sniff. The officer grunted with what could only be annoyance and nudged the dog with his leg. The dog snapped into a heel but whined again.

"Sir, do you want this to end?"

His eyes jerked up at the unexpected respect he heard in the officer's voice. He stared at him hard, judging his soul in those moments. The officer's intense stare never wavered.

He held out a hand. "Gordon." Always a man of few words, he waited for the officer to respond.

The officer didn't hesitate in grabbing his hand in a tight grip, pumping it with purpose. "Walter. Sergeant Walter Regitnig. We've never formally met but you did elude my dog."

Gordon nodded slowly, matter of fact, still keeping eye contact. "We haven't. And I did." He released the officer's hand. "I judge a man by his handshake."

"As do I, sir."

The Sergeant's gaze was keen; Gordon guessed he didn't miss much. The sizing up of each other was serious business. He stared at the Sergeant for several long breaths, blinking, taking in as much of this officer's spirit as he could. A calm washed over him, taking doubt away with it as the wave pulled back out into the vast sea of his feelings. This was the time. This was the man.

"You've been looking in the wrong spot." He took another sip of his coffee. The officer tensed but he never moved; never broke eye contact.

"Yes, sir. I gathered that. Seven months is a long time." The officer shifted in his seat, clenching his hands together. The dog whined at his side and the officer dropped a hand to the dog's head, absently stroking his fur.

Gordon closed his eyes but opened them again in the same breath. "Not quite seven months. Not until tomorrow."

The officer didn't respond. He just waited. Gordon respected the way this man conducted himself. He didn't rush, didn't threaten. He just…waited.

"South East corner of the Nelson property." The officer's eyes went wide, recognizing the name, but Gordon waved him off. "No, not that Nelson. John Nelson's land borders ours. There's a Jack Pine." He didn't say another word. Draining the rest of the coffee in a couple smooth swallows he stood and walked to the counter without looking back. He retrieved the one rabbit Fran left neatly wrapped up and walked out the door.

Soon, he could rest.

ON SCENE

Robertson's uncle, *who lives about three miles from the Robertson farm, told the Leader-Post he wasn't at all worried about his nephew. "If I could only find him, I would walk up to him and tell him to give himself up." He said. "He must have gone out of his head, I don't know. He had a big fight with his wife that day (Friday). He never drank and wasn't drinking that day. Something must have happened in his mind."*

Excerpt, Regina Leader Post (Wednesday, October 14, 1970)

Chapter Thirty-Six

```
Saturday, May 8, 1971
On Scene
1228hrs
```

That damn tree.

When Robertson Senior walked out the door of Fran's Café that morning, Wally knew his search was over. There was no need for maps. No more compasses. He knew exactly where he was going.

"Regitnig to base." He cranked the volume on his radio so he could hear it over the roaring engine as he pushed the vehicle to its limit, tires spinning on the loose gravel.

The box blasted a line of static with a reply but Wally couldn't hear over Bruce. The dog knew when the hunt was on.

"Be quiet!" he yelled, smashing the side of the box with the microphone. Bruce stilled in time for Wally to hear the end of the transmission.

"Send backup out to MacDowall. I've got a 20 on Robertson." One heartbeat of silence on the radio then Cavello came back to him.

"Say again, Sergeant Regitnig. Missed your last."

"The hell you did, Cavello. Tell Mosher. We've got him."

ON SCENE

Cavello had depressed his mic button but didn't speak and Wally heard Mosher's voice, far off, through the speaker.

"Regitnig, stand down—" he was cut off by Cavello's blundering, disbelief making him useless on the radio.

"Uh, the Staff Sergeant is, um…he says…"

Wally pressed the button on his radio, but Cavello hadn't let go of his and a squeal set Bruce to barking again.

"Okay, that's enough." Wally threw the mic down on the seat and put his hand up to the metal cage separating him from his partner. Bruce nosed Wally's fingers while he waited for the chaos to settle on the radio.

"Regitnig, come back." No mistaking Mosher's commanding tone. Cavello had given up the mic.

"10-4."

"Do not engage. We'll be there."

Wally struggled with that order.

"Regitnig, acknowledge."

Wally put his foot down harder on the gas pedal and swore at the ceiling of the cruiser, letting out every foul word he'd ever learned. There was no way he could sit on his hands and wait.

"Goddamn it, Regitnig, that's an order." The urgency in Mosher's voice did nothing to sway Wally's resolve to rush the tree the second he got close enough.

"Wally!" Mosher screamed his name, a pleading tone stabbing Wally right in the heart. Al had seen enough death on his watch.

"10-4, sir."

An audible sigh pierced the airwaves. Wally waited for clearance to speak again.

"Make it fast. Remember that Jack Pine tree? There."

"10-4, on our way. Do not leave your car."

"Yeah, yeah," Wally muttered to himself. He blasted down the back road, letting Bruce bark as much as he wanted now. It didn't take long to turn off onto a side road but it felt like an eternity. The road was little more than a cattle trail, and he had to slow down or risk losing his oil pan to a hidden pile of rocks. Mosher would love that.

He trundled along over the rough terrain, keeping an ear on the radio activity. Everyone in the vicinity was responding but the nearest backup was still fifteen minutes out.

Not one of them wanted to miss the arrest of the most wanted man in Canada.

He turned into a field beside a long treeline. The fence was still down here, even seven months later. There were no markers but he knew exactly where he was and parked the car in the tall grass before the trees, concealing it the best he could under the circumstances. He'd come in through the back and saw the hill from the side, not the straight on deer path that ran through the front part of the field to the shallow valley filled with water.

Bruce barked off and on, pacing. Wally strained forward to see the top of the hill from the car. It was a ways off; the only thing he could see clearly was the top of the Jack Pine above the much shorter poplars. The fifteen seconds he sat in the car looking around was far longer than the amount of time he assumed he would obey Mosher's orders.

He got out of the car, leaning against it with the open door between him and his mark. Bruce's barking became frenzied. Even though he had a great vantage point to see anyone trying to escape, their element of surprise was completely gone. It wasn't Bruce's strong suit. There was no point in waiting. He wasn't alone.

As if Mosher could read his mind, the radio crackled with his voice, "Stand down, Regitnig. You on scene?"

Before he even heard Mosher's voice, Wally knew he wasn't going to answer.

"We're coming Wally, do not approach. We're coming."

Wally never took his eyes off the top of the tree.

"Answer me, Regitnig."

He opened Bruce's door and grabbed his collar when the dog tried to shoot past him. He ordered Bruce to sit beside him, but didn't let go of him. Generally, Bruce had excellent self control but today Wally only expected as much self control from the dog as he could muster himself. Absolutely zero.

ON SCENE

"Listen, you stay low. You don't have to wait for me but you hold him, okay?"

The dog strained against Wally's grip when he leaned over and turned off the radio. Mosher's voice died with the volume and there was no regret when he stood up, patted Bruce twice on the side and let his collar go.

Breaking into an easy jog, he followed the dog through the trees, keeping his eyes up on the Jack Pine. This was the closest he'd been to it since the day he marked it on the map. He still had that map, even though he didn't need it anymore. He'd keep that map forever.

Bruce had long since disappeared, but Wally kept up his run. It felt good to stretch his legs again after the long, cold winter. They hadn't had a good run yet this spring. It seemed a fitting time for it.

He came out of the trees and into the small valley just in time to see Bruce lap water from the pond as he streaked past it and up the hill. He wasn't running for the pleasure of it. There was a difference in his gait that Wally well recognized.

He had a scent.

Wally changed his pace too, double timing it up the hill, pulling his revolver from the holster. He stopped just before the final rise so he still had some cover, flattening himself to the side of the hill. When Bruce grabbed Robertson, he could approach. He just had to wait.

His stomach clenched, waiting for the satisfying sounds of someone being grabbed by his dog. Any second now. His head spun with the anticipation of putting his hands on Robertson. He clenched his free hand into a fist. He could feel the smash of bone on bone. Nowhere near the satisfaction he needed, but it was a start. Could he control the vengeful rage he just now realized was still building inside him? He couldn't kill him, that wasn't right.

He only wanted justice.

Not hearing any screaming or growling, he pushed himself up to peer over the rise. Had Bruce gone up and over, to track Robertson down the other side of the hill?

Wally gathered his feet underneath him and rose into a crouch, duck walking the rest of the way up the hill, gun ready. He startled when he heard Bruce bark once, then growl and whine.

"Robertson, this is the RCMP. Come out with your hands up," he yelled as loud as he could. Dumbfounded as to why Bruce hadn't attacked the man, he stuck to arrest procedure. It wasn't the first time a Robertson had bewitched his dog.

"You're surrounded. There's no escape. Surrender now," he said, not allowing his mind to go to a place where Robertson escaped…again. He wasn't going to let it happen.

Bruce was still under the tree, barking, then came running out with something in his mouth.

Wally relaxed his stance a fraction.

The dog dropped the lump at his feet and he scooped it up. Holstering his gun, he turned the item over in his hands. It was a wet and worn lump of leather.

A wallet.

He pried it open, and peeled some of the papers out of it. He already knew what he would find inside.

"Find him," he said, pointing and ordering Bruce back under the tree.

He followed and ducked under the branches that swept the ground.

There was a body face down in the thick pine needles. Returning to the earth.

This wasn't the first body he'd come across in his career, and it probably wouldn't be his last. It would, however, be the one he remembered most, if only for the sake of his friendships with Bob and Doug.

There wasn't a doubt in his mind that it was Robertson.

He didn't know how long ago he died, but from the looks of him, he'd been under the tree for some time. How long had he and Bruce chased the man? How long had they been chasing his ghost?

There were so many questions, so many things unsaid.

Wally crouched at the base of the tree, head in his hands. "Why?"

ON SCENE

Bruce nosed his arm when he spoke out loud and he stroked the dog's head. "Why'd you do it?"

Seven months of stress came flooding out of him. Seven months of trying his damndest to keep his promise to Connie. Seven months of missing his family. Seven months of being there…but never really being present in any moment that didn't involve this search. This stranger. The pain started low in his belly and blazed its way up into his throat. His eyes burned and his mind collapsed with relief. He could let go of his heavy burden.

This quiet, lonely place was the only spot he would give free rein to these feelings. Bob had always been better with this stuff.

```
"Buddy, it's okay to cry sometimes." Bob clenched Wally's
shoulder as the coroner covered up the body lying on the
side of the road. The mother of three had no chance against
the moose in her path, and Bob and Wally had the unfortunate
luck of having to inform her family. Their only consolation
had been that none of the children were with their mother in
the vehicle at the time of the accident. One of them played
hockey against the twins.

"Not on the job, it's not." Wally cleared his throat gruffly
and Bob was warmed by the sound of his best friend's
nervous habit.

"Later, then. We'll go deal with this the best way we know
how, then we'll talk about it later." Bob stared into Wally's
eyes, both nodding.

"Yeah, later." He cleared his throat again. "You're a good
man, Bob."

"Only as good as the company I keep."
```

Wally's body heaved at the memory of every time Bob helped him, every time he'd reassured him, and counselled him. Taking advantage of his lowered guard, his body expelled as much of the anguish as it could, an involuntary purge of emotion that he needed whether he liked it or not. The gentle wind that slipped under the branches of the tree cooled his face and took with it some of his guilt and pain. At least he'd been able to keep his promise. But there were still too many questions.

Kate Kading

He looked at the non-descript lump, half consumed by the earth and piled pine needles.

"Why kill the people you did, instead of the ones you wanted to?"

The corpse didn't answer.

> *"During this period, seven patrols were made into the MacDowall area to conduct further searches of the creek, swamp, brush piles, bush areas, and also investigate two complaints of strange smells. By the end of this period the snow had melted and search conditions were again favourable.*
>
> *Excerpt from RCMP report dated 15 April 71 to 1 May 71*

Chapter Thirty-Seven
```
Tuesday, June 1, 1971
Fran's Cafe
Early
```

After the strain of a seven month manhunt, finding Robertson's body, the recovery operation, and the autopsy seemed almost trivial. They called off investigations across four provinces and amended their most wanted list immediately, but the mountain of paperwork that followed took weeks. Wally was ordered to take a week off but he knew that wouldn't last. He'd see how long it took for his restlessness to drive Dolores crazy. He was planning to take her out for a nice supper that night, but in his prowling hours of his first official day off, he found himself sitting in the back booth at Fran's Café. The summer sun was just winking over the horizon, bouncing off the windows in a glittery flash of brilliance. It was one of the first days in a very long time he was in civilian clothes, and he hadn't yet decided if he was okay with that. It was also the first day in a year he'd left his partner at home. He was sure Bruce wasn't happy about that, and Wally felt exposed even though there was nothing to take cover from. It would take a while to recover from this particular case. If he ever recovered at all.

He'd become a fixture at Fran's, no longer a stranger who stopped conversations when he walked through the door. He was welcome like one of them. No cause for speculation or concern.

He sipped his coffee, trying to quiet his mind, but in the weeks following the last signature on the last piece of paper, he often wondered if he would see any of the Robertsons again. He hadn't yet given up his habit of stopping in at Fran's with the hope that he might. But to say what? Convey his condolences for their loss? The intention seemed dreadfully inadequate in comparison to what they'd all lost.

The bell above the door jingled.

Wally raised his hand to Fran, signalling for a second cup of coffee to be brought to his table.

The man who entered the café came directly over to Wally. Heads were turning, conversations stopped, whispers started.

"It's been a little while, sir," Wally said.

"It has." Gordon sat down. Fran slid the fresh cup of coffee onto the table, refreshed Wally's cup, and eased away silently, as only she could.

"I'm sorry for your loss, sir," Wally murmured, sipping at his topped up cup.

"And I'm sorry for yours," Gordon said, on an almost inaudible sigh.

Wally stared at the man's hands around the cup, brown and creased. They looked like aged leather. He thought back to what he knew about this man. Those were the hands that had taught Stanley Robertson all he knew. Those were the hands that provided food for the table in Stanley's childhood. They were the hands that had disciplined him and applauded him. Staring at those work worn hands, then staring at his own brought his children to mind. They had grown up well and were making their own way in the world; Wally's hands showed that work and wear as well. He couldn't yet muster forgiveness for what happened, but in his heart, he found a kernel of understanding for the pain this father was feeling.

The silence stretched on forever, each man's eyes wandering from hands to coffee cup, out the window, and back again. It wasn't an uncomfortable silence.

Gordon clasped his hands together in front of his face, pressing his lips into his steepled forefingers. He sat like that for quite some time, and Wally wondered if he should say something. When Gordon finally moved, he reached into his front shirt pocket, took something out, and set it onto the table beside Wally's cup.

It was a bullet casing.

Sergeant Robert James SCHRADER (#15445) (Photo by RCMP-GRC)

Bob and Connie Schrader's wedding day April 24, 1954 (Photo courtesy of the Schrader family)

Constable Douglas Bernard ANSON (#21129) (Photo by RCMP-GRC)

Doug and Vallarena Anson's wedding day August 8, 1970 (Photo courtesy of Vallarena Blum)

Sergeant Walter J. O. REGITNIG (#17364) (Photo by Derek Sidenius – Victoria Times 1977. Formatting support by Peter Mieras)

Wally and PSD "Flash" (Photo by Derek Sidenius – Victoria Times 1977. Formatting support by Peter Mieras)

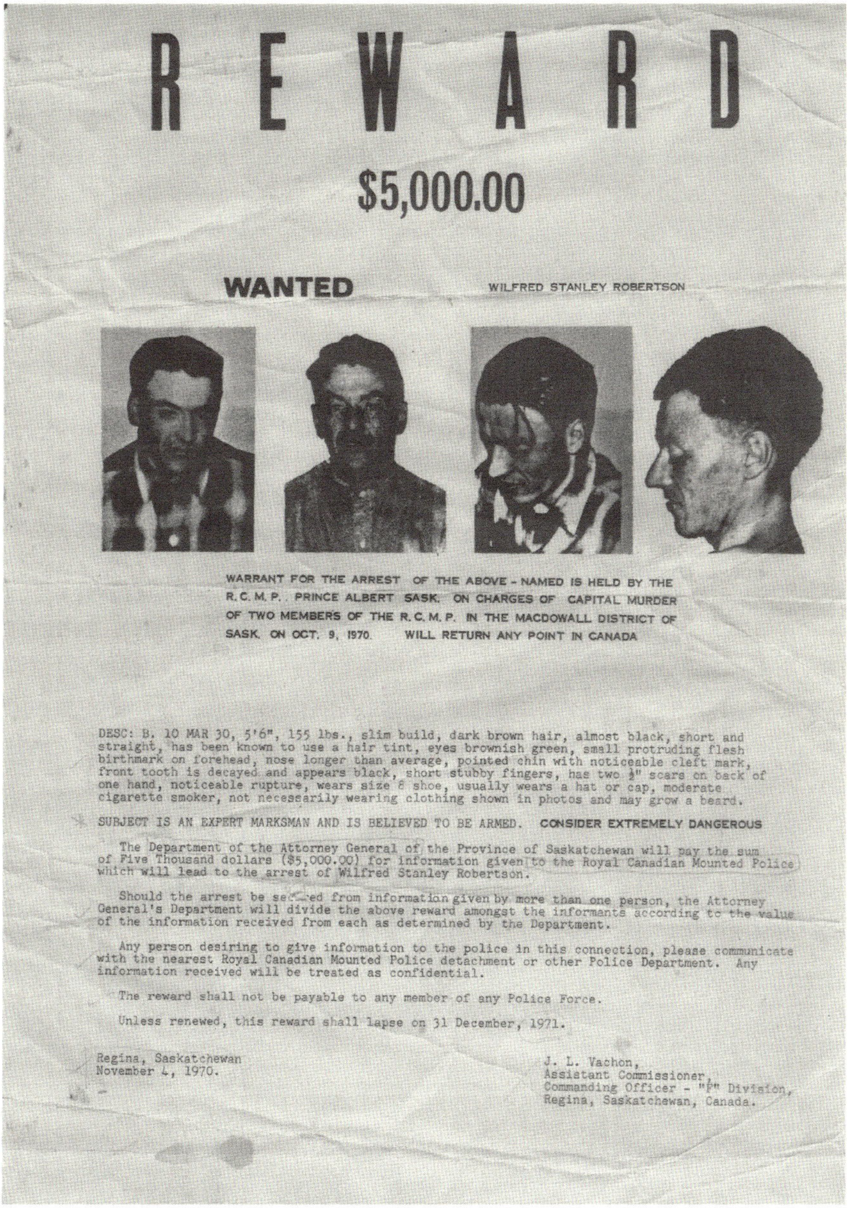

Pencil marks, coffee stains, and all…an original wanted poster for Wilfred Stanley Robertson on charges of capital murder. With my thanks to the source.

Notes from the Author

This is a work of fiction.

There are three sides to every story: your side, my side, and the truth. This book is made up of all of these, and more.

Although based on actual events, all characters and details resembling real life people are purely coincidental, unless otherwise noted with permission from the person in question. Some names, dates, and details have been changed for privacy purposes.

A great many people contributed their own personal accounts and for that, they have my deepest gratitude. Those interviews, along with newspaper articles, and police reports helped fill in the story. Speaking with so many retired RCMP officers was a pure pleasure. They want to remember their colleagues for the great men they were. The effort and coordination that went into this investigation is a piece of Saskatchewan history and is deserving of more than a mere cursory glance.

It is also important to note that Wilfred Stanley Robertson was *not* the Mad Trapper. Early in 1932, Albert Johnson (alias) shot at RCMP officers. Johnson was nicknamed the Mad Trapper and led police on a 240km foot chase through Northern Canada, lasting more than a month. Johnson was killed in a shootout in the Yukon and to this day, even after extensive investigation by RCMP, his true identity remains unknown.

In several publications over the years, these two manhunts have been mixed up, and details intermingled. The two events happened almost forty years apart, involving completely different people and circumstances.

There are many stories throughout history deserving of our recognition.

Kate Kading

This is one of them.

Chapter One

MacDowall or...Macdowall? In this book I used the spelling they used most commonly in 1970-MacDowall-but in modern publications and on provincial maps you will see Macdowall. My thanks to journalist Terry Pugh for his willingness to discuss with me the finer points of Small Town Saskatchewan Spellings and pointing out the example of his own hometown of LeRoy (Leroy) and the same debate of the spelling there. Both are correct, used at different times.

Wilfred Stanley Robertson delivered a double load of cord wood to Saskatoon, Saskatchewan earlier that day. He did unexpectedly head back to MacDowall that night.

All local interviews reported the Robertsons as a quiet, hardworking family.

In a Regina Leader Post news story it was reported that "Don Nelson" (name changed to protect privacy) was Stanley Robertson's cousin. Interviews with relatives and close friends confirmed this.

Police interviews revealed Stanley had come home in the wee hours of Friday morning and found the house cold and the children alone causing him to drive the back road into MacDowall to find his wife.

Chapter Two

Staff Sergeant (retired) Walter J.O. REGITNIG (#17364) December 6, 1931-July 2, 1992.

In 1970, officers carried a wooden baton, handcuffs, and a gun. Now, the RCMP has a 'use of force' model and they abide by the Charter of Rights and Freedoms (1982). They have several use of force intervention options including handcuffs, OC Spray (pepper spray), a baton (asp), and a taser. These options can be used prior to drawing a firearm. Training that has not changed from then to today are hard body (a strike) and soft body (a hold) controls.

Police Service Dogs (PSD) were (and still are) referred to as such "PSD Bruce", but I tried to keep the technical jargon to a minimum. You will see the acronym PSD throughout the police reports and statements for this case.

RCMP Ten Codes used in this book are as follows:

10-4: Acknowledgement (OK)

10-17: En route

10-20: Location

10-23: Arrived on scene

10-33: Help me quick

More often than not, the 10 is dropped in regular use. "I'm 17." "What's your 20?"

Connie Schrader always took in a boarder or two when a young officer needed a place to stay. Many officers I interviewed mentioned they had lived with the Schraders at some point in their career. The family was welcoming and made lifelong friends in the Force.

Barry Schrader recounted stories about playing hiding games with PSD "Bruce" in his childhood. "But he always found us." The middle Schrader twins, Barry and Garry, turned fourteen a few days before their dad was killed. There are a lot of Schrader family birthdays in October.

Chapter Three

In the interest of full disclosure, the entire character of Gordon Robertson is fictional, except his name. There is no evidence that I came across that shared anything more than him being a quiet man, small in stature. There were a few personal interviews that confirmed these traits but nothing substantial enough to base an entire character on. Wilfred Stanley Robertson's parents were listed as Wilfred Gordon Robertson and Helena Robertson.

Old records at the RM office confirmed multiple houses on the Robertson farmyard but the details here are fictional.

The series of events and the corresponding timeline after the domestic on the back road are well documented in the case file through interviews with witnesses. All dialogue between the Robertsons in this chapter is fabricated except a few details of Stanley being "moody and brooding all morning." (Gathered from an excerpt of an RCMP interview with Mrs. Robertson.)

There was speculation from a few officers that Mrs. Robertson was a victim of domestic violence but nothing is documented. A close personal friend of the Robertsons said she'd never witnessed them argue and that Mrs. Robertson wasn't a meek woman.

The Prince Albert, Saskatchewan RCMP Detachment was located above the local post office. It was not unusual at the time for detachments to share space with other public services.

The officers named in this book are a mixture of fact and fiction, taking stories from dozens of different officers and attributing them to only a few characters. Chronological order, who experienced which event, names, ranks, and locations may be altered.

One Regina Leader Post article stated Doug and Vallarena Anson had been married for eighteen months. This is a typo, as they were married two months when Doug was killed. They'd previously known each other for two years.

Chapter Four

It was ultimately decided that Anson would continue with the file as he was the one who took the original statement from Don Nelson (name changed to protect privacy.)

At the very beginning of the research, the story was that Robertson was such an expert marksman he had clipped "Don Nelson" on the ear with the warning shot. Interviews with officers who were at the detachment the day Nelson came in to report the incident revealed that the officers couldn't recall him being injured or bandaged at all. Interviews with local friends of Nelson's said he was. The part of this that causes the most speculation on the part of officers then and now is that if Bob and Doug were absolutely certain a firearm was involved, maybe they would have approached the situation differently? As it was, there was nothing that indicated they were walking into any danger whatsoever.

The dialogue between Doug Anson and Bob Schrader is fabricated with the help of countless hours of interviews with their colleagues, each lending their professional opinion on what the officers may have discussed on their way out to the Robertson farm.

The Ansons had a small wedding on August 8, 1970. The Thanksgiving weekend beginning Friday October 9, 1970 was a special one for the newlyweds. Vallarena's parents were throwing them an impromptu wedding dance in Pierceland, Saskatchewan where she was from. Doug was to have three days leave for this trip, which was extremely rare at the time.

The bar owner interaction is pure fiction. It is documented that the two officers interacted with locals prior to investigating the site of the domestic altercation, but with whom and what exactly was said is still buried in the remainder of the redacted case file, so I attributed it to a fictional bar owner. The actual bar owner at the time of this incident did not witness anything unusual that night, as told to me in a personal interview in 2017.

What Schrader and Anson found on the back road near MacDowall is listed in the police report along with the interviews to substantiate the theory that the altercation was physical between Stanley and his wife.

Chapter Five

Dialogue between Robertson and the officers during the shootings is documented from interviews performed during the original investigation. The words varied a bit from person to person so I did my best to piece it together.

The actions and movement during the shootings are speculation on the part of investigators paired with interviews with witnesses. The overwhelming theme in these interviews was Sergeant Schrader didn't run for the bush because there were children to protect and he wouldn't leave his partner. His internal turmoil in this situation is fabricated but according to his children, his former RCMP partners, and other friends, it wouldn't be at all off base and spoke to his true character.

There were five shots. Two hit Anson, one hit a tree, and two hit Schrader.

Chapter Six

Stanley Robertson was said to be an excellent marksman. The shots are all documented in autopsy reports as well as maps of the scene drawn by members.

I struggled the most with Robertson's wife's character. Interviews with close friends of the family differed from the interviews performed by police during the investigation. Both of those differed again from the personal accounts I got from retired members. Was she a fearful abused wife, or a master manipulator who finally drove her husband to an extreme reaction? We may never know. For this reason, and many others, the entire character is fiction. I can't pretend to know what it was like to witness something like this, so it's best to leave Ruth Robertson in the world of fiction.

Chapter Seven

Reports are extensive at this point but with the redactions I am still unclear on who called the police directly after the shooting, Robertson's sister, mother, or wife. The official police summary alluded to the sister, but when I received the full case file from ATIP, the interview with Robertson's father says he and his wife drove to the gas station to call it in. I wonder if the sister was with them as well? Personal interviews with officers did mention it was Robertson's sister and there could have been multiple callers. These may seem like picky details but just for a moment put yourself in any one of these people's shoes.

Who took the calls, who arrived on scene with whom and when is all fabricated for the sake of brevity. Every officer I spoke with relayed their intense fear and concern for their comrades as they all descended on the Robertson farm with no idea what they would find. I drew on my husband's modern experience in describing a scene like this but any errors in procedure are purely my own, with my apologies to the fine men who lived this.

RCMP Ten Codes vary from different decades and sometimes now even province to province. According to officers of the time, 10-33 wasn't used in Saskatchewan in 1970, but it is used now, so I included the nationally recognized call for help.

Chapter Eight

Lynn Schrader clearly remembers holding down the fort while her mother was in the hospital that week. She has fond memories of the close relationship she shared with her dad. She mentioned they heard the sirens that evening of the ambulance and police cars going by the house but had no idea it was for their dad.

Chapter Nine

Constable Douglas Bernard ANSON (#21129) born December 26, 1939, was pronounced dead on the scene at 2000hrs Friday, October 9, 1970. Officers arrived on scene at approximately 1915hrs, but due to the dangerous and uncertain circumstances, they were unable to recover his body until the scene was secure. At this point, they had no idea where Bob Schrader was.

Chapter Ten

Several reports, as well as interviews with officers involved, say the "Nelson" statement that had been taken by Constable Anson earlier that day and taken to the Robertson farm that evening was probably removed from the scene by Stanley Robertson in the hopes that the information wouldn't be made public. I would find out more about this statement as the research wore on.

"(Daddy) shot two police." was stated by a Robertson child and documented by police in interviews. It was the innocents in this case that certainly suffered the most.

Extensive personal interviews with locals revealed that Stanley Robertson could have easily lived in the bush for any length of time using the skills his father taught him.

Chapter Eleven

Sergeant Robert James SCHRADER (#15445) born June 24, 1929, was found behind the house near the bush line and pronounced dead at 2030hrs. For the purposes of this story, Sergeant Regitnig is the main searcher but in reality there were many officers involved with locating and recovering Bob Schrader's body.

Chapter Twelve

The relationship between Stanley and his father Gordon is fabricated for the sake of the story. Personal interviews gave me a good idea of how the family lived and as I live in the area, I am familiar with Metis culture and their respect for the land. No amount of research can properly convey the private relationship between a father and a son so this should all be taken as fiction. Any resemblance to actual persons, living or dead, or actual events is purely coincidental.

Chapter Thirteen

Schrader and Anson's police car was taken by Stanley Robertson but was actually recovered the following Saturday morning when ground searches began.

As with many things in the news, all it takes is one typo, a piece of evidence taken out of context, or personal speculation on the part of a reporter for details to go askew. In police reports, Stanley Robertson's gun was a .30-06, but some news outlets reported it as a .308. There are no reports of him ever firing the RCMP service revolver he took from the scene.

Chapter Fourteen

The story of an officer shooting at the side mirror of the recovered police car as they surrounded it to see if Robertson was still hiding there was relayed to me in several interviews. "It was a hell of a shot." Every other detail of this scene is fiction.

From this point on, Robertson's movements are pure speculation on the part of investigators, friends, and family. Everyone seemed to have a different opinion on where he would go and what he would do.

Chapter Fifteen

Connie Schrader was discharged from the hospital when word came in about her husband. Again, who told whom and when has been condensed for brevity. Details regarding the hospital, chaplains, etc, are all fiction.

ON SCENE

Chapter Sixteen

Interviews with the Schrader children were by far my most poignant. Lynn Schrader recounted in great detail what happened when she was told her father was dead. She came home from her sixteenth birthday party organized by friends to find her brothers all waiting for her at the window. "There was no sugar coating" but she remembers they were well taken care of. In the days following she wanted to see her dad, completely against her mother's wishes. The Prince Albert RCMP officers made sure it happened, though. When Lynn arrived to see her dad's body, she said she couldn't bring herself to get out of the car.

The story of Bob Schrader cooking breakfast for his family while they were at church is true. In Bob's estimation, church was only needed for *Hatch, Match, and Dispatch*. Connie Schrader took the children every Sunday, and they would all come home to a big breakfast. It is a fond memory for Bob's children to this day.

Wally did, indeed, promise Connie Schrader that he would find her husband's murderer. The circumstances and wording are fictionalized but the Schrader family recounted a moment between their mother and Wally Regitnig that stands out in their minds to this day. They were shaken by the ferocity in their mother's insistence and in the vehemence of Wally's promise.

I asked Larry Schrader point blank why, as just a young teenager, he felt the need to make sure Vallarena Anson was okay. "Dad was that type of person. He would have gone out of his way to see how the other family was doing. He would have gone to Val to talk to her. I sort of felt like I had to take over as head of the household."

Chapter Seventeen

Vallarena Anson remembers the shock of it all, but some details are lost. "It was so long ago, it's almost like a dream now. When someone dies, you go into a different state of mind. You forget things in the days following that you should remember. Details about the funeral, things that were said, or people who were there. That happened when my second husband passed away, too." Now Val Blum, she married RCMP officer Tom Blum in the years following her first husband's death. Val is now a widow again, but has always stayed in close contact with her RCMP family through the Veterans' Association.

Val didn't recall the exact timeline but fondly remembers Larry Schrader coming to sit with her. She was new to the area and didn't know anyone very well but experienced good friendships despite the tragedy of it all. With my apologies to Larry, I've taken creative license with the timeline in these scenes.

Again for the sake of brevity I have omitted a lot of people from the process of how and when the families were told about the shootings. Someone to note is Joan Halcrow, then just 18 years old, and still a good friend of Val's to this day. As events unfolded, RCMP higher-ups asked around as to who could immediately be sent to Vallarena Anson to wait with her until official word was brought. Dating an officer at the time, Joan was quickly identified as a friend of Val's and she was instructed to go over and wait with her until officers and family arrived. Fifty years later she said "I remember it like it was yesterday. We were so young but she was so strong. Val was very, very strong."

Val mentioned that Joan was specifically told to keep the radio off when she arrived that night. "That was the only thing that was different. Joan always turned the radio on when she came over and that night she didn't." We discussed how she very well could have accidentally heard on the radio that her husband was shot before anyone had a chance to tell her in person. Much like the speed of social media today.

Chapter Eighteen

These side scenes are fabricated in detail but were all told to me through the course of the interviews. The investigation left no stone unturned and one theory was that Stanley Robertson followed the railway tracks from MacDowall to Saskatoon trying to make his escape. Officers set themselves up on the tracks south of Duck Lake to intercept him should their theory be correct. (Then) Constable Ron MORIER gave me permission to use his name and he has my deepest thanks for his genuine recounting of his experiences. Any errors in the retelling of his parts of the story are entirely my own and I must beg his gracious forgiveness if my creative license with the character doesn't capture his true nature.

ON SCENE

There was a Constable D.B. ANTONSON at Prince Albert Detachment at the same time as Doug Anson. He was also young and newly married. When the news came out about the shootings there was some confusion regarding which of these two men it was. I never record my interviews but I do make jot notes in a book as I talk with people. Speaking with "Skip" Antonson I noted "Excellent to speak with, deep resonating voice. Very sharp. Personable." Both my ear for a good radio voice and my heart for a dedicated officer were engaged with this interview.

Chapter Nineteen

Back in 1970, there was no central dispatch like there is now. The radio room was the hub of information, relaying messages from radio and phone to officers on the correct channel in the vicinity.

Roadblocks were set up immediately following the officers arriving on scene at the Robertson farm, and over the course of the next 24 hours rippled out across the province. Many locals remember being stopped at each roadblock and searched thoroughly no matter how many times those same officers had seen them that day. Several people said there wasn't a lot of fear, just curiosity. "We locked our doors like they told us to, but we didn't have any fear that Stanley would hurt us."

Frederick Johnson is a made up character to represent several interviewees who recounted stories about Stanley Robertson, his quiet demeanour, and his attitude about law enforcement and living rough if he had to. Local friends said they were more afraid of the unknown officers than of Stanley. A Regina Leader-Post newspaper story quoted Robertson's father in law, Mr. Dallman, as saying Robertson could live in the bush forever, but in his estimation, the situation wouldn't end well. "He will never come out of the bush alive."

Chapter Twenty

Members of the army from Shilo, Manitoba flew in on Sunday, October 11, 1970. They brought two personnel carriers with drivers, planes, and pilots who helped out with the air search. A personnel carrier could knock down anything, including small trees, bushes, and fences. Basically anything in their way on the Saskatchewan prairie. (Then) Sergeant Bob HEAD from

Rosthern Detachment said "We were mending fences in more ways than one" in reference to the many relationships the RCMP had to smooth over following the search. Retired officers interviewed about their working relationship with the army mentioned how they appreciated the personnel carriers and the small amount of security they gave a tense situation.

Chapter Twenty-One

I can't stress enough that all internal struggle with Stanley Robertson is fiction. Nobody can guess what was going on inside his head at this time.

Newspapers had vastly differing information over the course of the first week of the investigation. There was one particular detail that has plagued me from the beginning, originally appearing in a newspaper story, and later recounted in two places (that I could find): on a Facebook page and in a Saskatchewan crime anthology (unrelated). It stated that after shooting the officers, Stanley Robertson sat down and ate a meal before dressing warmly, arming himself, getting into the police car, and fleeing the scene. There are perhaps a few people who do know the truth of this, but this piece of information, put out as fact, has never been substantiated in any documentation I found in four years of research.

Chapter Twenty-Two

"Joe Greenslade" is actually (Retired) Staff Sergeant Barry GREENSLADE. I already had a Barry (Schrader) and asked if I could change his name to suit the story. My deepest thanks for his agreement. As a constable, he spent the search directly assisting Wally.

Chapter Twenty-Three

There are no reports of Wally and Bruce ever coming upon someone in the bush. It must have driven him crazy to be an expert tracker and not be able to come up with a confirmed sighting.

ON SCENE

Chapter Twenty-Four

The coffee percolator story is true, although happened to different officers. Retired members recounted it with a chuckle, "Damn thing scared the hell out of us. Everyone was on edge."

Some locals speculated, and some newspaper stories quoted the speculation, that Stanley had returned to the house later in the evening on the day of the shooting to gather supplies. According to police reports, members arrived on scene at 1915hrs and never left. Officers spent the night on the property, prepared for an arrest if Stanley Robertson did come back.

The story Wally Regitnig tells Staff Sergeant Al MOSHER about the little girl in British Columbia in this chapter is fabricated. Sergeant Regitnig had a long and illustrious career as an RCMP dogmaster, and no doubt saw many things that nobody should ever have to witness. This particular story is merely an example of something that could happen to an officer.

Chapter Twenty-Five

The names of Fran's Café and the '66 Garage are well known in the area and Fran really did run the café for many years. The Schrader boys remember stopping in at the café to have breakfast before playing ball in MacDowall in their late teens and twenties. But my character Fran is fictional and her interactions with Wally the dogman are fabricated. Any resemblance to a real person or real events is purely coincidental.

It was the personal interviews that revealed how much time Wally Regitnig spent forging friendships with the locals. By the end of the investigation he had the respect of more than just a few of them. The details of every run-in with people at Fran's Café are fabricated but I learned from people's personal stories that it happened quite a few times. As with the officers, I have taken dozens of local accounts and condensed them down to be included in the story.

Chapter Twenty-Six

The bit about the loud, inexperienced constable is true but as with everything else, is attributed to different characters as it suits the story. With anything that involves this many people, there were a lot of personal details revealed in interviews; too many to include every single one. I feel privileged to have listened to so many fantastic people with superior memories for detail. Their personal accounts added much more depth to the story than they will ever know.

"Depot" is the name of the RCMP training academy in Regina, Saskatchewan. (Pronounced DEH-poe)

Many officers pointed out what a tight ship the superior officers ran, and how much planning an investigation of this magnitude takes, but there were a few things that went south, so to speak. The idea to lay down toilet paper when an area was searched was true, and discarded early on in the investigation. It was cold and wet, which destroyed the toilet paper and just left a mess.

Chapter Twenty-Seven

Through all my interviews, I was regaled with many stories about "Corporal Fuck-Fuck." Names have been changed to protect the innocent, but he was described as quite the character. I have embellished this part for a little bit of comic relief. The army was a serious lot that ran their equipment with efficiency. Many RCMP officers said how much they appreciated the safety the personnel carriers provided in an extremely dangerous situation, even when engines broke down or they got stuck.

Darby's Dirty Dozen came up in the interviews several times. An excellent crew on the ground search.

Chapter Twenty-Eight

The Schrader's trip to Ottawa to visit the Cunnin family is true. Several of the Schrader children provided me with detailed accounts of their cross country road trip and one theme rang throughout all of them. In their early childhoods, none of the Schrader children were ever aware that money was tight. Bologna sandwiches and Kool-Aid on the side of the road. Trying to sleep seven people in their old camper that only slept six. Camping their way to and from Ottawa, and setting up their camper at the Cunnins house to see that everyone had a spot to sleep. It was all normal and fun. The Schraders always had fun. Barry Schrader described it as such, "Dad was the perfect dad, always playing catch with us, taking us for walks, building campfires. And Mom was the perfect mom who stayed home with us, made the meals, took us to church, and made sure we were clean. They were very warm and loving. Back then, we had everything we wanted, and we were all very happy with what Mom and Dad were providing for us. We never realized money was tight."

Shirley Cunnin was one of the first interviews I did for this book back in early 2015. I didn't know what to expect, but she is a loving and gracious lady. Bob Schrader stopping the car to run back and hug Des Cunnin is true. Shirley recounted the story with such depth of emotion that I have great difficulty, even now, retelling it to people. I cried when I did the interview, I cried when I wrote that scene in the book, and I've cried through every edit since. I can only hope I adequately captured the spirit of the friendship between Bob and Des. May they both rest in peace.

Chapter Twenty-Nine

The beginning of this chapter is fabricated. There is no substantiated evidence that Gordon Robertson ever found his son. However, several interviews with local MacDowall families revealed a commonly accepted theory that Gordon did set out to find his son, and succeeded. One friend of the family stated "When he came back later that morning (Saturday), we asked if he found him, and he said no. But he wasn't acting right, and he never talked about it again."

(Then) Constable Brent JETTE is a real person and was stationed in Tisdale, Saskatchewan at the time of the shootings. I have taken considerable creative license with this character as it pertains to posting and his interactions with Wally but this particular scene of hearing a shot in the middle of the night on roadblock duty is true as relayed by the officer himself. The details of his partner, the stopped truck, and the location are fabricated.

Chapter Thirty

Businesses in MacDowall shut down for a day or two after the shootings occurred and RCMP spread out their resources to perform dozens of interviews. To protect the privacy of the people involved who are currently living, I decided against fabricating a bunch of police interviews. All the scenes in Fran's Café are fictional, but include a lot of the speculation Wally Regitnig heard from locals throughout the investigation. Wally was a regular in the area during the search and locals got to know him well.

Chapter Thirty-One

The entirety of the Anson's house is fictional. Val laughed at the memory, "We didn't have carpet in the River Street house!" Typical for newlyweds, their first home in Prince Albert was modest but serviceable.

Officers arrived unannounced at the Anson residence to retrieve Doug's work items and at one point Vallarena Anson did, indeed, destroy a file at the Force's direction. But the timing, circumstances, and details in this scene are all fiction. Val said, "I was so young, maybe a little bit naïve. I don't know why I did that. But I just thought that if I couldn't have it, neither could they." Val was 20 years old when her husband was killed. She didn't want to give up Doug's personal file so was asked to destroy it. She obliged.

I had the privilege of visiting with Val Blum at her home and saw several photos of her and Doug with their horses, their dog Lobo, and their house on River Street. She put two photo books in my hands that were "exactly as Doug left them 50 years ago." These books are filled with mementos of his time at Depot, a few newspaper clippings of him as a teenager winning awards, and some beautiful landscape photos. He had an eye for photography.

Chapter Thirty-Two

Over 700 people attended the regimental funerals of Schrader and Anson at Depot with an honour guard and procession, and every officer wore their RCMP ceremonial uniform— the iconic red serge. Regimental funerals can vary from member to member, and I was obviously not present for these in 1970. I described it as it may happen today, to the best of my ability, with my apologies to those in the know for any inaccuracies and accidental blunders in terminology I may have made. I have witnessed the march and sharp salute as officers pass the cenotaph in the parade square. It is unlike anything I've ever seen. Bob Schrader and Doug Anson's names appear on the monument.

Everything in this chapter is fabricated with the help of personal accounts. I wrote that Wally felt a crushing obligation to imprint his friends on the memory of every officer that came after them. This happened, in a way. The lessons learned from the murder of Schrader and Anson have been taught for decades at Depot through case studies and scenarios surrounding the shooting. My husband learned about them long before I wrote this book. He went through Depot in 2000-2001 and their memory was still living on in these teaching tools. Members are better prepared because of the tragedy of this loss. May Bob and Doug rest easy in that.

Chapter Thirty-Three

I learned from interviews that they did have members in boats on the river to possibly draw Robertson's fire. I've attributed it to Ron Morier here but it may have happened to other members as well. The interaction between Wally and "Anderson" is fabricated based on the fervent testimony of some higher up officers who would never have ordered their men to do that and, in their opinion, whoever did had made a grave error in judgement. My thanks to them for their candour.

Roadblocks were cancelled within the week, and the major ground search halted within the month. Newspapers lost interest after a week as well, as this was the same time the FLQ Crisis was happening in Quebec. That is one of the main reasons I took on this project. This manhunt is one of the longest in Canadian history and few people know about it.

One member recalled a day when someone came running across a field dressed similar to their description of Stanley Robertson. "Have you ever heard the safety go off on 12 rifles at the same time? It's deafening." The details attributed to Wally and Al Mosher are fabricated but the incident did happen. The members initially thought it was Robertson coming across the field until someone realized different and yelled to hold fire.

The story of the juveniles breaking through roadblocks between Regina and Saskatoon is true. I first learned of it during interviews so I made a note to research it further. I found a single story in the Regina Leader-Post highlighting the details and those details were mingled in with the Robertson story in a Saskatchewan crime anthology. The RCMP never believed the stolen car held Robertson, as the crime anthology noted. As told to me by members who were directly involved, this tragedy was separate and had nothing to do with the Robertson manhunt.

Chapter Thirty-Four

Wally Regitnig never stopped looking for Stanley Robertson, but he wasn't the only one. There were many dedicated officers working together to solve this case. Wanted posters spread out from Winnipeg, Manitoba to the coast of British Columbia. Each potential lead was investigated thoroughly.

The investigation did make its way out to British Columbia and Constable Lorne LOWE, a troopmate of Doug Anson's, got involved. "Doug was the only one in our troop stationed in Saskatchewan. We were watching the news that night and saw that two members were shot and killed in Saskatchewan and I said to my wife I hope that's not Doug. Turned out the next morning that it was." A family member of Robertson's ended up moving out to British Columbia in early 1971, leading investigators to believe Robertson had gone out there, too. After more than a month of surveillance they discovered the relation had no knowledge of Robertson's whereabouts. "I never took a more serious approach to any investigation."

My chats with Barry Greenslade were filled with tidbits about his working relationship with Wally, the search wearing on into the winter, and other incidents that came along with the frustration of not one sighting of their suspect. Barry was familiar with the terrain, comfortable with the firearms, and had no trouble keeping up with the dogmaster and his partner so he was taken off detachment work and put on the search full time for two months. He and Wally were the last two on scene when the heavy snow came and the official ground search was called off but you'll notice I took creative liberties with the search timeline to show that members searched through the winter as well, mostly in their spare time unless a specific tip was being investigated.

According to Wally's personal notes there were five dog teams involved with the investigation. When it was all said and done he gave each of them a small book with a typed synopsis of the case, complete with photos. It was a treasure to hold one in my hands.

Chapter Thirty-Five

Countless people described the relationships Wally forged during this investigation. The meetings and conversations between Wally Regitnig and Gordon Robertson are fabricated as far as this book is concerned. As of publication date, no evidence pointed toward Sergeant Regitnig interviewing Stanley's father at any time.

Chapter Thirty-Six

Everything in this chapter leading up to Wally finding Robertson is fabricated for the story. All reports just say he located Robertson, with no details on how that happened. Not even in a personal synopsis written by Wally himself that I had the privilege of reading. Some locals think he was located by a farmer fixing fences. Some said the body was found by a hunter and reported to police. But the most reliable accounts of how Wally and Bruce actually knew where to look for Robertson that day in early May said it was his knowledge of the area and the trust he'd earned from the locals that led him to the location.

Chapter Thirty-Seven

After the body was recovered, the investigation wrapped up fairly quickly and there was only the mountain of paperwork to deal with. There was no more to discover, and they could finally let Bob Schrader and Doug Anson rest in peace.

The bullet casing is significant as it represents several things. Robertson was well known for always collecting his shell casings when he shot, as he did on the Friday morning. It is well documented that he left his house for a brief time late in the morning, and family members interviewed speculated that he went to the scene of the domestic dispute he had with his wife on the MacDowall back road to collect up the shell casing from the shot he took at "Don Nelson". All documented evidence and pathology reports show that Robertson shot himself with a .22 rifle. In interviews with local families, there were rumours (as there always are) that he was shot by the RCMP or by his own father, so he wouldn't have to go to jail. There is no evidence whatsoever that points to either of these scenarios being true but I wanted to leave that bullet casing on the table between Stanley's father and Sergeant Regitnig to further point to the amount of speculation we are left with at the end of this case.

Late in the process when this book was long complete I received the entire case file (redacted) from ATIP. A friend of Mrs. Robertson's recounted how they were in the beer parlour with her the night before the shootings and how they heard about Stanley shooting at "Don Nelson" late that night. They went on to say "I was supposed to go and pick Stanley up and take him to Prince Albert in the afternoon. He had ordered a new motor for his car from MacLeod's in Prince Albert. I was scared, so I didn't go out to Stanley's place on Friday (October 9, 1970). I stayed home all day." Imagine if circumstances had been different and Stanley wasn't home when the officers came knocking at the door.

In an interview with a retired RCMP officer I learned this officer was called out to the Robertson farm just a few days after Stanley's body was recovered in the spring. Robertson's wife had called Prince Albert Detachment and said she had something for them. The young officer happened to be on patrol in the area and was sent out to retrieve what she had but he never read it. He simply followed orders, went to the farm as requested and brought back what Mrs. Robertson gave him. "It was neatly folded and had been kept flat all those months. Almost like it was pressed in a book. I was totally surprised. There was policeman handwriting in the standard format we used to take statements. She was meek and I felt there was a lot of remorse from her when she gave over the statement." Upon receiving the full case file from ATIP in digital form, nothing resembling this statement was included in the scanned (and redacted) pages. Perhaps these mystery pages are still tucked into the file somewhere. There is a good chance that the pages this officer was sent to pick up is the statement "Don Nelson" provided around noon on Friday, October 9, 1970 to Doug Anson. There was speculation that Stanley took the document with him when he fled the scene, but it just as likely could have been picked up by Mrs. Robertson and tucked away until she was sure her husband was found.

"I just heard a single shot and that was it. (It was) dismissed as a car backfire. But afterwards when they found the body and the pathology report said he had probably died on the first day, I felt vindicated. I still maintain to this day that that was the shot that killed Robertson." Brent Jette has a sharp mind for the facts of this case. Everything in his interview cross checked with the police reports and my other interviews. In my personal opinion, seeing on a map how far he was from the location of Robertson's body, talking to officers (including my husband) about how far away you can hear a .22 shot on a cold, clear night on the prairies, I believe Jette really did hear the shot that killed Robertson. What do you think?

RCMP Discover Robertson's Body In Dense Bush-It is possible that Robertson watched the searchers during the October manhunt, moving out when the search grew close, and returning to his look out after the searchers had left the area.

>Headline and excerpt, Prince Albert Daily Herald
>(Monday, May 10, 1971)

>"The area where the body was found had not been previously searched by any parties."

>Excerpt from RCMP report by Sgt. W.J.O. Regitnig
>#17364 (12 May 71)

Yours Truly,
Walter J. Regitnig

Acknowledgements

I'm always fascinated by an author's acknowledgements. The people on the page are strangers to the reader, but are of the utmost importance to the person who wrote the book. This is who is important to me.

My husband and boys first, for never complaining when we had hotdogs or pizza several nights in a row and their enthusiastic help when I needed demonstrations on police procedure. They are my biggest fans. My husband deserves his own medal for emotionally cheering me on for the six years it took, from start to finish, to research, write, and get this book into print. He has my undying love and gratitude.

Fellow Author and Editor Extraordinaire Katherine Johnson is not only a beautiful soul but has a talent for never sugar coating the fact that I wasn't done yet. Her comments are gold as is the value of her friendship.

Every person who contributed their personal experience with this case has my deepest and most profound appreciation. Without the interviews, this story would not be as whole as it is. Thank you for the kindness you showed in wanting me to provide as many real details as I could, even in a work of fiction.

The Surrey International Writers Conference, hands down the best conference in the world, for creating a venue where beginner writers, been-published-a-million-times-over authors, and everyone in between come together to share, learn, and grow. There is something magical in the air at Surrey when you get to hear from Diana Gabaldon, Jack Whyte, Robert Dugoni, C.C. Humphreys, and more all in the same weekend. It was there that I scribbled notes, learned from my mistakes, and refined my writing year after year. They have my loyalty forever and I will never stop supporting this wonderful conference.

This book would not exist as it is today without Table 30. Thank you for every critique, every read through, every rowdy, loud editing session in the hotel lounge that decided what my first page actually was. Thank you for every gentle nudge, and every not-so-gentle poke in the eye when something was absolutely no good at all. Thank you for letting me feel part of something grand. To list everyone would be impossible – you know who you are – but a special nod to author Tom Bont, fondly referred to as "Tom from Texas" whose wise words I will remember always. "What do you want, Sugar? A book or a hundred and fifty page newspaper article?" I've been a reporter half my life and love newspaper writing but I wanted a book. And now I have one.

Printed in Canada